My Time In The Affair

STYLO FANTÔME

My Time In The Affair
Published by Stylo Fantôme
BattleAxe Production, First Edition
Copyright © 2015

Editing Aides:
Barbara Shane Hoover

Cover Designed by Najla Qamber Designs
http://najlaqamberdesigns.com/

Formatting by Champagne Formats

ISBN-13: 978-1511709798
ISBN-10: 1511709790

Mission Statement

I not only write, I read. A lot. Probably more than is healthy. There are a lot of things I love about self-publishing/indie authors, and a lot of things I'm not a fan of. Just personal preferences, no disrespect meant. So when I decided to self-publish, I made some promises to myself to try my hardest to avoid doing those things I didn't like seeing/happening in other stories. Now I would like to make those promises to you, the reader:

I promise to never leave you hanging. If I write a story with a cliffhanger ending, I will only publish it when the second part is completely written.

I promise that all **cliffhanger sequels** will be published within 16 weeks—*maximum*—of the previous part (i.e., part **two** will come within four months of part **one**. Part **three** will come within four months of part **two**, and so on, and so forth). You will never have to wait six months, or a year, or *years,* for a sequel to any **cliffhangers** that I might write.

I promise that, while I am an **unsigned indie** author, I will never raise the price of any part of a **series** above $2.99. I will not "hook you" with book one, two, and three at $1.99 and/or $2.99, and then suddenly book four is $4.99. I refuse to pay for series that are like that, so I will never do that to you.

I promise that if I am lucky enough and blessed enough to have fans, I will interact and communicate with them as much as possible—you are who this is all for, after all.

If at any point in time, I fail to live up to any of these promises, you have my permission to tar and feather me, beat me, leave me for dead, or worst of all—call me out.
No work is ever really completed, no story ever completely told, but I will always try my hardest to bring you my best.

Thank you for reading.

Other Books

Dedication

To anybody who has ever felt bad for feeling
a way they knew they shouldn't . . .

Mischa

I MADE A CONSCIOUS DECISION to cheat on my husband.
Now, before you judge me, hear my story. Hear how much I'm like you, how similar my thoughts are to your own. Yes, I'm a horrible person. Yes, I've done horrible things. Yes, I don't deserve forgiveness. Yes, bad things happened because of my actions.

But I'm willing to bet I've done things that maybe, just maybe, *you* have thought of doing.

Maybe, just maybe, you're not as innocent as you'd like to think.

Or maybe I'm not so guilty . . .

Falling Out of Love

FALLING IN LOVE IS kind of easy. Two people meet. They're attracted to each other, or maybe they're not. But they connect. Friends, a connection, whatever. It leads to something more—flirting, then dating, then sex. Then LOTS of sex. Move in together, live together, love together. Happy wonderful times, and then *voilà*, marriage.

Mischa had known Michael for a long time, since right after high school. They had both gotten jobs at Target before college, met while bagging up cheap home décor. They went to school together, stayed friends, hung out all the next year. Then at the end of that following summer, after a drink too many, Michael kissed Mischa. Pause. She kissed him back.

And they lived happily ever after . . .

That's what made her so mad. They couldn't blame it on being young—they had started dating at nineteen, but didn't get married till they were twenty-four. Five years together, that's a long time to get to know each other, and twenty-four isn't that young of an age to get married. That's an adult. Capable of making semi-intelligent decisions, once in a while.

They couldn't blame it on not really knowing each other—they were best friends. "*The Mikes,*" as they were affectionately known to their friends. They had started as best friends, and she could honestly say that they were *still* best friends. Not a day went by that they didn't speak to each other, about everything and anything. Anytime anything happened in her life, Michael was the first person she wanted to talk to about it. Promotion at work, gossip with the girls, the next door neighbor that she battled over parking spots with; all of it. They almost had their own language.

Worse than falling in love. Worse than hating someone. Falling out of love was much, much harder. How does a person say that?

*"Hey, I love you—I really do. I want you to be a part of my life. I can't bear the thought of not seeing you and talking to you every day, but I just don't want to be romantically or sexually involved with you anymore. I'm not **in** love with you, and have thus become increasingly less physically attracted to you."*

What a horrible fucking person. She hated herself. She found herself hoping, *praying,* that Mike would cheat on her. At least if he cheated on her, then they could break up, and he wouldn't hate her, and of course she wouldn't hate him. It would be her release, she could *thank him.*

I just don't want him to hate me. Please don't hate me.

They had talked about it. Multiple times, so Mike could never claim that she hadn't tried. She suggested therapy. Shot down. She pointed out their problems. Denied. Michael had a rich fantasy life; everything seemed to be fine in his mind.

But in her mind, there was nothing fine about a married couple not having sex in almost six months.

"Don't you want more than this?" she would ask him.

"I'm just stressed, we're both busy," he made up excuses.

And being best friends *just made it worse,* because she knew him so well. She knew he genuinely believed that, that he honestly thought there wasn't a problem with what was happening between them. He didn't seem to notice the time that passed between their sexual encounters.

Oh, but she did, and the further and further apart their sexual encounters became, the less and less she wanted them. She got so used to satisfying herself, it got to a point where she didn't care. She started to prefer sex with herself over sex with him. At least with herself, she didn't have to shave her legs, she didn't care how much weight she'd put on, and she *always* came.

A brag that Michael couldn't share.

"What do you want to do for your birthday, Misch?" Mischa's best friend Lacey asked her, as they jogged down the street.

"I won't be here for my birthday," Misch huffed, picking up their pace.

"Oh, I keep forgetting! How does Mike feel about that?"

Mischa started jogging even faster.

"Eh. He's bummed, but he's excited for me," she replied.

Once upon a time, Mischa had been a dancer, had even gone to the University of Michigan for dance. Ballet, tap, and modern jazz. Later hip hop. She taught at a studio for a while, but a torn ACL put her out of commission. While recovering from her injury, she put on weight. At first just ten pounds. Not so bad, and she enjoyed the bigger ass. But then a year later, another ten pounds crept up on her. Before she knew it, she was fifty pounds overweight.

But why should she care? Not like she had anyone to get naked for, not like she could dance well anymore. She left the dance studio, got a job at an insurance office, and it turned out she was really good at it. Filing claims, selling policies, boring shit, but the money was excellent.

The company Mischa worked for was expanding at a rapid rate. They already had multiple branches all over the United States, and a couple in South East Asia. Now they were expanding to Europe. Misch's boss was being sent overseas to help start up offices in Italy, Turkey, and Armenia. Misch had been asked to go along to assist him. No worries, it wasn't happening immediately—she had a year to prepare. A year to plan.

So perfect.

Her friend Lacey was looking to lose weight, too, so the two of them came up with an exercise plan together. Now, a year later, both women had dropped a lot of weight. Mischa was giddy over having her body back, but she kept telling herself it had all been to help Lacey lose weight. That was it, no other reason. No other reason at all. Certainly not to get attention from other men. And definitely not to cheat on her husband . . .

Am I really gonna do this? Am I really gonna do this? Am I really gonna do this?

Misch's thoughts pounded around her head in time to her feet pounding against the pavement. Most of the time, she told herself no.

But other times . . .

"Hey! I didn't ask last week, but you must have met your goal weight," Lacey called out. Misch looked down at herself. She had actually hit her goal the month before—she'd lost another five pounds on top of that, and was working on toning up.

"Yeah."

"You look amazing, Misch! I can't believe we did it! Mike must be so proud!" her friend cheered.

I am going to the worst part of hell.

They separated at the end of the block, but made plans to go out for drinks later that same night. Misch was flying out on Friday, which was only two days away. This would be their goodbyes—she would be gone for two months, possibly longer.

At home, Misch went into her bathroom and turned on the shower, letting it heat up while she took off her sweaty running clothes. She stood in front of a full length mirror, looking over her naked body. The same time the year before, she had avoided looking at her body. Now, she was proud of it. She'd taken it for granted when she was younger, because it had seemingly stayed in shape without effort. Now she had worked for it, and worked *hard.*

There wasn't anything terribly exceptional about her body, she supposed. She was on the tall side, almost five-foot-eight, with a standard figure. B-cup boobs and hips that were built to proportion, she was lucky in that sense. When she was young, her dancing had given her strong thighs and an ass that defied gravity—she'd gone back to dancing, taking classes and renting studios at night to get that ass and those thighs back.

She had dusky nipples that matched her lips, and her dark brown hair brushed just past her jaw, teasing the sides of her neck. Her eyes were hazel, usually resting at a honey-moss color. She felt out of place a lot of the time, not quite fitting in with any color, with any race.

She hopped in the shower and scrubbed up. Washed her hair and body before jumping back out and getting ready. Mike got home while she was still putting on her makeup. He came into the bathroom, talking about his day at work. He walked up behind her and wrapped his arms around her waist, kissed the side of her neck. She leaned into him, wondering if it would go farther, for once. Wondering how she would feel about it, if it did.

But of course, it didn't go anywhere. He patted her on the butt, like a content dog, then leaned against the counter and babbled on about work, playing with a makeup brush. She laughed and joked with him, booped him on the nose with her foundation. They made fun of his boss, then her boss. When she was done getting dressed, they kissed goodbye and she headed out to meet her friends. It wasn't till she was halfway to the pub that she realized something.

He never even asked where I was going.

The *"boring shit"* at work was what started her snowball of misfortune. Her mind wandered. She thought about different things, possibilities, opportunities. For a long time, Mischa tried to think of ways to fix her marriage—hence the suggestions of therapy. She'd also attempted to spice up their marriage, set up romantic evenings, tried to get dirty and nasty. Nothing worked.

So her mind wandered further. Would she have sex with someone else if she could? She sort of casually asked Mike what he thought of the idea of an open relationship within a marriage. Maybe she could have the close friendship with her husband in marriage, and seek sexual and physical satisfaction elsewhere! Problemo solved. But no, that idea was SHOT. DOWN.

She felt trapped. Suffocated, yet alone. This is not a subject a woman can talk about with her friends, especially when she'd already expressed her own distaste of cheaters. Hello, hypocrite. How could she explain that to anyone?

I get along great with my husband, we're super pals! He's nice, thoughtful, caring, sweet . . . but I really, really want to fuck someone else.

It sounded awful, but Mischa found herself feeling guilty—not because she wanted to cheat, but because she'd judged other people for cheating. Now that she was perilously close to being in their shoes, she understood. She understood so much.

It started small. Just an idea, that she could sleep with someone else. But then no, no, no, she couldn't do that, she wasn't *that* person. Then . . . well, maybe she could be *that* person. But no, no, no, who would want her anyway? She was fifty pounds overweight and hadn't dated anyone else since she was nineteen—she was twenty-seven now!

Then she thought . . . maybe she *could* lose the weight. Maybe she could get her old body back, and if she could accomplish that, something that had evaded her for four years, maybe she could give herself a treat.

Like a Nordic ice god . . .

No, no, no, she couldn't do that. She *wouldn't* do that!

Would I?

"Bon voyage!"

All her girlfriends screamed and laughed as she entered the bar. Misch laughed as well and sat down at their table, ordering a vodka-tonic.

They got appetizers and did shots. Most of them had been friends for years—Lacey had been one of the Target-summer-job crew, and had known Misch and Mike since they'd met. They giggled and got loud and got a little drunk.

"I'm gonna miss you," Lacey whined, leaning close to her. Misch nodded and knocked back another Lemon Drop.

"I'm gonna miss you, too, chick," she breathed, wiping at her chin.

"But . . . but . . . who am I going to talk to?" Lacey continued, pretending to cry.

"Your husband. These losers," Misch joked, gesturing to the other girls at the table. She was met with a chorus of boos.

"But no one talks to me like you," Lacey groaned, then pressed her forehead to the table.

"Oh god. Okay, someone call her husband to come get her, I'm getting the rest of us another round!" Misch shouted. There were cheers, and she headed to the bar.

"Can I get four Washington Apples, and a vodka-tonic!?" she called out to the bartender. He nodded and began assembling their drinks.

"*Hey.*"

Misch jumped a little, startled. A guy had sidled up to the bar next to her, leaning against it. He looked young, or at least younger than her. He eyed her up and down very openly, his gaze lingering on her breasts before moving down to her hips and thighs.

"Can I help you?" she asked, glancing around to double check that he was talking to her.

"Oh yeah, you can. You live around here?" he questioned, his eyes finally making their way back to her own.

Holy shit, am I getting hit on?

"Uh, yeah."

"Nice. I noticed you ladies were celebrating. Birthday?" he kept going, chewing on his straw.

"Sort of."

"It's a sort of birthday?"

"Birthday slash going away party," she clarified, nervously running her fingers through her hair. She hadn't really been *out*-out in a long time. The more weight she'd gained, the more she'd stayed at home. Even when she'd started losing weight, she'd just spent all her time trying to lose *more* weight. She didn't even remember what it felt like to get hit on—she couldn't tell if that's what was happening or not.

I'm an idiot.

"Aw, you're going away? Bummer, I was hoping we could hang out," the guy mock-pouted, but his eyes were smiling.

"Really?" she laughed. "You don't even know me."

"I could get to know you a lot better tonight, back at your place."

Oh yeah, he's hitting on me.

"I'm sorry, I'm married," she automatically responded.

"I'm sorry, too. We could go to my place."

That moment. That moment was *the* moment.

Mischa blushed and said no, thank you. Paid the bartender and took her tray of drinks. Smiled politely at her admirer before making her way back to her table.

But as she took two shots back to back, then chugged down her vodka-tonic, she kept glancing at the bar. Glancing at the man. He would look back every now and then, sometimes wink. Chew on that straw. Misch knew she wasn't going to go home with him, wasn't going to do anything bad.

But not because it *was* bad.

But only because her friends would see what a horrible person she was.

I am most positively, definitely, going to hell.

"You sure you don't want me to come? I could get a ticket," Mike said, following her through the airport. Mischa rolled her eyes.

"We've been over this, Mikey. I asked if you wanted to go in the beginning. You said no. Now it's too late. You have your job. You're coming to visit me in a month," she reminded him, hiking her messenger bag up higher on her shoulder.

"I'm gonna miss you so much," he sighed. She frowned and glanced at him.

"Me, too, babe."

It was such a horrible feeling, because she would miss him. *So much.* Just not in the way she was supposed to miss him. Not the way a wife should miss her husband.

Before she could go through security, he hugged her tightly. She pressed herself against him, comforted by his familiar smell, his familiar body. He felt so comfortable to her.

Maybe that's our problem, we just got too comfortable.

He kissed her goodbye, a chaste pressing of lips. No tongue. Nothing overly emotional. Of course not. She clung to him, but he became embarrassed. Pulled away. She wanted to get angry. She was about to climb into a metal tube of death, that could fall five miles out of the sky, dropping her to a fiery grave—couldn't she get a little passion? A little emotion?

Just a little tongue!?

Once she was through security, she waved once more at him. He blew her a kiss, which she caught, then she walked away. Picked up her pace, dragging her carry on bag behind her.

She passed several gates before she realized she was crying.

Mischa

YOU HAVE TO UNDERSTAND, I wasn't trying to *"have my cake and eat it, too."* That wasn't what it was about.

I was a horrible person, who just didn't want to hurt her best friend.

Of course I had talked to him about it, of course I had broached the subject with him—but when you're shot down at so many turns, you begin to fire back. Sometimes in a not very noble way.

I'm not trying to make excuses. There is no excuse for what I did. I should have broken up with him. Point, blank, period. I know this. *I know this.*

But when you're looking at your best friend, a person who is a part of the fabric of your being, and you can literally see their heart start to break, well . . . it takes a lot of strength to smash that heart all the way. To disintegrate it.

It takes someone stronger than I am.

So then you *do* begin to make excuses.

Maybe I was meant to be a swinger, that's what it is. I'm just in an open relationship . . . that only one of us knows about . . .

He'll never know. He'll never find out. My heart can still belong to him—that's all that counts, right? I can get pleasure from someone else, desire from elsewhere, but still belong to him in a way he needs.

Fucked up. *So fucked up.* But it begins to make sense. Especially right around the time when you stop caring if *he* did the same thing. Cause that's what stopped me in the beginning, the ol' *"well how would I feel if he cheated on me?"* trick.

That worked for the first year or two. Then, slowly but surely, it went away. I didn't care. Mike could have gone and fucked half the neighborhood, and I would've been ecstatic—because it would've meant I could do the same. It would've meant my best friend was finally experiencing the pleasure and desire he had been missing out on for so long. It would mean that *I* could finally experience it, too.

Because experiencing it with each other was no longer a possibility.

He'll never know . . .

Italy

I T WAS HOT AND muggy in Italy—murder on Misch's hair. It was also go, go, go! From the moment they got there, she had to hit the ground running. They landed at night, went straight to bed, and she was woken up at six in the morning to get ready for the day. Jet lag was still very present as she muscled through the work, trying to explain coding and filing procedures to a translator.

The first few days took adjusting. Time changes, climate changes, cultural changes, and on top of all that—*her nerves.* She was a nervous wreck.

How am I going to do this!? I don't even know what flirting is anymore. I haven't even tried to pick anyone up yet, and I already feel like puking. This is such a bad idea. I'm not doing it.

If there was anywhere a woman would want to work on her self-confidence and man-getting abilities, Italy was the place. The men were very aggressive and very vocal. Misch didn't speak a word of Italian, but she didn't need a translator to tell her the kinds of things that were shouted at her, and every other woman on the street, on a daily basis.

Dinner was another exercise in being single. She dined alone, not really having much in common with her boss. She would sit at the bar in the hotel lounge, and men would come up to her and start prattling away in Italian. Same thing happened at the outdoor cafes and restaurants she went to; men would walk up and just start talking to her, switching languages when they discovered she wasn't Italian.

"Are you alone?"

The first couple times she heard that, Misch's standard response was, *"I'm married."* She'd been saying it for so long, it was a hard habit to break. Eventually, though, she got to where she could say *"yes"* back to them. She wasn't going to lie—it was bad enough that she was attempting to lie and cheat on her husband, she wasn't going to lie to anyone else. She wore her rings, and if they asked if she was married, she told the truth.

"I am, but he's not here."

Shockingly, this didn't deter most men. If anything, they became more aggressive. She wondered if it seemed like a challenge to them. Mischa didn't like it. She wasn't a prize to be won. She felt cheap enough as it was, she didn't need a man making her feel that way, too.

On top of that, the idea of actually cheating on her husband made her feel kind of sick to her stomach, *and* she was also simply *too nervous.* A man would sit close enough to touch her and she would practically jump out of her skin. Laugh like a nervous donkey, then scoot away. Finish her drink and run away. She would share drinks and laugh, and one man went as far as caressing her bare thigh, but she always psyched herself out. Found herself making excuses to get away, begging off for the night.

Maybe I can't do this.

Having sex with another person was all fine and dandy in her mind. But when it was time to put her "plan" into action, she had a realization. She couldn't do it. She just couldn't. She had planned and schemed and worked for a year, and when the "prize" was right in front of her, she didn't want it anymore. She had totally overthought it, watched too many rom-coms, read too many romance novels. That wasn't real life, *this* was—a boring, shadow of a marriage that she was too weak to get out of. She had to learn to deal with that, because she clearly wasn't able to be a heartless, cheating vixen.

How did I think I could do this? I'm not that person. I can't do that to him. I made my decision when I married him. I made my bed, and now I have to lay in it. For better, or for worse.

And so her first week in Italy went. Amazed at her surroundings. Overwhelmed by her job. Scared of her future. Regretful of her feelings. She was all over the place—definitely not the right frame of mind to start something that might ruin her life.

Oh, and the tiny fact that actually doing it would make me the worst. Person. Ever.

At the end of that first week, she felt better about herself. Better than she had in a long time. She wasn't going to cheat on her husband, she wasn't going to become that person. She was going to do her job, Mike was going to visit, and maybe being in Europe would reignite that spark. Reignite something, *anything.*

Life was good. She was a good person. Nothing bad was going to happen.

"You are alone?"

Mischa sighed and looked up from her manual.

"Yeah, but I'm busy," she replied, her voice terse. Her plan was over—no more flirting for her. No point in being a bundle of nerves all the time for no good reason. She hadn't even bothered dressing up, was just wearing a simple black sundress and sandals.

"Surely not too busy for a drink," the man in front of her said, a cheesy smile spreading across his face before he slid into the empty seat next to her. She put her manual aside.

"Look, I'm sorry, but I really am working," she tried to explain. He snapped his fingers in the air, summoning a waiter.

"Ah, just one drink. You can spare time for one drink," he insisted, his accent thick and his gaze heavy. The waiter approached and her unwelcome-guest ignored her, speaking Italian and ordering a drink.

"I'm sorry, I don't want to sit with you," she pressed.

"See? Is too late. Now you must drink with me," the guy teased.

Misch was tired from a long day at work. Tired from a long life. She glared at the man.

"I don't want to drink with you. I don't know how to get that through your head. So *you* can leave, or *I* can leave," she informed him.

"Or we can stay and you can get to know me, I am very fun guy," he assured her.

Misch snorted, stood up, and began collecting her paperwork. The man stood up as well, and next thing she knew, he was pressed up against her side. She started to pull away, but he wrapped his arm around her waist.

"What are you doing!?" she was shocked.

"The night is young, and you are very beautiful. Come, let us get to know one another," his voice was low as he leaned down towards her. She practically bent in half trying to get away.

"You're about to get to know my fist! Let go of me!" she snapped.

"American women are so feisty, I love it. I will show you -,"

"Babe! Sorry I took so long!"

Misch turned her head and stared in shock as a second man came up to her other side, grabbing her free hand and bringing it to his lips, kissing the backs of her fingers.

Am I releasing pheromones or something!?

"Excuse me!?" she squeaked. The new guy was tall, and though he blended in with the local scenery, his accent was American. He didn't look at her, just held her hand and glared at the other man.

"Can I help you?" he demanded.

"You know this woman?" the Italian guy questioned.

"I should hope so, I fucking married her," new guy snapped, then grabbed her left hand, holding it up so the other man could see her wedding set.

"I am sorry. She said she was alone," Cassanova began sliding away.

"Well, she's not alone anymore, so get the fuck out of here."

Misch's mind was blown, and she didn't say anything as the American man hugged her close to his side. She watched as the Italian gentleman glared at them for a moment longer, then walked away, cursing in the other language. A deep voice chuckled from above her, and she was let go.

"Did you just save me?" she asked, moving away from her new friend.

"Yeah, you looked like you needed it," he informed her, smiling down at her.

Oooohhhh, wow. And I picked tonight of all nights to not dress up . . .

"I'm sorry, who are you?" she blurted out.

"Your savior."

He was smiling, but she didn't feel like he was joking. His voice was low and his smile sly. He had incredibly thick, black hair, which almost shined and had waves on top of his head. His eyes were so dark, they almost looked black, matching his thick eyebrows and heavy lashes. His lips were on the fuller side, and he easily had two days worth of stubble on his jaw. Her heart started beating faster.

No, no, no. This can't be happening. I'm not doing this. I don't want this.

"I'm sorry," Misch said with a dry laugh, putting a hand on her chest. "I'm a little . . . uh . . . thrown off, by that guy. Am I missing something?"

Her savior finally held out his hand.

"I'm Tal," he introduced himself as she put her hand in his. She held still.

"Your name is '*tall*'?" she asked, surprised. He smiled, showing a wide expanse of pretty, perfect, white teeth.

"*Tal*," he corrected her pronunciation. "*T-A-L*. It's Hebrew. Means '*dew*'."

She felt stupid.

"Oh. I'm Mischa," she finally shook his hand, realizing she'd been holding it the whole time. He squeezed her palm and she felt her heart rate increase.

"Mischa. Russian, '*Who is Like God*'," he informed her.

"Are you a collector of names?" she tried to joke. Lamely. He let go of her hand.

"No, I've just been around a lot. Knew a Mischa. Please, sit," he offered, before pulling out her chair. Misch was sliding into her seat before she even caught on to the fact that she'd just been invited to sit at her own table. But she didn't say anything as he sat across from her.

"Where are you from?" she asked, wondering what she should do, what she should say. He obviously knew she was married, and he had saved her from a creeper—surely he wasn't hitting on her, as well.

"All over. And you?" he returned the question, then lifted his hand. Snapped for a waiter.

It didn't seem offensive when he did it.

"The states. Michigan," she told him.

"Ah. Detroit. Nice. Never been."

And that was it. A waiter came, and Tal ordered in what sounded like perfect Italian, albeit with an American accent. Then they sat in silence. He stared at her, his dark eyes wandering over her face. Misch shifted nervously in her seat.

"So, uh, what brings you to Italy?" she tried another question.

I sound like such an idiot. What am I still doing here? Thank him for saving you and go home, Misch.

"A little work. Mostly vacation."

"Oh, I'm here for work, too."

"I know."

That threw her for a second.

"How?" she asked. He gave a tight smile as a waiter came and set a cocktail in front of him.

"Your technical manual here on the inner workings of the insurance world," he commented, tapping a large binder which was sitting on the table.

"Oh, yeah, obviously," she laughed at herself, and some of her nerves abated.

"But I've seen you before."

Nerves made a U-turn.

"Huh?"

"I've seen you around, knew you weren't local. Clearly not a student. But I gotta say, you don't look like an insurance agent," Tal explained.

"Oh? What do I look like?" she was curious.

"A dancer."

"Really?" she asked, feeling short of breath. One year. It had taken her one year to get her body back. Mike had never said anything except '*good job,*' right after fist bumping her.

Fist. Bumping.

"Yes. You have amazing legs, good arms. And the way you hold yourself. Very graceful. Screams dancer."

Oh, this man. I'm in trouble.

They sat and chatted for a while. Mostly superficial things. The weather, the sights she'd seen. He managed to wiggle information out of her, but remained surprisingly tight lipped about himself. Misch ordered two more vodka-tonics, sucking them down quickly to help calm her nerves. Mr. . . . what was his last name? He'd never said it. *Tal* seemed to notice her nerves, and he kept giving her that sly grin, those dark eyes burning into her.

It got later, and he surprised her by calling for the check, then paying for the whole thing. It was just as well. She was slowly turning into a basket case. She felt like she was going to throw up, her wedding ring felt like it weighed a ton, and she was positive she was sweating *everywhere.* She kept telling herself that she wasn't doing anything wrong, that she *wouldn't* do anything wrong.

But that sly smile . . .

"Well, thank you for saving me, and for keeping me company," she sighed, walking out of the cafe with him.

"It was my pleasure. I live to save damsels in distress," he assured her, grinning down at her. He was all that was right with the Mediterranean—tall, dark, and handsome. She blinked rapidly and forced herself to look away.

"Good, that's good, cause a lot of us damsels need it here. I hope you -," she tried to say goodbye.

"Oh, you're not going anywhere."

She looked back up at him.

"Excuse me?"

"The night's still young, who goes to bed at this hour?" he asked her. Misch glanced at her watch.

"It's eleven," she pointed out.

"Early in Italy—look at all the people," Tal instructed. There were a lot of people about, dining and drinking and walking around. Rome was a busy place.

"I usually go to bed at this hour," she replied.

"How boring."

"Excuse me!?"

"*Boring.* Your life must be *boring,* if you always go to bed at eleven," he repeated himself.

She wanted to argue, but she couldn't. He was right. Her life was beyond boring. Had bored her all the way to another country, and what did she do once she got there?

Went to bed by eleven every night.

"What did you have in mind?" she sighed, tucking her hair behind her ears. His smile made a reappearance.

"Walk with me," he suggested, then he began strolling down the street.

They walked for a while. Tal was somewhat easy to talk to; or at least, he would have been, if Mischa hadn't been so anxious in his presence. She didn't know what it was—he hadn't hit on her, not really. He stared at her in a way that made her panties want to run away, and he was very charming, but he hadn't said anything to indicate he was attracted to her. Hadn't touched her since that first encounter.

Maybe he was just an American, happy to spend time with another American in a foreign country.

"Okay," she started as Tal led her into the lounge of a really nice hotel. "If I'm going to have another drink with you, you have to give up some more information."

"What do you mean?" he asked, taking them right up to the bar.

"Your Mr. Mysterious act is cute and all, but I don't feel like getting chopped up into pieces tonight," she explained. He rolled his eyes and waved for the bartender.

"I'll share if you share," he replied. She snorted.

"I've told you lots. You know what job I do, what town I'm from, how long I'm staying here, how -," she began to prattle off.

"I want to know why a married woman is standing in a bar with me," Tal cut her off.

Misch blinked at him as she felt the blood rush to her face.

"There's nothing wrong with having a drink with somebody," she defended herself. He smirked down at her.

"You say that, but I don't think that's what you're really thinking," he said in a low voice.

I'm entering a danger zone. This is too much.

"This is a bad idea. Thanks for the drinks," she grumbled, grabbing her tote bag from off the floor.

"Stay."

She'd been in the act of turning away, but she stopped. Looked back at him. He had grabbed her arm, was holding her in place, and his heavy gaze was once again searing her. He had such intense, dark eyes.

"What's your last name?" Mischa demanded. He let go of her arm.

"If I tell you, will you stay?" he responded.

"I'll think about it."

"Canaan."

"Excuse me?"

"My last name—Canaan."

20

Tal Canaan. So interesting. So fitting.

"Where are you from?" she continued. He shook his head.

"That kind of information, you have to earn," he informed her. A shiver ran down her spine.

"What are you doing in Italy?" she pressed.

"I told you, I was sent here on a job," he reminded her.

"Yeah, I meant what's your job?" she clarified.

"My job is . . . hard to explain. I work for the government," he answered evasively.

"U.S.?"

"No."

"Italy?"

"No."

"Somewhere in the E.U.?" she kept guessing.

"Misch," he sighed. "We were having a nice time. I'm sorry I fucked it up. Let's just shoot the shit and have a couple drinks. Be pals."

Not exactly poetry. Not exactly a pick up line. But it was nice to have someone to talk to, after a week of speaking only insurance lingo. Misch leaned against the bar, and took her drink when it was offered to her.

"To new friends," she toasted him, setting a boundary and making a statement. Tal smiled and clinked his glass to hers.

"New friends," he echoed, then took a drink. But when he moved his glass away, his smile had a decidedly sly look to it again.

They had more drinks, talked about football. Talked about Misch's dancing days. Talked about the year he'd spent in Thailand. Mr. Canaan had traveled quite a bit throughout his life, it seemed. He wouldn't say where he was from, or where he was currently living, but Misch began to think it was because he didn't have a home base. He seemed to be a modern day gypsy.

Conversation flowed between them, in an easy manner that somewhat shocked her. She felt comfortable with him, and was finding herself happy to realize she'd made her first friend. She would be in Italy for a while, so having a friend would help. It was looking like Tal could be that friend.

"What's the most exotic place you've ever lived?" Misch asked, vicariously living through him. He handed her another drink, her third since they'd been there. She was feeling a lot looser, most of her nerves gone. She was in a foreign country, having drinks with a friendly man. A very friendly, *very good looking,* man, but she focused on the friendly part.

"Hard to say. Everywhere is exotic if you look at it in the right light," Tal replied, pulling the straw from his whiskey-and-coke. He ran his tongue along it, capturing the excess liquid, before tossing it onto the bar. Misch ate up every movement.

Just a friend . . .

"Really?"

"Sure. I was in the tundra once, in Siberia—amazing sunsets, like you wouldn't believe. Like the snow is on fire. Also lived in Bosnia, great culture," he broke it down.

"I never thought of it that way. I was thinking palm trees. Jungle," she explained.

"Typical."

"Hey!" she laughed, coughing on the sip she'd been taking. "What's that supposed to mean?"

"That means I think you've led a very sheltered life, Ms. Rapaport," he told her, his voice low. She cleared her throat and took a gulp of her vodka-tonic. Mostly vodka.

"*Mrs.* Rapaport," she corrected him.

"Ah, yes. Of course. How could I forget," he gave another tight smile.

"Is there a *Mrs.* Canaan?" Misch tried to sound nonchalant. Failed miserably. Tal's smile got bigger.

"Would you care if there was?" he countered. Her blush was back, though whether it was from embarrassment or excitement or the liquor, she couldn't tell.

"I . . . I'm not . . . we're not . . . ," she stuttered. He narrowed his eyes, but kept smiling.

"Charming. Utterly charming. Will you excuse me for a moment?" he suddenly asked, putting his glass on the bar top.

"I, uh, sure," she managed to nod. He chuckled and leaned down close to her.

"Don't let any other men hit on you, I won't be here to save you," he cautioned her.

She snorted.

Misch watched Tal walk out of the bar. When he was out of sight, she let out a breath she'd been holding and sagged against the bar, downing the rest of her drink in one gulp. What was she doing? What in the fuck was she doing!? What was going on? She was a little tipsy, a little excited, but that was it. Nothing was happening, he'd actually been a perfect gentleman.

Would you care if there was a Mrs. Canaan?

She had to leave. Mischa had to get out of there. Before something happened that she couldn't take back. "*Just friends,*" who was she kidding? This wasn't a fucking game. When Tal came back, she would explain that to him. Hammer it into him. They were both adults—she was attracted to him. He seemed to be attracted to her. But that didn't have to mean anything. It didn't have to go anywhere.

"*Ciao,*" a soft voice said close to her.

Misch whirled around to find another gentleman standing close to her. Fuck, was she in heat or something!? Were "*cheating-whore*" vibes coming off of her in waves!?

"I'm with somebody," she snapped.

"Ah, American!" an Australian accent rolled out of the guy.

"*And* married," she continued, showing him her ring finger.

"I'm just being friendly," the guy claimed, holding up his hands. She cringed and felt like a bitch.

"Sorry, I'm sorry, it's just been a weird night," she sighed.

"Sorry to hear that," Mr. Aussie started, then leaned a little closer. "Maybe I can help cheer you up?"

"No thanks. I really am here -," she began, gesturing towards the door.

"What're you drinking? I'd love to buy you another," he offered.

"Oh no, I've already had too much. I'm with someone, I'm just waiting for him to -,"

"Well, if you've had too much, then one more can't hurt," he suggested, then winked at her. She actually laughed.

"Did you really just say that?"

"Bartender! One more for my lady friend!" he called out, pounding on the bar top. Misch waved the bartender away.

"No no no, I don't want another, I said -,"

"Baby, I can't leave you alone for a second."

Misch had barely turned towards Tal before his mouth was on hers. She gave a muffled squeak, completely shocked as he pressed his entire body against her, pinning her against the bar.

Eight years. It had been eight years since she had touched lips other than her husband's. Eight years since another man had touched her in an intimate manner. She didn't know what to do, didn't know how to respond. She'd automatically braced her hands against his chest, but then froze up.

Tal wasn't frozen. He was pressing against her so hard, the edge of the bar was painful against her lower back, and she was practically bending backwards over it. One of his hands had grabbed onto her hip, gripping the material of her dress in his fist. His other hand was on the back of her head, holding her lips to his, keeping them there.

He moaned and she gasped, and he took the opportunity to slip his tongue in her mouth. Her brain went into complete nuclear meltdown. She didn't know which way to turn, what to do.

Stop him! This isn't okay! You're married! You're not gonna do this!

This is what you want. This is what you came here for.

God, he's good at this. God, he tastes good. God, is this what kissing feels like!?

Hell. *You're. Going. To. Hell.*

God, he feels good.

Before she could sort those thoughts out, Tal pulled back a little.

"Can I help you?" he asked, giving a condescending look to the Australian man who was still standing next to them. Misch had already forgotten about him. Forgotten her own name. She just stared up at Tal.

"Sorry, I didn't realize the lady was here with somebody," the Aussie said quickly. Tal's hand moved from Misch's hip and his arm snaked around her waist, pulling her even closer to him.

She kept staring. She was pretty sure her mouth was hanging open. Her thoughts were still scattered all over the place. Tumbled about the bar, laying at her feet.

"That's funny," Tal started, "because I could've sworn I overheard her specifically telling you that she was here with somebody."

"My mistake. Sorry."

"Yeah, big mistake. Get the fuck out of here."

The guy got out of there.

"Wha . . . what just happened?" Misch panted, raking her hands through her hair. Tal leaned down and grabbed her bag, shoving it into her arms.

"C'mon," was all he said, then he was pulling her out of the bar. Misch struggled to keep up with his pace.

"Where are we going?" she breathed when she realized they weren't heading out of the hotel.

Tal didn't answer. They were moving towards a bank of elevators, and one had just opened up, depositing a group of people into the lobby. He picked up his pace, practically dragging her into the lift.

He let go of her and she lost her balance, stumbling into a corner. By the time she righted herself, he'd pressed a floor button. When she turned around, he was back up against her, flattening her against the wall. She held her breath, staring up at him. It was the best lighting she'd seen him—he really did have super dark eyes. Black whirlpools, intense as they swallowed her whole.

I never stood a chance.

"God, you tasted good," he echoed her thoughts from earlier, lowering his mouth to her neck.

"Tal . . . we can't . . . I'm . . . ," Mischa struggled for air. For thought.

"In another country, looking for something you aren't getting at home," he finished for her as his hands swept over her hips.

Am I that transparent?

"That doesn't mean I'm going to -," she ended in a gasp when his hands slid down to her butt and gripped her, hard.

"Yes, it does."

"No, I'm not -,"

"Yes, you are."

"Please," she whined. He chuckled.

"You'll be saying that a lot more tonight."

When his hands moved up to her breasts, she felt like she was going to jump right out of her skin—she actually jerked to the side involuntarily, her body so shocked by the contact. She started shivering and his hands stopped moving.

"My husband is the only one who's touched me like this in eight years," she whispered. There was a long pause.

"I'm willing to bet it's been a long time since *anyone* has touched you like this, *period,*" Tal called her out as the pressure from his hands increased, pushing her breasts together.

Correct.

"How do you know these things? How do you know me?" she asked. He finally lifted his head, looking down at her.

"I'm a very observant person, Mischa," he sounded serious.

She felt like shit.

"I don't know how to be this kind of woman," she said, her voice small. He chuckled.

"I'll teach you."

When Tal kissed her that time, it broke something. Broke *her.* Misch groaned and opened her mouth to his, pressed her tongue against his. She pushed her body back against his, wanting to feel every inch of him, every moment with him.

"God, oh god, oh god, oh god, what am I doing?" she panted when his mouth moved to her cleavage.

"Making two lonely people very happy," he breathed, his hands skating down to her legs. His fingers slipped against her bare thighs and began dragging their way up. Her shivering grew stronger.

"It's been so long, I don't know if I know how to do this anymore," she warned him. She choked on her voice when his fingers hit her underwear.

"You're doing fine."

"But what if I'm -,"

"Time to be quiet, Mischa."

Tal was a tall man, a lot taller than her, and he had long legs. Long arms. So of course, he had long fingers. They tapped out a rhythm against the pulse inside her thigh, made her pant in time. Then tiptoed to the side of her panties, his middle finger sneaking its way inside the material. Inside her body, inside her brain.

"God, I shouldn't be here," she groaned, moving onto her toes.

"Feels like you've been ready and waiting for this," he chuckled in a low, ominous sounding voice as his finger swam in her heat.

"Oh my god."

It wasn't at all like she'd imagined. Back in the U.S., when she'd been planning her little fling, Misch had figured she'd be a flirty vixen, with a thin veil of guilt over everything she did. But it wasn't like that. She was a shivering mess, incapable of speech, unsure of what to do, and guilt didn't exist anymore. Confliction didn't exist. Concern didn't exist. *Marriage* didn't exist.

The elevator came to a stop, but Tal didn't. He didn't pull away from her till long after the doors slid open. Then he pulled her out by her hips, walked her backwards down the hall with his mouth attached to her. He finally let go of her when he had to open his door, and they stumbled inside.

"Do you need anything?" he called out, striding across the suite. Misch shut the door behind her and slowly followed him.

The room was large. There was a kitchenette by the entrance, and she moved into the living room, which had huge picture windows with a stunning view. To the left were two large double doors, which Tal had pushed open and walked through, heading into a bathroom on the other side of the room. The *bed*room.

With a king sized bed.

I can't do this.

"What have I done!?" Misch hissed to herself, letting her bag fall to the floor as her hands went into her hair. How had she gone from a quiet drink alone, to making out with a stranger in an elevator? Granted, one of the sexiest strangers she'd ever met in her life, but still. Sexy didn't matter—*she was married.*

"Do you want anything to drink?" Tal's voice called out. She turned back around to face him. He was making his way across the bedroom, but he wasn't looking at her. He was focusing on his wrist, on taking off a large, complicated looking watch. Once he got it off, he tossed it onto a dresser, then stopped to look at her. She looked back at him.

"I can't do this," she stated bluntly.

He smiled. That annoying, smirky, sly smile.

Her panties got slightly damper.

"And why not, Mischa?" he asked, his voice low as he folded his arms across his chest.

"Because, I'm married. I don't want to hurt him. I like you, I really do, but I just . . . can't. I don't . . . I don't want this," her voice fell into a whisper.

"You don't want me?" Tal clarified. Misch looked away.

"It's not that," she sighed.

"You *do* want me."

"That doesn't matter. *I'm married.*"

"*That* didn't matter, two minutes ago."

"Well, it matters now."

"When was the last time he touched you like that?"

She looked back at Tal.

"A long time," she replied.

"*How long?*"

"Months. I'm not sure. Maybe six, maybe more."

Tal stared at her for a long moment. His eyes wandered over her face, then down her body. Clear to her feet. Back up again, lingering at her hips and breasts before locking onto her eyes.

"I would touch you like that *everyday,*" he said softly. She gave a sad laugh.

"Words are easy to say—I'm sure he felt the same way, at one point," she replied. Tal shook his head.

"No, I doubt he ever did, or else you wouldn't be here right now, about to get fucked by a different man," he corrected her. Misch shook her head.

"I told you, I can't do that with you," she stressed.

"Say you don't want to."

"What?"

"Say you don't want to. Say this isn't what you wanted when you went to that cafe tonight. *Every* night. All those bars, all those restaurants. Say this isn't what you're looking for," he commanded her.

"I don't want this," Misch's voice was barely a whisper. His eyes narrowed.

"And the rest?" he pressed, his voice hard.

It was pointless. She couldn't say it. Of course she couldn't say it. Everything he said was true.

He knew it, too. He stormed through the double doors, steaming up to her so fast, he literally swept her off her feet when his arms went around her. Her toes barely touched the carpet as he crushed her to him.

It was like he wanted to devour her. His tongue was rough and aggressive, plunging into her mouth, and the hand he'd moved to the back of her head pulled at her hair, hard enough to sting.

Just like in the elevator, there was no thought. No worry. She was pulled along by him, going in the only direction she could go—forward, at hyperspeed. There was no stopping, no shifting, no changing direction. This was it. This was *meant* to happen. This was *going* to happen. This was something she *wanted* to happen.

Misch moaned, wrapping her arms around Tal's shoulders, and eventually her legs around his waist. He carried her across the room, leaned them up against the door jam long enough for him to pull her dress straps down her arms. While she shimmied the material away from her chest, he held her close again, moving them into the bedroom.

"I don't even know you," she panted when he dropped her on the bed.

"You don't need to," he replied, pulling his shirt off. Her mouth went completely dry as she stared at his amazing body, and he took her moment of shock as an opportunity to move over her, forcing her to lay down.

"I've never slept with somebody I don't know," she babbled as he pulled her dress down her body before tossing it across the room.

"That doesn't surprise me," he chuckled, dipping his head and running his tongue over her hip bone. Her eyes rolled back in her head.

"I just can't believe I'm doing this," she continued.

"I can't believe you're still talking. Get naked," he urged, but then he took care of the problem himself—he yanked her forward and slid his hand around her back, flicking her bra open. A second later, and that item of clothing joined her dress on the floor.

His mouth immediately went to a nipple and she cried out, her hands going into his hair. She honestly couldn't remember the last time someone other than herself had touched her bare nipples, and now some gorgeous, mysterious, dark man was worshiping them.

I love Italy.

It was dark in the room, but not dark enough to hide her inhibitions. As Tal peeled her panties away from her body, Misch's shivering came back. His own pants hit the floor, then he was back on top of her, his fingers roaming over her skin, his mouth moving across her shoulder.

"How did you know?" Misch whispered, her lips close to his ear.

"Hmmm?"

"How did you know he hadn't touched me in a long time?"

"Because of this," Tal's voice was practically a hiss, and then his long finger was back between her legs, thrusting in and out. Her back arched off the bed.

"My reaction?" she gasped, hooking her nails into his shoulders.

"No, because you're so tight."

"What!?"

"*You're so tight.* You said you've been with him for eight years? No way is this pussy getting fucked on the regular. Pity, but don't worry. I'll make up for those lost years," he promised her, and a second finger joined the first.

Michael had never talked to her like that; *no one* had ever talked to her like that before. Sure, they had dabbled in some light dirty talk, but not too much. And not at all in recent times. So someone talking about her "*pussy*" so casually, it sent a thrill running through her body.

"How did you know I'd come up here with you?" Misch continued. Tal's tongue traced the outline of her nipple, then moved under the swell of her breast.

"I can spot lonely," he whispered back.

It would've been depressing, if his tongue hadn't felt so good, if his fingers hadn't felt so amazing. They erased everything. Her past, her future, her present. Gone, with one thrust. All that existed was this man, this room, this bed.

He brought her right to the edge of an orgasm, then stopped. While she moaned in protest, he moved to kneel between her legs. His hand gripped her knee, holding it up against his hip. She was still coming down off the high his fingers had given her, so it wasn't till he was pressing against her, pushing inside of her, that she realized what was happening. She froze, started to panic, started to say stop—"*wait, I'm not ready! This makes it real!*"—but then it was too late. He was already sliding his way into a snug fit.

Oh. My. God. I'd forgotten they come in different sizes.

"Wait, wait, wait," she breathed, pressing on his shoulders. His hips stopped moving.

"You're fine," he assured her, kissing and sucking at the sensitive spot under her ear.

"I don't think this is going to happen," she was now gasping for air, squirming under his weight.

"Why?"

"Because, your dick is *huge.*"

Tal laughed loudly, which made her laugh, and in that instant of distraction, he jerked his hips forward. Suddenly, they were flush. Misch's laugh turned into a cry, and she was pretty sure her fingernails drew blood from his skin.

"*Holy. Fuck,*" she managed to say. Her shivering was so bad, her teeth were actually chattering.

"You feel so good," he groaned, his hips twisting against hers. Making room.

"I . . . um . . . ," thoughts apparently didn't exist anymore.

She began to relax and Tal picked up on that, his hips gaining speed. Thrusting harder. She cried out in time to his rhythm, to his dance. She didn't remember the steps anymore—he was showing her. He pulled away from her, moving to lean back on his knees, and she closed her eyes, rubbing her lips together.

"Fuck, I wish you could see yourself the way I see you," he told her, his hands holding onto her hips and lifting her to him.

"I wish I could feel me the way you do," Misch replied.

"Open your eyes."

"What?"

His hand was suddenly gripping her jaw, almost painfully so, and he forced her head to face forward. She opened her eyes to find him staring down at her. He held her in place, his eyes boring into her.

"Keep your eyes open," he commanded, then his hand fell away.

Misch's eyes lingered on his shoulders, on his chest. On the sweat that was running down his body, getting caught in the lines and definitions of his muscles. Whatever Tal did, it must have required him to keep in shape. Her eyes followed the lines, down to his abs, down to the V cut into his hips. Down to where his pelvis met hers, where it thrust back and forth against her.

"God, you're amazing," she breathed, licking her lips. He chuckled.

"You're welcome."

He was pounding into her so hard, she couldn't think straight.

She'd never had sex like that, never been fucked like that before. It was scary and amazing and so much more than anything she'd ever expected. He hadn't even been inside her that long, and she could already feel an orgasm blooming low in her body.

"Holy shit. Holy fuck," she cried out, her hands moving to her breasts, squeezing them.

"Ms. Rapaport, I think you're about to come," he informed her.

She didn't correct his use of her name.

"Me, too," she panted.

"Hmmm, not yet," he whispered.

He pulled away from her and she actually cried out at the loss. She had been empty for so long, she never wanted to not be full of him. But before she could complain, he laid down on her, kissing her sloppily. She sighed against his mouth, tracing her fingers across his slick shoulders.

He kept moving, his mouth running over her chin. Down her throat. Down to her left breast. His teeth grazed the tightened nipple and she hissed. She felt him smile against her, then he was moving again. Tongue sliding down the very center of her stomach. To the very center of her legs. When he actually tried to press his tongue inside of her, she gasped so hard she choked on air.

"Please. Please, Tal, please," she whined, her fingers twisting in his hair.

"It's been so long for you, hasn't it, baby," he sighed, kissing the inside of her thigh.

"Yes, yes," she whispered.

"How often do you touch yourself?"

"A lot."

"Everyday?"

"Almost."

"From now on, you'll be thinking of me when you do this," he whispered, hooking his two fingers inside of her.

"I will," she agreed.

Then he was lapping her up like she was warm milk, and she was back in that timeless existence. She lifted her hips up, pressing herself against his mouth. She never wanted to be away from it.

He worked the orgasm out of her slowly, almost like it was a game.

Cat and mouse. His tongue would drive her to the edge, then he'd pull away, work his fingers. She couldn't remember if she'd ever experienced an orgasm from just penetration, but she was willing to let him have a go at it. But then he switched it up again, and his tongue and fingers were tag-teaming her.

She shrieked when she came, both her hands in his hair, holding him to her. He didn't seem to mind, just pressed his tongue completely flat against her as hard as he could. She shrieked again, the shivers taking hold of her once more. Then she completely relaxed, let every muscle in her body go limp.

When was the last time I did this? Just went limp? Ever?

"That was outstanding," he laughed, pulling away from her.

"Yes," she agreed, pressing a hand to her chest.

Her eyes were closed, so she wasn't aware of what he was doing. Just that he had moved far enough away that she couldn't feel him. Suddenly, his hands were on her hips. He flipped her onto her stomach, surprising her a little. She tried to ask what was going on, but then her hips were yanked up. As she tried to push herself up onto her hands, he slammed into her.

She actually screamed. She hadn't had sex in a long time, and he was a large man. She was almost uncomfortably full. But Tal either didn't notice or didn't care. She was assuming it was the latter, because he slapped her on the ass—two times, more for show. A third time, to sting.

"So fucking hot, so fucking good," he hissed, holding onto her hips and pulling her back every time he slammed forward.

She literally couldn't breathe. Or at least that's what it felt like to Misch. Her mouth was open, her face pressed against the mattress, her hands above her head. She pressed them against the wall, used that to shove back into him. It felt like his dick was brushing against the base of her brain. Interfering with basic thought process.

This is fucking amazing.

He roughly grabbed her left arm and yanked it behind her back. He pulled on it till she was forced up off the mattress, forced to arch her back towards him. Then he pinned her wrist to the bottom of her spine, just above her ass. His other hand worked its way to her front, squeezing her breast. Pinching her nipple.

"Oh. My. God. Tal. Please," she panted along with his thrusts. He gripped harder on her breast, pulled harder on her arm, forced her back closer to him.

"I'm gonna come soon, Mischa," he whispered, leaning close so his lips were at her ear, his teeth grazing it.

"Me, too. Me, too," she cried. She couldn't believe it. She'd only ever come twice during sex maybe a handful of times in her entire life—even with herself! Now a complete stranger was going to accomplish it like he had been training for it.

"Good girl. Very good girl."

His hand let go of her breast and slithered down her body, pressing between her thighs. Those long fingers, goddamn. She could feel a finger on either side of his dick, then he was pulling back, drumming his fingers against her sensitive skin. Then back again, sliding against his thrusts. So many sensations, so little time.

She screamed his name, coming hard enough that she couldn't maintain her balance. She fell forward and he let her arm go, let her top half fall flat on the mattress. She whimpered and shuddered and clenched, all while he slammed away. Then he let out a roar, and she could actually *feel* him coming, feel him pumping into her. He bent over her, his chest pressed to her back.

Misch wasn't sure how long they laid like that together. Long enough that her knees slowly slid out from underneath her. He went down with her and she laid flat on the bed, with him on top of her. He panted, his breath hot against the back of her neck. His hand rested on top of her arm, his thumb brushing back and forth.

"You do that like it's your sport in the Olympics," she managed to breathe. He snorted at her.

"Do I get all tens?" he asked.

"Fuck yeah."

He kissed her in the middle of her shoulder blades, then pushed himself off of her. She closed her eyes, ready to pass out, but he grabbed her arm again and began pulling her off the bed.

"C'mon, let me show you what I can do with a detachable shower head," he said in a low voice, pulling her towards the bathroom.

I love Italy.

There was an incessant chirping noise. Misch waved her hand at it, but it didn't go away. She groaned and tried to unbury herself from the blanket and pillows that seemed to be all over her. She didn't remember there being so many pillows on her bed before, she'd have to toss some onto the floor.

She finally broke free, and reality crashed in on her. They weren't her pillows. It wasn't her bed. It wasn't her room. Not even her hotel. In fact, she didn't even know what hotel she was in *at all*.

Oh fuck oh fuck oh fuck oh fuck. What have I done!?

"Answer your goddamn phone," a voice grumbled near her.

Misch jumped, a little startled, and turned to the lump next to her. Tal was laying on his stomach. She pressed her hands over her face for a second, then looked at him again. The sheet had been yanked away from him, only covering his legs up to his thighs, revealing the fact that he wasn't wearing any clothing.

Neither was she.

Misch slithered sideways out of the bed, taking the top blanket with her, leaving the sheet for him. When she had the blanket wrapped around her body, she tiptoed across the suite. Found her bag where it had fallen on the floor. She dug through it till she located the chirping noise. She pulled out her cell phone and looked at the screen.

Mikey Boy

She felt sick, to the point she pressed a hand over her mouth to stop herself from throwing up right then and there. To make matters worse, she heard movement from the bedroom. Tal was getting out of bed.

"I'm gonna take another shower. Wanna join me?" he asked through a yawn. She shook her head.

"No," she managed to answer, though her voice was coming from somewhere near the middle of her throat.

"You sure?"

His voice sounded sly, and out of the corner of her eye, she could see him strut past the bedroom door, still completely naked.

She refused to take a second look.

"I'm sure," she replied. Her phone stopped chirping and she looked down. She had a new voicemail.

"Your loss. I'll be a couple minutes, order us breakfast," he called out. Then she heard the bathroom door shut, quickly followed by the shower turning on.

Misch went into full blown panic mode. She ran around the hotel room, searching for her shit. She wiggled her panties back on, but couldn't find her bra anywhere. She gave up and slid her dress on without it. Glanced in the mirror. She actually had pretty good breasts, she didn't really need a bra, but she felt like when she didn't wear one and it was obvious, like it was with that dress, it screamed "*slut.*"

Well, technically, if the slutty shoe fits . . .

"Oh god," she moaned out loud, digging her shoes out from underneath the bed.

She rushed across the hotel room, swiping a pair of sunglasses on her way out the door. Her hands were shaking as she put them on in the elevator, but by the time she got out at the lobby, she was almost in control of herself again.

Almost.

It wasn't till she got to her own hotel that she realized she'd left her purse back at Tal's. There really wasn't much of importance left behind—thankfully her wallet and passport weren't in it. Just some necessities for spending a day out and about were in the purse. But it also had her insurance binder, and her hotel room key card.

Fuck.

"I'm sorry, I misplaced my key," she said in a low voice at the front desk. She felt like the clerk was staring at her.

Can people just tell!? Does it say "heartless cheating bitch" on my forehead!?

But no one said anything, and she was issued a new key. Her phone started ringing again on the way up to her room, but she still couldn't talk to Mike.

No, that would have to wait till the tears stopped. They had started on the elevator ride up, and weren't showing any signs of stopping. Not when she got into her room. Not when she crawled into her shower. And not when her husband called again, an hour later.

Mischa

SOMETHING I HAVE LEARNED in life is that things are never as they seem.

You think love is one thing—turns out, it's whole big barrel of fucked-up-ness.

You think marriage is one thing—turns out, it's an even bigger barrel of fucked-up-ness.

You think you can plan something down to the letter—but really, things will go down however they're going to go down, regardless of your planning.

You think you've made up your mind—but someone can make it up for you.

You think you're resolved to do something—and then you do the exact opposite.

God, everything I've ever thought is wrong. *Every. Fucking. Thing.* Mike. My feelings for him. Our marriage. How I could fix it. How I couldn't fix it. How I could cheat to feel better about myself. How I could keep it a secret so he could continue feeling good about himself.

Wrong.

I had resigned myself to *not* cheat—then it had happened.

I thought it would make me feel better—it made me feel *amazing*.

I thought I could keep it secret—there was no way I couldn't tell him.

Telephone Speak

"*H*^{*I.*}" Misch twisted a lock of hair around her finger. She'd given herself many hours to calm down, to think of what she would say. In her original "plan," she had been ready to keep it a secret. Just a one time fling she could keep to herself, a memory to keep her warm. Having actually gone through with it, though, she quickly realized there was no way she could keep it a secret. There was no way he could never know.

For starters, she was feeling an odd combination of amazing and wretched. Tal had fucked her into another plane of existence—part of her had stayed there. She had never had sex like that; Tal had made her feel things that no one else had ever made her feel. It was like he'd owned her body, yet had given it back to her. She was a Rubik's cube, and Tal had solved her.

Wretched because it wasn't right. She knew it wasn't right. Mike was still her husband. Still her best friend. It was so fucked up, but when she'd been reliving some of her moments from the night before, she'd had the strongest urge to call Mike, to talk about it with him. Like they did with everything.

It made her feel sick.

She couldn't keep that from him. Couldn't keep something so monumental from her best friend. *Couldn't lie to her husband.* She didn't know how she had ever convinced herself it was even a possibility. She felt like she was drowning. It was awful.

She had slept with someone. Let another man fuck her. Now it was over, she'd gotten it out of her system. She would throw herself into her work, she would tell Mike the truth, and she would get on with her life.

Whatever kind of life it will be . . . please, don't let him hate me.

"Hey, babe! How are you? I was getting worried," Mike's voice sounded scratchy over the line.

"Sorry, I was kind of out of sorts today. Took a shower, took a nap," Mischa told him.

Fucked myself with my fingers, pretended they were another man's—someone with dark eyes and a strange name.

"Rough life," he laughed.

"Look," she sighed, "I wanted to talk to you about -,"

"Oh, hey! I meant to tell you, my mom is coming to stay here while you're gone," he interrupted her. She scowled.

"What? Why? You know I hate it when she messes with my stuff," Misch complained.

"C'mon, it's not so bad. She'll take care of me while you're gone," Mike pointed out.

"I don't like it. I don't like that she -,"

"Oh! And Roger scored tickets to a basketball game, I'm finally gonna see . . . ," he interrupted again, and that was it. Misch was staring out the window, watching the breeze ruffle the gauzy curtains. While her husband prattled on, her mind wandered. Made its way back to a moment in time that involved long fingers and a tricky smile.

She shook her head.

This isn't right. He never listens to me, just wants to talk, and I never listen, and don't care what he has to say.

"*Mike*," she said his name sharply.

"What's up?" he responded, chewing on something.

"We need to talk," she gentled her voice.

"I thought that's what we were doing," he laughed. She glared again.

"No, that's what *you* were doing. I haven't opened my mouth in ten minutes," she snapped.

"Babe, I've told you, you gotta speak up. You get mad, but how can I know you want to talk if you never say anything?" he chuckled. The urge to throttle him was strong.

Calm down. You're a lying, cheating, slut-bag—he's allowed to be a dick.

"We need to talk about *us,*" she stressed. There was a long pause.

"What about us?" he asked.

"We've got some problems, Mikey. Some *big* problems," she sighed.

"It's not that bad, babe. It just seems like that cause you're so far away," he tried to convince her.

Soooooo far away, you have no idea.

"It's seemed like that for a while, Mikey. Look, is there anyway you can bump up your trip?" she asked. She couldn't tell him over the phone. She had to tell him to his face.

"You know I can't. I'll be there in three weeks, babe. I miss you, too," he told her.

"Alright. But when you get here, we are going to have a *long talk,*" she informed him.

"Whatever you want. Look, I gotta go, mom just rolled up. Love ya," he prattled. She rolled her eyes.

"Love ya."

The phone went dead.

Misch spent the day in bed, trying not to feel sorry for herself. Failing miserably. The whole thing had been like . . . sky diving. It was all fine and dandy for a person to say they were gonna jump out of a plane, but a mile in the air, it was a little different. She'd told herself she wouldn't do it. She'd told the plane to turn around. In the back of her mind, she'd really thought she'd never leap.

Boy, did I leap.

She took another shower, cried some more. Ordered room service for herself. She knew she had to get her shit together, she had to be back in the office the next day. Which that thought only reminded her of something else—she had to get her purse back from Tal. She needed that insurance manual.

Fuuuuuuuuuuck.

Night Games

"LET'S GO, GO, GO! We ain't got all day!"

A hand beat against a car roof top, and Tal looked up as he walked out of his hotel. A black Range Rover was parked at the curb. A man was standing on the other side of it, now drumming his fingers on the roof top.

"Be careful with my baby," Tal warned as he slid into the vehicle. "I let you borrow my car—that doesn't mean you get to abuse it."

"Someone's in a peachy mood. What the fuck happened to you?" the other man, Ruiz, asked as he got in the car as well.

"Nothing happened to me."

"Really? Cause I called you a dozen times last night. Why didn't you answer?"

Tal finally smiled.

"I was busy," was all he said, but Ruiz smiled as well.

"Aw, shit. I knew it. Can't leave you alone for a second. You gotta slow down, man, leave some Italian hotties for the rest of us," he joked. Tal shook his head.

"She wasn't Italian. American," he corrected his partner.

"Whoa. Switching it up. Where'd you find an American?"

"I've seen her around."

"You've been scouting this chick?"

"Eh. She wound up in my line of sight," Tal answered sideways. The car roared down side streets, earning curses and shouts from locals.

"Sounds dangerous. Was she any good?" Ruiz questioned. Tal closed his eyes.

"Yeah. Yeah, she was pretty good."

Mischa, *Mrs. Rapaport,* had definitely been a pleasant little surprise. The first time he'd seen her up close, she'd been in her own hotel's bar. All dressed up, with nowhere to go. She had seemed skittish, and whenever men talked to her, she'd looked ready to have a nervous breakdown. But she'd been dressed up like she wanted to get fucked.

What was the deal? He had to know more.

Saving her from her unwelcome guest the night before had been a calculated move—Tal had only been at the cafe because he'd walked by and had seen her sitting at a table. Helping her, well, that had just been a treat from fate. A way in, an excuse to talk to her.

She was good looking, but had no clue, which was usually the best kind of woman. Dark hair, hazel eyes, amazing body, fan-fucking-tastic legs, great tits. She was racially ambiguous, he couldn't quite tell what all was going on there. Maybe Spanish. Definitely some Caucasian. Possibly Asian. *Exotic.* She looked exotic, and Tal *loved* to visit exotic places.

He didn't give two fucks that she was married. Clearly, Mr. Rapaport wasn't taking care of his business at home. Tal was more than happy to look after his interests abroad. She'd been nervous, and scared, and at war with herself, but Tal knew he was a hard man to resist. He was used to getting what he wanted.

God, I wanted her so bad.

Despite her nerves, she'd been incredible. So eager, so ready, so excitable. Wet at just a look from him, he loved women like that. Loved it when they spread their legs and said *"please, sir, I want some more"*; he was ever so happy to oblige. She was a little lost, and had been willing to let him guide her. Gave him the excuse to be bossy—not that he needed one, but it was so much better when it wasn't a battle. There had been hesitancy in her eyes, but she'd always done as she was told. Got down on her knees in his shower, bent over the railing on his balcony, rode his face in the bedroom.

Charming. What an utterly charming woman.

He would have gladly gone for round two and a goodbye fuck the next morning, but she snuck out while he was in the shower. He had halfway expected her to, but a small part of him had hoped she wouldn't. She was gorgeous, and great in bed, and clearly was only looking for someone to remind her what sex was like—they were a perfect match. Doubles tennis, they could pass away the summer days batting each other back and forth.

Apparently, Mrs. Rapaport doesn't like to play.

"You gonna hit her up again?" Ruiz interrupted Tal's thoughts. They finally broke out onto a dirt road, and the Rover ate up the kilometers.

"I don't know. Depends on how busy we get," Tal replied, shaking the steamy memories out of his imagination.

"But you would?"

"Yeah. Sure. She was nice."

"Nice!?"

Tal cleared his throat.

"A nice fuck. Do you know where we're going?"

"Chill, I know what I'm doing. Do you know what *you're* doing? Eyes on the prize, man. I don't want things getting screwed up cause you're thinking about pussy," Ruiz cautioned. Tal glared at him.

"Don't forget who you're talking to, asshole, and just drive," he snapped.

Ruiz didn't respond, but he smiled as he looked out the windshield.

The night was completely black, stars twinkling high above. Tal knew he needed to get his head in the game. They had an important job, and a limited amount of time to do it in, and he certainly *did not* need to be thinking about Mrs. Rapaport. Had no right to be thinking about her. Still, his mind kept wandering back to a nervous dancer with amazing legs.

I wonder how flexible she is . . .

The Affair

*Y*OU CAN DO THIS, *Misch. You got this. You're a confident woman. You're a strong, self-assured, confident woman. You're a take charge, take no shit, strong, self-assured . . . who am I kidding. I'm a pussy. Somebody help!*

Misch took a deep breath and barreled through the doors to the hotel. To *Tal's* hotel.

She'd avoided it for two days. Had gone to work, then straight back to her hotel. She didn't know his phone number, he didn't know hers. He didn't know where she was working, what hotel she was staying in, it should have been perfect. She would've never had to see him again.

If I wasn't such a fucking idiot.

She'd coasted along without her binder for those couple days, but it was too hard. She needed her rules and regulations guide, and her boss was demanding to see it, as well. She had to get it back.

So there she was, walking back through Tal's hotel, in the harsh light of the morning. She'd figured going before work was best—she had a great excuse to dash in and out. She could say hello, thank him for his amazing pussy pounding abilities, then get the fuck out of there.

Like an adult. Yeah. Totally.

"Hi," she said at the front desk, and cursed her voice for sounding nervous. A clerk smiled at her.

"Can I help you?"

"Yes, I'm trying to reach one of your guests, Mr. Canaan? In suite 405—could you call and see if he's available?" Misch asked.

The clerk said yes, then picked up the phone. But there was no answer on Tal's end. He must not have been in the room. Ug, Misch didn't want to have to make the trip again in the afternoon. She explained her plight to the clerk, hammed it up, tried to appeal to the other woman's feminine sensibilities.

They finally reached a deal. Misch couldn't be allowed to go walk around the room willy-nilly, but a housekeeper could go with her and they go in together and could locate the purse. If there was identification in the purse showing that it belonged to her, then Misch could take it. Perfect!

As she rode the elevator up, she couldn't believe her luck. She'd be able to get her things back, and not have to interact with him. Her impending heart attack started to fade away. She was embarrassed by the way she'd behaved with him, embarrassed that she'd slept with him after knowing him for only a couple hours, embarrassed by the way she'd run away, and if she was honest with herself, she was nervous about her performance. She hadn't had sex in a long time. What if she hadn't been very good?

Couldn't have been awful, he barely let you sleep.

Misch was a little surprised to see his suite door standing open. It couldn't have been more than a minute since she'd left the counter, and the housekeeping manager had said it would be a few minutes. How had the other woman gotten there so fast? Oh, well. The faster Misch got out of there, the better.

She was halfway across the suite when she realized something wasn't right. There was a housekeeping cart parked inside the door— why would the manager have brought that? And there were also noises. Like someone was panting. And something else. Something like . . . something like . . .

She got to the bedroom doors and froze. They were wide open, like they'd been the last time she'd been there. And much like the last time she'd been there, Tal was naked. And fucking somebody.

Just not her.

He was standing at the foot of his bed, and a woman was laying underneath him. Her legs were splayed in the air, and he was holding her by the ankles. Misch assumed it was a maid, based on the sensible white sneakers and ankle socks the other woman was still wearing. The panting gave way to moans and shrieks. Familiar sounds.

Oh. My. God.

Mischa turned in a couple circles, looking for her bag. Freaking out. She spied it on a couch and dashed over to it. Clutched it to her chest, then whirled back around, peeking in the bedroom. They were still going at it—Tal had even moved so one knee was on the mattress, allowing him to thrust even harder. Misch chewed on her bottom lip and couldn't deny that it was pretty hot.

Cheating slut-bag AND a pervert, my evolution continues. Shoot me now.

She tiptoed across the doorway, turning as she went, watching them to make sure no one saw her. But she hadn't looked before she turned, and she rammed into an end table, knocking over some glasses. She spun back around, trying to grab them, but only succeeded in knocking more over. Fuck. She leapt upright and bolted for the door.

"Mischa?"

Busted.

"Hey, Tal, I just had to get my . . . oh, muh . . . uhmm . . . ," Misch began to stutter as she turned around.

He was still completely naked, walking towards her, his dick pointing the way. She tried not to stare. Couldn't *not* stare. Finally pressed her lips together and looked over his shoulder. She couldn't look at him. In clothes, he was one of the best looking men she'd ever met, but naked, he was unbearable. All muscle and mocha skin and dark outlines—black hair, black eyebrows, black eyes. One flash of his naughty smile, and she knew she'd be done for.

"Oh yeah, your bag. I was wondering when you were gonna show up," he chuckled, stopping a couple feet from her. Misch shifted from foot to foot.

"I needed it," she replied.

Awk-fucking-ward.

"You ran away so quick the other morning. Did I scare you?" he asked, folding his arms across his chest.

"No."

"Then you didn't come back for the bag, it's been a couple days."

"Been busy."

"Your vocabulary was a lot bigger the other night."

"The vodka helped."

Before they could go back and forth anymore, his afternoon delight made an appearance.

"Are we done?" the maid snapped, walking into the living room. She was wearing a cute uniform, a short dress, but almost all the buttons down the front were undone, revealing a racy red bra. Her hair was a messy bush around her head.

"Oh yeah," Tal said in a low voice, his eyes never leaving Mischa's. "We're done."

Misch swallowed thickly.

"But I wasn't finished!" the woman had a thick Italian accent, and she stomped over to Tal.

"*I* am," he replied, then he ran his teeth over his bottom lip. His gaze was making Misch heat up. Sizzle. Catch fire.

"I have to go," she said softly, hugging her bag tighter to her breasts.

"I don't think so," Tal's voice was equally as soft.

"*What is going on in here!?*"

The voice behind them was shrill and Misch turned, stepping to the side as she did so. It was the housekeeping manager, and she looked *pissed*. She strode into the room and began yelling in Italian, steaming up to the maid. The younger woman held up her hands, gesturing at Tal. He turned towards both of them, and the manager shrieked, just then noticing his nudity.

What the fuck did I get into!?

Misch practically ran from the room, hurrying to the elevators. She pressed the down button, over and over again. Prayed for it to open up. Of course it didn't. Footsteps came down the hall behind her.

"Wait, wait, wait, no running away," Tal sighed, then he grabbed her shoulder, slowly turning her around. He'd wrapped a towel around his waist, thank god.

"I'm not running away," she said quickly. "I came for my purse. Now I'm going home."

"Babe, I don't think you know what home is anymore," he laughed. She glared at him.

"Don't be cute, we don't know each other well enough."

"We know each other pretty well."

The elevator pinged open and Misch hurried onto it.

"I'm sorry I interrupted you, back there," she blurted out. Tal braced his hand against the door, keeping it open.

"Is that why you're upset?" he guessed. She snorted.

"I'm not upset. Really. Just . . . caught off guard. You can do any maid you want. I just don't particularly want to watch," she even laughed as she said it. He smiled, and she felt warm inside.

He had a great smile, very wide, showing lots of teeth.

"Good to know. So when can I -," but Tal was cut off, by the housekeeping manager screeching at him. He stepped away from the elevator, turned towards the commotion.

Saved.

The doors slid shut, and Misch was quick to hit the lobby button. Then she fell back against the wall, closing her eyes. Went over everything she'd just seen.

Tal was not her boyfriend. For god's sake, *she was married.* She had no claim on him, no ownership. In fact, she'd ditched him, after he had given her an amazing night. Had given her exactly what she'd been hoping for, and so much more. So his private life was his business, and absolutely none of hers.

But it still hadn't felt very good, watching him do to another woman what he'd been doing to her only a couple nights ago.

I deserved it.

As she walked down the street, Misch slid on a pair of sunglasses and slipped her purse strap over her shoulder. That was a chapter in her life that was closed. Thankfully. She wasn't cut out to be a cheating vixen. The persona hadn't suited her at all. Best to leave it back in that hotel room, with a man who was far sexier than Mischa would ever be.

Her back pocket began to vibrate. Misch grimaced; she'd been avoiding Mike's phone calls. She couldn't talk to him, not with her secret weighing down her soul. But when she pulled her phone out, it wasn't his number. It wasn't any number, technically. Just *0–0–0–0,* scrolling across the screen. She frowned and brought the phone to her ear.

"This is Mischa Rapaport," she answered in a brisk tone, sounding professional. Maybe it was her boss, calling from a local line.

"What's your maiden name?"

She stopped walking, completely shocked.

"How did you get my number!?" she asked, automatically glancing around her. Tal's deep voice chuckled in her ear.

"I'm a man of many talents," he replied.

Not creepy at all . . .

"Did you go through my purse?" she demanded.

"Wouldn't dream of it. Besides, your number wasn't on anything that was in there," he answered.

"What!?"

"When can I see you again?" he ignored her. Misch sighed and moved into a small alley.

"Look, Tal. I like you, and you did a really nice thing for me. But it can't happen again," she told him, keeping her voice down.

"Why not?"

"Because I'm married. Because it was a mistake. Because I thought it would make me feel better, but I just feel worse," she tried to explain.

"I call bullshit. You were feeling pretty amazing the other night. I could make you feel like that *every* night," he offered. She cleared her throat, fanning her hand in front of her face. Was it hotter than normal?

"Looks like you have other women you can make feel '*amazing*'," Misch called him out.

"Ooohhh, jealousy, I like it," he teased. She snorted.

"I'm not jealous," she lied. "I'm just not that kind of girl."

"Oh really. And what kind of girl are you referring to?"

"I'm not like her, I'm not some . . . some . . . some slut," she tried to explain. He chuckled again. It came from deep in his throat, and was like an electric jolt that shot from her ear straight to between her legs.

"You're a married woman who, three nights ago, *begged me* to fuck her. Several different times. Mrs. Rapaport, I'm pretty sure you're the definition of a '*slut*'."

Misch hung up on him. She gasped in air, glancing around again. Why, she wasn't sure. It wasn't like anyone could have heard him, or would have cared. She waited for her phone to vibrate, for him to call her back. She would throw her phone away if he did. But he didn't. And after a couple minutes, she caught her breath. Crept back out of the alley, like some sort of creature of the night.

Almost.

Slut. Misch could honestly say she'd never been called that before, had certainly never done anything that would earn her that name. She'd lost her virginity at fifteen, to her boyfriend. Second guy she slept with was a guy she'd dated during her freshman year of college. And of course after that, Mike. Only Mike. Slut was a word that belonged on other women, she'd always thought.

Now it belonged on her.

She should've been angry at Tal. It should've offended her. But truthfully, it kind of turned her on. He hadn't sneered it at her, he hadn't said it in a mean way. His voice had been low, and she could practically hear his sly little smile, wrapping itself around his words. Picture his dark eyes, narrowing on her. His long fingers, teasing her. He made her want to be slutty. Made her want to do slutty things, with him.

But it wasn't meant to be. She'd had two full days to go over her reaction to her indiscretion. The moment had been great. Beyond great. *Amazing.* But the afterwards had been like the hangover from hell, and she still wasn't free of it. She had an acute sense of what an alcoholic felt like; sobriety was hell. She wouldn't put herself through that again.

*Oh, yeah, and there's the little fact that cheating on your husband is **bad**. Fuck, I'm such a bitch.*

Work was torturous, and to make matters worse, at the last minute before leaving work, she agreed to dinner with her boss and some of the Italian people who would be running the office after they left. All she wanted to do was curl up in her bed and think about what an awful person she was; she didn't want to press palms and talk about how awesome insurance was. Barf.

They were going to an upscale restaurant, so she took care getting ready. Slid on a tight black dress, did her makeup, blew out her hair. Italians all seemed to have amazing fashion sense, everyone looked like they'd stepped out of the pages of a magazine, and she didn't want to look schlumpy in comparison.

She stared at her reflection in the mirror, and she had to admit, she looked good. Really good. *Sexy.* Tal had done that for her, reminded her that she could still be sexy. Reminded her that other people thought she was sexy. It was nice. Nice to feel attractive. Nice to feel wanted. She tried to cling to that and pushed away the bad feelings. She would have enough of those when she had her talk with Michael.

Mischa got to the restaurant early, no one else was there yet. She was shown to a large, semi-circle booth. She slid towards the center of the seating and ordered a glass of pinot grigio. It was brought to her, and she sipped at it while she waited.

And waited. And waited.

Twenty minutes late was her cut off, and she started to turn in place, wondering if she'd been seated at the wrong table. But as she twisted to the left, looking over her shoulder, someone slid into the booth at her right.

"You clean up good," Tal's voice was in her ear.

Misch yelped and jumped about a mile high. She turned to face him.

"*What the fuck are you doing!?*" she squeaked, pressing her hand to her chest.

"I told you, I wanted to see you again," he answered, squeezing in close to her side. She gaped as he reached across her and grabbed her wine glass, taking a sip from it.

"You can't be here! You have to go!" she hissed, shoving against his ribs, trying to get him to move.

Oh my god. Oh my god. My one-night-stand that wouldn't die. Why can't he just disappear!?

"Why? Goddamn, Misch, you really look amazing," he complimented her, leaning back so he could look her over. She blushed, but refused to be taken in by his flattery.

"I'm dressed up because I'm having dinner *with my boss,*" she explained, sweeping her gaze across the restaurant, paranoid that they were about to be caught.

"Wow, lucky guy. You screwing him, too?"

She gasped.

"*Fuck you,*" Misch swore, standing as best she could and starting to wiggle away from him. He grabbed her hip and yanked her down.

"*I'm teasing you.* You need to loosen up," he chuckled at her. She shook her head, trying to shake him out of her brain.

"What are you doing here? How did you know I was here?" she asked, pushing at the hand he still had on her hip.

"I told you, man of many talents," was all he replied, then he took another drink of her wine.

Misch stared up at him, simply amazed. She couldn't believe he was there, sitting next to her. Bubble, officially burst. Mr. Canaan was a real life man, flesh and blood, not some fantasy to be locked away in some hotel room, shoved to the back of her brain. And the fantasy-come-to-life sitting next to her happened to be dressed up, as well, in a pair of slacks, a blazer, and an off white dress shirt. He had looked sexy the other night, in just a t-shirt and jeans, but now, holy hot damn, her panties had just combusted. Sexy didn't cover how he looked that evening.

Though to be completely honest, he looked best in the towel.

"Tal, we can't do this," Misch lowered her voice. "You did me a huge favor the other night, really. I appreciate it, more than I can say. But it ended in that room."

His hand moved off of her hip and across her lap. Came to rest on her bare thigh. Her voice caught in her throat.

"Oh, no. No, I don't think so. I don't think it ended at all. I think it's still very much going on," he breathed, sliding his hand up, moving the skirt of her dress out of the way.

"Tal, please," she whimpered.

Whimpering. The man makes me whimper.

"Ah, there's that word I love."

"My boss could walk up any minute," she hissed, pressing herself back into the cushioned booth, trying to gain some distance.

"Don't worry about your boss," Tal whispered, dipping his head and kissing her temple.

"*We can't.* He knows I'm married," she whispered back, squirming as Tal's hand pushed the last bit of material out of the way. If a waiter popped up, he'd have a great view of Misch's hot pink underwear.

"I told you, don't worry."

"Don't worry!? How can I not -,"

She gasped as his thumb slid under the crotch of her panties. While her lips were parted, he dove in, kissing her hard. She moaned, welcoming him. Fuck, she'd cook him dinner and rub his feet, if he'd just keep touching her. Just keep wanting her.

"I love that you're always so ready for me," he pulled away to laugh at her. She gripped onto his arm.

"Oh my god, I'm gonna get fired," she panted, but made no move to stop him. His thumb was ridiculously dexterous; she wondered if he was double jointed. It swam in circles, making her dizzy.

"You won't get fired, I promise," he had his sly smile on, and he actually rested an elbow on the back of the booth, propping his cheek against his fist. His relaxation actually made her more aware of their surroundings. She was sitting in the middle of a nice restaurant, waiting for her boss, and she had a man's thumb in her crotch.

Slut.

"Someone's going to see us. Please."

"You know what's funny," he ignored her. "This really wasn't my plan when I decided to come here. I thought we could have a drink, talk. I could watch you laugh. You have a great laugh. But then I sat down, and you're wearing this amazing dress, showing those amazing legs, and well, here we are."

"I don't want to be doing this," she begged.

"Why not?"

"Because," she couldn't finish the sentence. Didn't want to say it out loud. Wanted to pretend that she was begging him to stop for the right reasons.

"Because *why?*"

I'm such an awful person.

"Because, you were fucking that maid. I don't want to be just another lay in your daily rotations."

He chuckled again.

"I wanted to be fucking you," he whispered. "Since our night together, that's all I've thought about. All I've wanted to do. From this point on, you're going to be the only person I fuck while I'm here."

"Tal, please, I'm going to . . . I'm about to . . . ," she couldn't catch her breath. She was too busy trying to stave off a huge orgasm.

"*Shhhh,*" he shushed her. Then his thumb was gone. He pulled his fingers free of her underwear, ran it up her body. Rested his hand against the side of her jaw. She was breathing heavily through her nose, staring up at him. He stared right back and pressed his dewy thumb against her bottom lip. Traced it back and forth.

Resistance is so fucking futile.

"What are you doing to me?" she whispered. He smiled, then stuck his thumb in his mouth, sucking her wetness away.

"Anything you want, babe. *Come find me,*" he whispered back.

Then he was sliding out of his seat. Walking away.

Misch dropped her head back on the booth, tried to catch her breath. She pressed a hand to her chest and gulped in air. She had thought the night was going to be boring. Shmoozing their international partners, talking about insurance, trying to tell bad jokes in broken Italian. Getting off in the middle of a crowded dining room hadn't been part of the plan.

Mr. Canaan had never been part of the plan.

"*Rapaport!*"

Mischa sat upright. Her boss was waving at her, making his way towards the table. There were people trailing behind him, smiling and laughing. Misch quelled a panic attack and hurriedly shoved her dress back into place. She managed to stand and shake hands. Even smiled. Didn't say much of anything.

One minute. If he had walked in one minute earlier . . .

Her boss spoke Italian, and most of the conversation took place in that language. Mischa drank what was left of her wine and tried to think about home. Thought about Tal instead. Thought of that naughty smile and those talented fingers.

Come find me.

Bold man. Brash man. He was supposed to be a one night stand. He should just fade away. Isn't that what men wanted? A night of no strings attached, anything goes sex? Apparently not that man. Well, that's what *she* wanted. Nothing more. Right? *Right!?*

Come find me.

She didn't want to be *that* woman. The woman carrying on an illicit affair. Acting scandalous while her husband was oblivious in another country. How wretched. How horrible. *How cliché.* She didn't want to hurt Mike more than she already had; it would be bad enough telling him everything that had happened. Did she really want to add more sins to the pot?

Come find me.

"Excuse me," Misch murmured, shoving her way out of the booth. Appetizers had just been delivered. She had a while before dinner. She smiled her thanks as she walked away from the table.

Come find me.

The decision had been made, she'd had no say in it. Resistance *was* futile. Tal had flipped a switch, and she was revved up and pointed in one direction. *His* direction. There was no other course of action, no option. She couldn't see anything but him, couldn't think past him.

Mischa slowly strolled past the bar, trying to look like she wasn't looking. But he wasn't there. Despite having features that made it look like he'd been born and bred on the Mediterranean, Tal actually stood out a lot. Maybe his height, maybe his smile. Most likely the sex-god vibes that rolled off of him.

As she headed into a dark hallway, she glanced back across the restaurant. He didn't seem to be sitting at any of the tables. She ran her fingers through her hair and made a beeline for the bathroom. She could go in there and dunk her head in a sink full of cold water. Get her priorities straight. Remember who she was, and what that night had been all about; fulfilling a very bad fantasy. *Not* continuing it. She just needed to remember that.

But she never made it to the bathroom. An arm reached out of the darkness, grabbing her. Pulling her into the shadows. She was pushed against a wall and a tongue was pushed into her mouth. She raked her fingers up his chest, working her hands under his jacket.

What was I supposed to remember?

"I thought you said this was over," Tal breathed against her.

"I thought it was," she replied, nibbling on his earlobe.

"It's not."

"No."

He yanked her up against him and shuffled them down the hall. They burst into a room and she was put back up against a different wall. She gasped and moaned, yanking his shirt out of his pants. His own hands weren't idle, they moved over her body, massaged her breasts, then went back to her panties.

"Scusi!"

Misch's eyes flew open, and over Tal's shoulder, she saw a man standing with his back to them. He was looking over his own shoulder, his face very red. Probably because he was peeing—he was standing in front of a urinal. They were in the men's bathroom.

Slut.

She wanted to push Tal away, to tell him to stop, to ask to go somewhere else. But he had two fingers thrusting in and out of her, so thought was pretty much not an option. She pressed her lips together, pulled them between her teeth and bit down to keep herself quiet, and tapped him on the shoulder.

It was the least she could do.

"I'm very sorry, sir," Tal chuckled, glancing at the man once before staring back down at Misch. "You see, my lady friend here is very wet, and really wants to be fucked. You understand how it is."

The man prattled something in Italian, and Tal actually laughed. Misch couldn't believe it. Couldn't believe what was going on.

Tal wrapped an arm around her waist and actually picked her up that way, hugging her body to his, his hand trapped between them. He moved them into a stall, shoved her into a corner, then slammed the door shut behind them.

Misch had never felt so charged up in her life. She didn't even question what was going on, didn't even ask what to do. As he ripped his belt apart, she wiggled her panties over her hips. Dropped them to the floor. Kicked them into a corner. By then, Tal had shoved his pants down his hips, and they met in the middle of the stall, pushing each other around in their want and desire.

He braced her against the door. She kept an arm wrapped around his shoulders and stretched out her other arm, pressing her palm against the wall. As her legs went around his waist, his hand worked between them, guiding her onto his dick. It was that same sensation, of too uncomfortable. Too full. Too much. *Too perfect.*

"Oh, god, you feel so perfect," she moaned, struggling to keep her ankles locked behind his back as he moved up and down. Back and forth. Rocked her world.

"I had to feel this again. *I had to,*" he told her, picking up the pace. "*I'm glad.*"

He began pumping so hard, the door started to bang in its hinges. She cried out and let go of his shoulder, moving her hand to grip the top of the stall, holding herself up a little for him. This allowed him to remove one of his arms from around her waist, and his hand immediately went to her chest. He yanked at her dress, pawed her breast out of her bra, then cupped it in his hand. Lowed his mouth to it, sucked on her nipple.

I've never had sex in public before . . .

In the back of her mind, Misch knew she should be quiet. Anyone could walk into the bathroom—including her boss. Or a waiter. And there was a restaurant full of people right outside, potentially listening to every screech, every cry, every groan coming out of her mouth.

Keeping quiet was definitely a *failed* mission.

"*Mischa,*" Tal grunted her name, licking a trail up the side of her neck.

"Yes, yes, yes, yes . . . ,"

"We're leaving after this."

"Okay."

"I'm coming back to your hotel."

"Okay."

"You're going to blow me during the cab ride."

"Okay."

"If I want to finger fuck you in the lobby, you'll let me."

"Okay."

"*Such a good girl.*"

Misch shrieked, an orgasm pouncing on her, taking her by surprise. She let go of the stall door, all of her weight dropping onto his shaft, and that just intensified the feeling. Her arms were around his neck as she sobbed into his shoulder, every muscle she had clenching and unclenching. He groaned, managed to lower himself a little, then he drove his hips home one more time, as hard as he could, before he came, as well.

"Oh my god. Holy fucking shit. *Oh my god,*" Misch's lungs were begging for air.

"Lovely mouth you've got there," Tal panted.

"Where did that come from!?" she asked, letting her head rest against the door.

"This damn dress, your damn legs. I couldn't help myself. I almost crawled under the table so I could eat you like you were the main course," he told her.

"God, I wish you would've."

"We've got time."

Tal finally backed away from the door, helping her to stand as he went. Her legs felt like overcooked spaghetti. He cleaned himself up while she straightened out her dress. As he was doing his belt up, they heard something. A man, clearing his throat. Then the bathroom door opening and closing. The guy who had been there when they'd first stumbled in, he'd stayed for the whole show. Misch turned flaming red and Tal burst out laughing before he pulled her close, giving her a big kiss.

"I have to go back out there," she said, her voice husky as she smoothed her tongue over his bottom lip.

"I know you do. To make your excuses, so you can leave," he reminded her as he speared his hands into her hair, holding her in place.

"And what am I supposed to say? '*Sorry, have to go have sex, ciao*'?" she laughed.

"Whatever. I don't give a fuck. Meet me out front in five minutes, or I'll come find you," he warned her. Then he was moving out of the stall, adjusting his jacket as he went.

Misch stood there for a second, breathing heavy. What was wrong with her!? Over the last few days, she'd told herself that her little adventure-in-cheating was over, but then one look from him, one whisper, and she was pinned against a bathroom stall. He had a magnetic pull on her, something she couldn't deny. He wasn't a one-night-stand. She wasn't sure *what* he was, but he wasn't going away. And she was beginning to think that she didn't want him to go away.

*You're already in trouble, you can't get in **more** trouble . . .*

Misch crept into the hallway, paranoid that she'd bump into her boss. Luckily, she didn't. Still. She felt like she'd been gone forever. She'd just been fucked stupid up against a stall in a bathroom. She wasn't wearing any underwear. Surely they would be able to tell, as if "*cheater*" was branded onto her chest.

Turned out, Tal had pounded her to an orgasm a lot quicker than she'd thought—when she got to her table, dinner was just being served. Everyone stood up, but she begged off, claiming a stomach ache. And a headache. And nausea. And a chill.

Might be overdoing it.

When she walked out of the restaurant, she didn't see Tal at first, and thought he'd played a cruel joke on her. She ran away from him after great sex, now he was running away from her after amazing sex. But she finally spotted him, standing on the corner at a four-way. Well away from the front of the restaurant. From where anyone would see him.

How thoughtful.

As Mischa made her way to him, she looked him over. He looked completely unruffled, it was impossible to tell that he'd just had sex in a public bathroom. Or maybe not—he kind of already had that look, just all the time. Tousled, wavy hair, sly smile, and a naughty glint in his eyes. He was pretty much every woman's fantasy. Or wet dream . . .

What is he doing with me?

Maybe that was it. He was just so dashing, so sexy, that she was swept away with it. A beautiful man, paying attention to her. Wanting her, desiring her. It was a novel feeling. Something she hadn't experienced in a long, long time.

He was talking on a cell phone, but he stared at her as she approached. His dark eyes roamed over her body, and it was such an interesting sensation. Knowing that when he looked at her, he was picturing her naked. Not just picturing her, but *knowing* what she looked like naked.

When she reached him, he didn't get off the phone, but he wrapped an arm around her waist and began walking down the sidewalk, pulling her along with him. Her first instinct was to panic. He couldn't touch her like that, not in public! Someone might see them!

But then she relaxed. She was in another country. No one knew her. No one knew *them*. They probably looked like exactly what they were, a couple of people who had met in a bar and were going home to have some fun. She was already going to hell. Cuddling on a street wouldn't get her there any quicker.

I'd forgotten how good it feels just to be touched.

"No, no, I know . . . I'll be there . . . when do we . . . ," he was almost barking out his responses to whoever he was talking to. His voice was deep, and gravelly, and very serious. *Sexy.* She decided fuck it, if she was gonna be with a sexy man, she was going to show her appreciation. She walked on her toes, stretching up so she could lick at his neck, suck at the spot where it met his shoulder. He kept on talking, but his hand moved to her ass, squeezing it hard.

I can do this. I can totally do this. This is who I am now. Bold. Confident. Sexy. Slut-bag.

They waited in a queue for a cab. Pawing and kissing each other. An old woman tutted at them and Tal blew her a kiss. Misch laughed and worked on giving him a hickey. Then it was finally their turn and they tumbled into the backseat of a taxi. Tal gave the name of her hotel, and they took off.

"How do you know where I -," she began to ask, but then his fingers were pinching her lips closed.

"No talking. Remember what I said? There's a good girl."

Sex in a bathroom, check. Blowjob in a taxi, check. I'm crossing all kinds of personal boundaries tonight.

Why Am I Here

TAL WAS IN ITALY for work. Work was slow, though, and Rome was beautiful in the summer, so it was kind of like a vacation.

But he still had to work.

Mischa Rapaport was a distraction. A beautiful distraction, who had an uncanny gift for making it impossible for him to think of anything but sex. Hence the little snafu at the restaurant the night before; he'd been there for work, Mrs. Rapaport had simply gotten in the way. When he'd realized she was there, he'd figured talking to her wouldn't hurt anything. In fact, it might lead to something else, he'd just have to finesse it a little.

Thumbing her almost to an orgasm at the table, not exactly finesse. Fucking her in a bathroom stall, while awesome beyond all words, *definitely* not finesse.

Of course, no one had ever accused Tal of having finesse, anyway.

It's probably overrated.

Tal stood next to the bed, looking down at Mischa. She was sleeping on her back, one arm raised above her head, her other hand resting on her stomach. She had put on a long t-shirt before falling asleep—he found her modesty adorable. He'd licked just about every inch of her skin, and yet she still tried to hide pieces of herself.

He found a lot of things about her adorable. She was supposed to be a one-night-stand, a fling, a moment in time. He wasn't sure when he'd decided it should become more, but all of a sudden, *bam.* It was. The moment he saw her in that restaurant. The moment she went into that bathroom stall with him. The moment she got in that taxi with him.

Something about this woman. She makes me want more. All of her. All the time.

He wanted to wake her up, pick back up where they'd left off, but he decided against it. He slowly moved away from the bed, made his way over to her luggage. She'd hung up a bunch of clothes in the closet, shoved some things into the dresser, but he could see that there was still stuff in her bags. He sat at the foot of the bed and pulled the luggage tray close, pushing the top of her suitcase open.

It didn't take much digging to realize it was her makeshift hamper. He dug in the side pockets, found some jewelry. Some hidden money. He left it all alone, flipped the lid closed. Then he rummaged through the large pockets on the front. Found a tour guide for Rome, some brochures for her insurance company. He finally found what he was looking for in the smaller pocket, shoved way down to the very bottom.

It was a small frame, maybe five-by-seven inches. Mischa was younger in the picture, though not by too much, and *very* tan. She smiled widely at the camera, one hand holding the fedora she was wearing down on her head. She looked good—Tal was willing to bet she'd always looked good—but she wasn't what he was interested in.

No, it was the man standing next to her, the man she had her arm around. Michael looked to be around five-foot-nine, or ten. Not a whole lot taller than Misch. He had sandy colored hair, almost with a hint of red in it. Or maybe it was just in contrast to his face, the man had a ruddy complexion. Along with his dark blue eyes, his appearance was overwhelmingly . . . *normal.* If Misch was an exotic locale like Bali or Indonesia, then Michael was Akron, Ohio. *Bor-ing.*

And more so than that, it was apparent to Tal that whenever the picture had been taken, they were already struggling as a couple. Maybe they hadn't known it, but he could tell. He was a very observant person, his job required it. The way their arms were around each others shoulders, not their waists. The way there was a space between them, big enough for a balloon to fit. The way they were smiling, so broad, more like a grin, no hint of mischief. They both were wearing tank tops, both non-sexy. It all spoke leagues to Tal.

Why on earth did you marry this man, Misch?

Not that he cared, it was none of his business. He just wanted to know what made her tick. What made an exotic, sexy dancer settle down with some boring, country tax accountant. Or whatever white-bread did for a living.

What made a woman settle down with a man who couldn't please her in bed?

And why do I care? Why am I even here? What is this woman doing to me?

Being there was wrong. He knew it was wrong. It wasn't allowed. Sleeping with her the first time had been a challenge. Breaking the rules *and* seducing a married woman? Yes, please—Tal loved trouble. And when he'd seen her in that restaurant, just a chance to push the boundary even further. See how close to the edge he could take both of them.

The only problem with edges, though, was either a person had to step back or step off.

He was no longer sure which step he was going to take.

And *that* meant trouble for everybody. Trouble Mrs. Rapaport didn't need, nor deserve, simply because Tal had been stupid enough to forget his place in the world. Stupid enough to grow a crush on a married woman who was off limits.

"What are you doing?" Misch's voice was sleepy behind him. He faked a yawn and dropped the frame to the floor, scooting it under the bed with his foot.

"Just woke up," he replied, then he stood up and stretched. Reached over to the windows and pulled back the curtains. Sunlight spilled into the room.

"No, too early," she moaned, and when he glanced at her, he saw that she was burrowing under her pillows. He laughed and crawled onto the bed, moving so he was hovering over her.

"Not too early. What time do you have to be at work?" he asked, pulling the pillows away. She blinked up at him.

"Oh yeah. Work."

That earned her another laugh.

"You could play hookie, spend the day with me," he suggested, lowering himself so he could kiss her chest.

"No, I can't do that, that wouldn't be right," she replied. But her voice lacked conviction.

"Sure you can. You begged off sick last night—this will just make it more believable," he pointed out.

"Hmmm. And what did you have in mind?" she asked, stretching underneath him.

"Several things."

"Not winning me over," she snorted.

"How about," he began, rolling to lay on his side next to her, "I take you to lunch, then we go do some tourist shit, then we see if we can sneak in a quickie at the Colosseum."

"You're trying to break my vagina, aren't you?"

"Wasn't my intention, but I could try. We'll get you a t-shirt made—'*I went to Rome, and all I got was my lousy vagina broken,*' sounds great."

"Tal," she wasn't laughing as she turned her head to look at him.

"Yes?" he responded, reaching out and brushing hair away from her forehead.

"What are you doing?"

"Excuse me?"

"What are you doing here? With me?" she asked.

I have the same question, Mrs. Rapaport.

"I thought I was trying to talk you into committing more acts of public indecency," he joked.

"You could do that with anybody. I walked away, I was gone. You were off the hook. Why did you want more?" she pressed.

It was a great question. How was he supposed to answer? "*You've got one of the most amazing pussies I've ever fucked*" just didn't sound right. "*I could learn to live to see you smile*" also sounded wrong.

Both were correct.

"Because you're pretty," he answered, keeping his voice soft. "And you smile at me. You're smart and funny. Because I kinda like you, Mischa."

There. Sweet and simple. But she frowned at him.

"I like you, too, Tal, but I guess I'm just . . . confused. Are we going on a date today?" she kept questioning. He rolled his eyes.

"I don't think you can call it a date when one of us is married," he pointed out. She pressed her hands over her face.

"God, don't say it out loud," she groaned.

"I won't mention the M-word again. How about we don't give it a title, and just say it's two friends hitting the town," he offered. She didn't move her hands, and a shaft of sunlight bounced off her diamond. He looked down at her wedding set. Frowned.

"Friends don't break each others vaginas," she pointed out, her voice muffled by her palms. Tal began pulling at her fingers.

"Well, I'm a really good friend. You should thank me. With your vagina," he encouraged her. She moved her hands away and started pushing back the covers.

"I don't thank my friends with my vagina. At least not usually."

"What a waste of a vagina."

"Can we stop saying '*vagina*'?"

"What a waste of a pussy."

Misch finally laughed as she padded into the bathroom. She stood in front of the sink and stretched, raising her arms above her head. The hem of her t-shirt lifted, revealing her bare ass. Tal cocked up an eyebrow, then followed her into the small room.

"No, no, no, you go wait out there," she instructed, turning and pushing at his chest. He grabbed her hand and something bit into his palm. When he let her go, he saw that it was the rings.

"One rule for today," he started, raising her hand towards his face.

"What's that?" she asked, following his movements with her eyes.

"Today, you don't wear these," he informed her, then he wrapped his lips around her ring finger, all the way at the base. He laved the cool gold with his tongue, then used his teeth to drag the set over her knuckle. When he pulled them free from her finger, he stuck out his tongue, showing her the rings before he dropped them into his own hand.

"Okay," she whispered. He smirked and leaned down to her.

"Today, you're *mine*."

Mischa

WHEN SOMETHING FEELS SO good, you find a way to convince yourself that it's okay. Over-eaters and drug addicts know what I'm talking about. You make excuses, you claim it's because you're weak, a million things.

For me, it was the feels. Sure, I felt bad afterwards. But I felt *so good* during, that I couldn't stop. I couldn't back down. I couldn't back away.

And even if I wanted to, I wasn't allowed to. He couldn't back away, either.

I had planned on cheating on my husband.

I had never planned on having an affair.

Tal paid no attention to plans. Plans didn't exist in his world. He colored outside the lines, and he dragged me with him. Handed me a brush and said, *"here, paint me as you like."*

I wanted to paint him with my aura, stain him with my shades.

Who the fuck needed plans, anyway.

Opening a Door

MISCHA CALLED IN SICK. Tal took her to lunch. They looked at tourist shit. He tried to screw her in a bathroom at the Colosseum. She resisted.

At first.

"How long are you in Italy for?" Misch asked as they strolled down a street.

"How long are *you* in Italy for?" he turned her question around on her.

"Just over three weeks, then we head to Turkey," she answered.

"Nice. I love Turkey."

His arm snaked around her waist, pulling her into her side. She flushed. She wasn't used to so much physical contact. Her own husband didn't touch her as much as Tal did—he *always* seemed to be finding a way to touch her. On top of that, there was the naughty aspect. It was so bad, so wrong, so illicit. It made her blood pressure skyrocket.

My left hand feels so much lighter. Like my spirit.

"You've been to Turkey?" she asked as they turned a corner.

"Yeah, I have a home in Istanbul," he told her. She was shocked, and judging by the look on his face, Tal had surprised himself by letting go of that snippet of personal information.

"You're from Turkey?" she went ahead and questioned. He shook his head.

"No, I just live there sometimes. Want an ice cream?" he asked, but before she could respond, he let her go and he jogged to an ice cream cart on the curb. When they both had ice cream cones, they started walking again.

"Are you going there after whatever it is you're doing here?" Misch tried to keep the questions light.

"I go wherever my job sends me," he answered.

"When do you have to leave?"

"Not sure. Could be next week, could be the week after."

"Oh."

Even she could hear the drop in her voice, and Tal laughed at her.

"Don't worry, plenty of time to work on that whole broken-vagina thing," he assured her.

"Always thinking of others, aren't you?" she sighed. He snorted.

"I'm like Mother Teresa."

"Tal, what is it you do?" Misch asked. She watched his eyebrows move into a scowl and she expected him to change the subject.

The night before, in between rolling around in her bed, they had talked about some things. Questions were okay, but digging around wasn't encouraged. Mischa refused to talk about Mike with him. Tal refused to talk about his personal life. So they called it even and agreed not to pry.

"It's . . . I'm a photographer. Sort of," he tried to explain.

Except it didn't explain anything.

"I thought you told me you worked for a government, or something," she replied.

"Sometimes. Sometimes not. It takes me all over, it's a nightmare sometimes. But this time it brought me here, and you're here, so it's good," he said, and his arm was back around her again. With sweet words like that, she couldn't bring herself to pry anymore.

They found a little cafe and Tal held the door open for her. Waited for her to sit first. Little things that probably came naturally to him, but were still foreign and exciting to her.

"This was a good idea. I've been so uptight lately," Misch sighed, letting her head fall back.

"I could tell," Tal agreed. Without looking, she threw her napkin at him.

"So you're probably leaving in the next week or two," she began as soon as their iced coffees were delivered. "And I'm definitely leaving at the end of the month."

"Yup," he concurred.

"We'll go our separate ways," she added. He glanced at her.

"You sound upset about that," he pointed out. She shrugged.

"Not upset. But I will miss you," she was honest. He smiled big.

"I'll miss you, too. At least we'll always have Rome," he reminded her.

"That's true. And what about tomorrow?" she continued with her questions.

"What about tomorrow?"

"Figuratively. What are we doing here, together, us? Are we gonna separate, say goodbye, but then a week later, you show up at my job, or at my hotel room? I can't handle that," she explained.

"Hey, I didn't even get a goodbye last time, you just ditched out—I had to come find you. Aren't you glad now?" he teased her, and she rolled her eyes. "How about we just play it by ear. Who knows, I may have new orders to go somewhere else tomorrow. I'm not making you any promises, Misch. I picked you up in that cafe because I'd seen you around, and I thought you were hot—not because I'm looking for a girlfriend or anything."

Mischa cleared her throat. Looked away.

"Good thing, because I can't be anyone's girlfriend. I'm married."

"That's why you're so perfect for me."

"I don't think I'm perfect for anybody," she whispered.

"Let's make this easy on each other. If I want to see you, I'm gonna come find you. If you want to see me, come find me. We're here now, with each other. You and me. There's no jobs or life or . . . *husband*," he said the word carefully. "Just you and me, and this time together in Rome."

She wasn't sure if it sounded awful or perfect.

"A year ago, when they offered me this job, I started working out. Lost a bunch of weight, psyched myself up. Told myself I would get here and I would find somebody and I would sleep with him. Only once I got here, I sucked at it. I was scared and nervous and I hated it, hated myself, so I stopped. Told myself I wouldn't do it. Then *you* found *me*. I want to feel awful, and I did the other day, but right now, I'm . . . ," her voice trailed off into the afternoon sun. Tal scooted his chair over so he was right next to her.

"Right now you belong to me, and that's all that matters," he whispered, his breath hot on her ear. She closed her eyes and leaned into him.

This is a very dangerous man.

They spent the day together and it was amazing. They laughed and talked, acted silly and touristy. He even danced with her in front of the Trevi Fountain, then kissed her in a way that made the locals cheer for them. They shared and they learned about each other and they bonded. Then they ended the evening at his hotel room.

But she didn't stay the night—Misch absolutely *had* to be at work the next day. He said he understood. They kissed goodbye before she got in the taxi, and she waved at him as she pulled away. Smiled the whole way to her own hotel. Fell asleep smiling.

Then three days went by and she didn't hear a peep from him.

He said I belonged to him. Did he only mean for that day!?

She felt sick. She felt stupid. She felt used. She felt worried. She felt . . . just about every emotion a person could have—except for guilt. Thankfully, all those other feelings squeezed guilt to a backburner, and it only reappeared when a certain name scrolled across her cell phone screen. And even then, she only felt guilty *after* she realized she was disappointed it wasn't Tal's number.

By the end of that first day, she was pretty sure she'd covered all the five stages of grief, possibly several times over. She went to sleep worrying her lower lip, wondering what had happened to change things.

But the next day, it was like she woke up with a whole new attitude. She wasn't that girl anymore, the one who was always worrying about what was wrong with her. She'd spent the last couple years doing that in her marriage, she didn't need to do that with Tal. Nothing was wrong with her. Nothing was wrong, *period.* He had a job, she had a job, they hadn't promised to spend every waking moment together. A man she liked hadn't gotten into contact with her. Big deal. What was she going to do about it?

"If you want to see me, come find me."

So she decided to do just that. The worst thing that could happen was he told her it was over. Or really, he just wouldn't be there. Skipped town. But at least she'd know, and she could get on with her life. She'd be sad, she wouldn't lie to herself, but she wouldn't be heart broken. And she certainly wouldn't beat herself up. She was done doing that.

After work on the third day of no contact, Misch went back to her hotel room and changed into a pair of cut off shorts and a black tank top. She decided against taking a taxi. His hotel really wasn't too far from her own, and she was feeling so good about herself, she wanted to burn the excess energy.

It took her about half an hour, but she enjoyed the walk. She'd stopped in at a cute little furniture store along the way, and an old man had given her a flower. She hooked her glasses onto the front of her tank, then used them to pin the flower in place. He kissed her on the cheek and then sent her on her way.

It made her day.

She went up to the front desk of the hotel to see if they could ring for Tal, but the only clerk that was available didn't speak a word of English. Misch leaned against the counter, propping her head in her hand. She'd been there about five minutes when she heard a familiar voice echoing across the lobby.

"*. . . next time, you're gonna be the one in the dirt,*" Tal was laughing.

Mischa turned around and was surprised by what she saw. Tal was filthy, his clothing covered in dust. His hands were disgusting, coated in dirt almost clear up to his elbows, and it was all smudged on his cheeks and forehead. He wore a button up shirt, but it was untucked from his slacks, and the top three buttons weren't done up. He looked dirty and disheveled.

He was walking next to another man, who looked messy as well, though not quite as much, and was wearing cargo pants, combat boots, and a skin tight black tank top. He had all the right equipment to pull off the look, with an incredibly built physique. He looked Spanish, or some kind of Hispanic, and he was carrying a large duffel bag as he walked alongside Tal.

It's funny, when you spend so much time alone with someone, you

71

forget that they have a life outside of you.

Misch wondered if maybe it was a bad time—she didn't want to bother him while he was hanging with his buddy. She considered just sidling off and calling him later, but right then his eyes locked onto hers, and any doubts she had about his feelings towards her, flew away. His smiled broadened, showing all his perfect teeth.

"I don't believe it!" he called out to her. She smiled back and walked towards him.

"Don't believe what?"

"I didn't think you'd do it," he responded, which made no sense.

"Do what?" she asked, coming to a stop in front of him. But he didn't stop. He walked right up to her and wrapped his arms around her, lifting her off the ground.

"*Find me,*" he breathed in her ear before giving her a wet kiss on the side of her neck.

"You told me to," she reminded him, feeling a little light headed at his response to her.

"Yeah, but you're a scaredy cat. I thought you'd be hiding in your hotel room and I'd have to come hunt you down again," he said. She swatted him on the shoulder and he sat her down.

"No, no more of that," she replied.

"Ah, good. Very good girl," he teased.

"Am I just supposed to keep standing here like a frickin' perv?"

Misch had forgotten about the other man. Tal's presence made her stupid. She went to step back, but Tal kept his arm around her, kept her pressed up against him. He nodded at his friend.

"Misch, this is Claudio Ruiz, my partner. Sort of. Everyone calls him Ruiz," Tal introduced them.

"*You're* the chick?" Ruiz clarified. Misch blushed and again tried to push away from Tal. He had probably told his friend all about her, about what she was doing.

"The one and only," she mumbled, pulling at Tal's arm.

"Thank god, cause if there were more of you, I'd probably never see my '*partner*' here ever again," Ruiz teased. He smiled and laughed, but there was an edge of hardness underneath it. His eyes didn't smile at all, and they stayed trained on her face the whole time.

He doesn't like me.

"Sorry, I'm not trying to be a Yoko," she offered.

"Oh, no, he just talks about you. A lot. Like non stop. Never shuts up. Can't get a word in edgewise. Won't -," Ruiz began prattling off. Tal slapped him in the back of the head.

"Shut up, Ruiz. Look, give us twenty minutes, and we'll meet you in the bar," Tal suddenly said, and with his free hand he grabbed the duffel bag out of Ruiz's.

"What? But I thought you wanted to -," his partner began to argue.

"No, no, it's okay, I can come back, Tal. I just wanted to say hi, really -," Misch chimed in.

"Shut up," Tal snapped. Everyone shut up. "You're not going anywhere but upstairs, Misch. Ruiz, we can handle that shit later. Meet us down here. Twenty minutes."

Then Tal was practically dragging her into the elevator.

"Honestly, hang out with your friend. I'm not trying to be that chick, I just wanted to say hi," she said quickly, once they were alone.

"I want you to be '*that chick,*' and you're gonna do a lot more than say '*hi*' to me," he assured her. He raked his fingers through his hair and shook his head. Dust flew everywhere—his black hair almost looked salt-and-pepper.

"What were you two doing!?" she demanded, her eyes wandering over his clothing again.

"Hmmm, wouldn't you like to know," he teased, grabbing her hips and pulling her close.

"Yeah, I would. And stop touching me, you're filthy," she pointed out.

"Oh, c'mon, you love a filthy boy," he cooed, leaning in to bite on her ear.

"Filthy, not dirty. You're gross," she informed him.

"Filthy, dirty, nasty, raunchy; I'm a man of many talents," he whispered, running his tongue along the inside of her ear.

He looked like he had been rolling around in a dried up mud pit, but when he kissed her, Misch didn't stop him. She couldn't resist him. He could've told her to get on her knees for him—in the elevator, dirty as he was—and she would've done it without hesitating.

Why can't life be like a dirty man who kisses good?

"Your friend doesn't like me."

It was closer to forty-five minutes later when Tal and Misch made their way back downstairs.

"No, he's just . . . closed off," Tal tried to explain.

"Your '*closed off*' friend doesn't like me," she repeated herself. He rolled his eyes.

"He doesn't know you, so how can he have an opinion?" he pointed out.

"Um, it's called '*judging*' someone. Is it because of . . . you know . . . my thing," she stuttered around what she was trying to say. They still weren't saying the M-word.

"Ah, '*my thing,*' how perfect. Like a cancerous growth," he chuckled, though it sound angry. Evil.

"*Not funny,*" she snapped.

Mike was completely innocent, a victim of her little infidelity. Well, not so little, anymore—and that just made it worse. She would never let Tal, or anyone, say a disparaging word about him.

"Sensitive. And *no,* it's not cause of that—Ruiz doesn't have morals, I'm pretty sure he *prefers* married women. He's just worried that you're too much of a distraction for me," Tal told her. She bit at her bottom lip.

"Am I? I don't want to get you in trouble," she replied. Suddenly, his hand was on her ass, grabbing her roughly, yanking her up against his side. He seemed to prefer her that way, always pressed against him. She didn't think she'd ever get used to it, someone needing to touch her that much.

"Baby, you are the biggest distraction I've ever had in my entire life. *I love it.* Let me worry about my work," he assured her.

"That would be easier if I knew exactly what it was."

They strode into the lounge, and he ignored her statement as he said hello to his friend.

Ruiz still looked at her in that smiling-not-smiling way, but didn't say anything. They ordered dinner and drinks. Conversation flowed. Tal was cheeky and witty, but Ruiz was more laugh-out-loud and slapstick funny. He had a slight accent, and it was finally revealed that he was originally from Cuba.

They finished dinner and moved up to the bar, ordered some real drinks. Ruiz seemed to loosen up with her, and he regaled her with stories of Tal. Places they'd been and stupid things Tal had done while there. He had a penchant for getting caught in public doing nasty acts that were better left to be done in bedrooms. Apparently, Mischa wasn't the only one he liked to indulge in that fetish with.

She eventually let go of the feeling that Ruiz didn't like her, she was having such a good time. She couldn't remember the last time she'd laughed so hard, had felt so carefree. With her friends, she was always hiding her shameful secret—with these men, it was open, and it was accepted. With her husband, she was always walking on eggshells because he was easy to offend and always wanted to be the center of attention—with these men, they could dish it *and* take it, and even encouraged her to be the same.

"You guys are too much," she struggled to breathe, she was laughing so hard. Tal was walking away, going off in search of the bathroom.

"Yeah, we get that a lot," Ruiz's laughter died down.

"I haven't laughed this much in a long time," she sighed, wiping at her eyes.

"Tal's good for a laugh."

It was said in a dry voice, and it sobered her of her giggles.

"He's pretty funny," she attempted to lighten the mood back up.

"He is. So tell me something," Ruiz began, leaning against the bar, getting closer to her. It was funny, but when Tal got in her personal space, even that very first time, she hadn't minded. With this man, she minded very much.

"What?" she asked, crossing her legs. He was standing close enough that her knee brushed against his waist.

"What's your deal with my friend?" he questioned.

Phew, he's just worried about his buddy.

"No deal. He's a great guy, we bumped into each other one night," she started to explain.

"That's it? You just '*bumped*' into him?" Ruiz clarified.

"Yeah. I promise, I'm not trying to break up the band," she assured him.

"I get it. So it's just, like, sex. Right?"

Whoa. This one isn't shy at all.

"Well, I guess so. Sort of," Misch responded, though that didn't cover it. Not at all. She'd been trying not to think about it, but it was now obvious they were so much more than that—she could never say that's all they were, would never call what they did '*just sex.*'

"You flew all the way to Italy just to get some ass. Man, things must be *rough* at home," Ruiz said, his eyes wandering down her body.

"Excuse me!?" she was a little shocked.

"Hot little thing like you? Who wouldn't want to give it to you good. Who else are you doing while you're here?" he kept on with the questions. Mischa felt her face burning up.

"Nobody, it's not like that. I'm not like that," she snapped.

Only . . . you kinda are.

"Woman cheating on her husband with a dude she doesn't know. You are definitely like that, baby. Why not give me a crack at that pussy?"

Misch jumped off her stool and went to push past him. He wrapped an arm around her back and held her in place. Meanwhile, his other hand ran up and down the side of her body. She felt sick.

"Get the fuck off me!" she all but yelled, shoving and hitting at his chest.

"C'mon! If you think Tal can show you a good time, wait till you see what -,"

"*What the fuck are you doing!?*"

Tal was a big man with a dark complexion and intense features—picturing him angry was easy. Seeing it and hearing it, though, was a whole different ball game. Even Mischa was scared at the tone of his voice, at the sight of him walking up to them.

"Hey, it's cool, man," Ruiz laughed, letting go of Mischa. She stumbled backwards into Tal, who practically shoved her behind him.

"It's not fucking cool—what the fuck!?" Tal demanded.

I'm so the Yoko. God, I'm horrible.

"I'm gonna go, you guys can work this out," she said, backing away. Tal turned and pointed at her.

"*You stay.* And you," he turned back towards his friend. "You have five seconds to tell me what the fuck you were thinking."

"You said she was a good time. I wanted to see for myself."

All hell broke loose after that; Tal stormed right up to the other man, got right in his face, started yelling at him. Ruiz rolled his eyes and was a smart-mouth right back. The bartender started yelling at everyone. People were shoved. Threats of violence were made.

Misch turned and scurried out of the bar.

It was one thing for her to destroy her own relationships. She wasn't about to destroy anyone elses.

What Are We Doing

"*M*ISCHA!?" TAL SNAPPED, WALKING across the lobby.

"She's gone, man, let it go," Ruiz groaned, following a short distance behind him.

"Shut the fuck up," Tal growled back before heading outside onto the sidewalk. But Ruiz was right, Misch was long gone. She'd snuck out while Tal had been threatening to shove Ruiz's head up his ass.

"You can go find your hot piece of ass later. We need to talk this shit over," his partner called out.

"I don't have to talk about shit with you! You seem to keep forgetting, *partner,* who outranks who," Tal reminded him.

"Oh, I haven't forgotten a thing. You seem to have forgotten a lot. What are you thinking, fucking around with her!? Why didn't you say anything!?" Ruiz demanded, walking up next to him. He was holding his nose, trying to stave off the bleeding. Tal had punched him, a clean jab to the center of his face.

Call her another name, fucker.

"Cause it was none of your damn business. It doesn't mean anything, it doesn't change anything," Tal stressed.

"Are you fucking with me!? It completely compromises the integrity of our mission! So you need to remember what the fuck we're doing here! And remember that we're not gonna be here for long, either," Ruiz snapped.

"What's that supposed to mean?"

"It means you were looking pretty fucking cuddly with this bitch, which isn't necessary if you're just in it for the pussy. She's fucking married, bro. As in *not yours*. She's using you, too. You don't live here, you're here for a job, and you need to fucking remember everything that job entails. Remember what we're here for."

Well, when he lays it all out like that, it sounds fucked up.

Tal glared at him and walked a few feet away. Of course, he knew Ruiz was right. They were in Italy to do a job, and then they would be gone. Assigned elsewhere. It wasn't like he could take Mischa with him—for a whole bundle of fucked up reasons he didn't even want to begin to get into. And even if by some magical way he *was* able to, *she* couldn't go. She belonged to someone else.

No. Not while she's here. Something about this woman . . . while we're here, she's mine.

"Look," he sighed, turning back to his partner. "I get it, alright. Your little act was super cute, trying to piss me off, trying to scare her off. Don't worry about me, okay? I know what I'm doing. I know what's going on, I know what the mission is. You know me, you know I wouldn't do anything to compromise that. I'm just having a little fun."

This stopped being "fun" a while ago. How did I not notice? She's more than just a "fun time."

Ruiz stared at him for a long time, scowling. Then he took a deep breath and nodded.

"Fine. *Fine.* I trust you, man. And you were right, she's a knock out. A sweetheart. I just . . . don't want your little crush ruining all our months of hard work," he said.

"It won't."

Ruiz gave a curt nod, then walked off down the street, running his hand over his head. Cursing in Spanish.

Tal turned the other way and snapped for a hotel valet to get him a taxi. When he slid into the back seat, he pulled out his phone. Called Misch's number. But just like he'd assumed would happen, she didn't answer.

He chewed at his thumb nail while the car raced across the city. He hadn't really taken the time to think about it before, what was going on between them. He'd told her they were just winging it, just having fun. That's really all it could be, fun . . .

But it was already more. Somehow, in their small space of time, it had become more. He'd felt it before he'd left. He'd felt it even more while he'd been gone. And he felt it now more than ever, as he worried that Ruiz had possibly ruined something amazing, before it had even really started.

What am I doing, chasing a married woman all over Rome? I'm a stupid, stupid man. Only me. I'm the only man on earth who, when I decided to fall for a woman, she's fucking married. Figures.

He didn't bother stopping at the front desk or trying to call her again. Just went straight up to her room. Knocked on the door. It took her a while to answer and he was leaning against the door frame when she opened up.

"I told you not to move," he said, smiling down at her. She frowned up at him, her bottom lip being worked between her teeth, and she kept the door mostly closed.

"When it's just us, Tal, it's kinda like a dream, as cheesy as that sounds. But being around other people, makes it real. And reality is horrible," she said, her voice barely above a whisper.

God, don't say that. Nothing about us is horrible. I'm beginning to think we're the only "right" that's going on in our lives.

"Ruiz was being a dick, he's just . . . work has him worried," Tal tried to explain. Tried to reassure her. Tried to remove that worried look from her face. He knew it was lame, but he wasn't in a position where he could tell her more. Her eyes slid away from his, stared off down the hall.

"It's not just him," she replied.

Oh.

"What happened? Did *he* call?" Tal asked bluntly. She'd never really talked about her husband, wouldn't say a word about him, and still. In his own mind, Tal had grown to hate the man. Hated sharing something with him. Mischa still wouldn't look at him. She just frowned and nodded.

Tal didn't know what had happened to Mischa's relationship, couldn't wrap his brain around it. She was sexy. Beyond that, she was beautiful. Captivating. Something. Something big. Like the sun, just pulling him into her gravitational field.

He reached for her, tracing his fingers down the side of her face, and her eyes slowly closed. She had amazing hazel eyes, one of them a slightly darker shade than the other. He kept moving, slowly slipping his fingers into her hair. Moving his hand around her head, attempting to pull her forward. She held her ground.

"Tal," she whispered his name, not opening her eyes.

"Just let me be with you," he whispered back. He didn't know where the words were coming from, but there they were.

Let me make you feel whole.

He continued pulling, and she finally moved. Allowed him to pull her out into the hall. Allowed herself to be pulled into him. Allowed him to kiss her. Kiss her like how she deserved to be kissed. How she should *always* be kissed.

What the fuck am I doing?

"How about school?" Tal threw out. Misch glanced at him.

"I went to the University of Michigan, studied dancing," she replied, kicking her leg up for effect. He smiled.

"I knew that."

"What about you?"

"Didn't really go to school. I was in the Israeli Army for a while," he told her. Misch was surprised. Not just that he'd been in the army in Israel, but that he'd actually answered the question.

After he'd talked his way into the room, things had calmed down. He'd made himself comfortable while she'd gone into the bathroom and tried to clean up her face. When she'd come back out, he'd been sitting at the foot of her bed. She had a standard hotel room, not a suite like him. There was only a queen sized bed, and two cushioned chairs pulled up to a small, circular table, and that was it for furniture.

Misch had stretched out on the bed, upside down, and rested her feet against the wall. Tal laid down from where he was sitting, and both their heads were near each other. Then they started talking.

Something they'd said they wouldn't do.

"Military man, I should've guessed. Is that what you do now, take pictures for the military?" she continued, dropping her feet so they were on the pillows, her legs bent at the knees.

"No, I haven't been in the military for a while. I left when I was twenty-three," he explained. With him saying that, she realized for the first time that she didn't even know his age.

"How old are you now?"

"Twenty-nine."

"How'd you get into photography?"

"Long story."

"I've got time."

"Maybe I don't."

"Testy."

"I'd rather hear about you. You're more interesting. How old are you? How'd college work out for you?"

"Twenty-seven. I graduated with a liberal arts degree, but I always wanted to be a dance instructor. I was in a studio for a long time, but then I tore my ACL. I went to work in insurance, never went back," she filled him in.

"Why not?"

She shrugged.

"I don't know. It just wasn't . . . I almost didn't want to dance anymore. I mean, I did, but I gained a lot of weight. I always felt like shit, my marriage was horrible, everything. Dancing just made it worse. So I didn't do it," she tried to explain. There was a small pause, then Tal cleared his throat.

"So what was your plan?" he asked. It was vague, but she knew what he meant.

"I was gonna come here and be a heartless vixen. I had given up when you found me," she reminded him.

"I'm glad I did."

"Me, too. I never meant for it to be more, though," she spoke slowly, not wanting to spook him. "Maybe a one night stand here and there. It sounds awful, but I just wanted to cheat, just wanted to sleep with other people. I just . . . *wanted to be touched.* I wasn't looking to have an affair, I didn't want to do that to him. Physically cheating is bad enough. Emotionally cheating . . . that's even worse."

"Why did you marry him?" Tal questioned. She'd been waiting for it.

"Because I loved him. I *love* him, as hard as that is to believe. We started dating when we were nineteen, and it was so awesome, you know? We had been best friends, and we got along great, and then hey, throw sex in the mix, and it felt like the jackpot. But after a couple years, it kinda cooled off. I just chalked it up to how relationships go or whatever. He had started a new job, I was busy at the studio. I don't know, maybe I shouldn't have spent so much time there," she finished with a sigh.

"No. If that was the only problem, then it would've changed when you stopped dancing," Tal pointed out. She shrugged.

"Maybe. I thought getting married would change things. Like, maybe he was all stressed out about proposing. Then I told myself it was the stress of planning the wedding. I just kept making excuses, kept thinking things would be different once we got married. That things would get better. But they didn't. They just kept getting worse. Both of us stopped caring about each other, at least in that way. We're still friends, though," Misch assured him.

"Hmmm, *friends*. I can't think of anything worse than being married to a girl who '*friend zoned*' me," he said. She frowned.

"But it wasn't always like this, really. We used to have such great times—we still do. You'd probably like him, he's a lot like me, only funnier. Always up for a good time, always wants to be laughing, or doing something," she described her husband. Now it was Tal's turn to frown.

"I don't think I could ever like someone like him," he replied.

"That's not really fair—just because I'm unhappy, doesn't make him a bad guy or something," she argued.

"That's not why I wouldn't like him, I don't think he's a bad guy."

"Then what is it?"

"I don't think I could like any man that has touched you the way I get to touch you," Tal's voice was low. Mischa felt a flush spread across her body.

Heelllloooooo, new territories, new boundaries.

"Oh. Well. I doubt you'll ever meet my husband, anyway."

"*Good.*"

"Stop it."

"You know what the problem is?" Tal suddenly said. Misch turned her head towards him. He was a little lower on the bed and she was looking into his dark hair.

"Enlighten me."

"You married your best friend," he said in a simple voice. She rolled her eyes and looked back at the ceiling.

"That's stupid. Everyone should be friends with the person they marry," she argued.

"Friends, yes. Of course. But you didn't say that, you said he was your *'best friend.'* I think when you guys started having sex, you got confused about what you really were. You thought sex meant he was your soulmate. No, sex just meant you were banging your best friend," Tal explained.

Misch stayed silent and stared up at the ceiling. *Best friends.* She'd always been so proud of that fact, that she'd married her best friend. That they had such a great friendship. She knew a lot of married couples who barely knew each other. Not her and Mike, they were besties, could finish each others sentences.

But what Tal was saying, it felt *right.* She and Mike had been best friends for a long time, since before they started sleeping together. She had always been attracted to Mike, he was an attractive guy, and when they'd started sleeping together, that attraction had only grown, because he was good in bed.

It was kind of stupid to assume that having funny jokes and good moves in the sack equated to lifelong marriage material. But that's what had happened. She had loved him, because he was her friend, and somehow, she had mistaken that for being *in love* with him. She loved her friend Lacey, but she wasn't going to marry the woman.

Yet she'd done just that with Mike.

Oh my god.

"So many years," she whispered, and a tear slipped down her cheek, ran sideways towards her neck.

"What?" Tal asked. She shook her head and wiped at her face, trying to stop the armies of tears in their forward march.

"Nothing. I just feel stupid," she managed a laugh.

"Why?"

"You've known me a week, and you've already figured out why I sucked at being married—something I wasn't able to figure out in three years," she replied.

"Don't say that, you don't suck. You're both to blame, but you're not a horrible person. He's not a horrible dude. He just wasn't supposed to be your husband," Tal told her.

"No, just my best friend."

"Everyone needs their proper title," he joked.

"Then what's your title?" she asked.

"Huh?"

"'*Everyone needs a title.*' You're not Mr. One-Night-Stand. You're certainly not my boyfriend. What are you?" she continued.

He was silent for a long time, then she felt him rolling over. He crawled up the bed and moved so he was leaning over her, kneeling at her side. She stared back at him, trying not to sniffle.

"They have a word especially for people like me," Tal said softly, reaching out and wiping her tears away.

"And what word is that?"

"*Lover.*"

Mischa

HOW MUCH I WANTED him took me by surprise. I didn't want to feel that way—I'd been telling the truth. I wasn't looking for another relationship. Clearly, I wasn't good at relationships, and had no business entering into an already-fucked-up-relationship without ending my last totally-fucked-up-relationship.

But it was like he understood me. I could say anything to him, literally anything, and he just got it. He didn't think I was a horrible human being for cheating on my husband. He didn't care that I was married. Didn't care that I was emotionally stunted most of the time, and physically inhibited some of the time. All he cared about was being with me. Everything else, that was just background noise.

I hadn't ever known that kind of freedom, to just be myself, one hundred percent. Say whatever I want, do whatever I want, in all situations. You just can't be like that with most people, there's always a filter that needs to be in place. But not with Tal.

Not in *any* situations.

I was drunk on him. High on him. I wanted to swallow him down, inhale him, inject him. I wanted him to live under my skin and change my DNA. I wanted to live in his air and breathe his passion.

I thought maybe, just maybe, I could overdose on him. If I could just take him one more time, and shut my eyes, and it would be the last time, with anyone, with anything, that would be alright. Guilt would be gone. Hurt would be gone. Confusion would be gone. Oppression would be gone. *Obsession* would be gone.

My memory would be his, I would only exist in his mind, and that was fine.

It was the only place I wanted to be anymore.

Done Pretending

THERE WERE NO MORE *"let's see where the day takes us"* days. No more *"just two friends hanging out"* talk. No more ignoring the large, married elephant in the room.

Mischa only had nine days left in Rome. After that, she would spend five days on the Amalfi coast, in Positano—a sort of mini-vacation, given as a reward for all the hard work they were doing.

Positano was where Michael would be meeting her.

Where her marriage would end.

She and Tal talked about it a lot. They were honest with each other—they didn't know what was happening between them, neither had been looking for a relationship, nor could either make a commitment at that time. Tal had work, Misch had life. He wanted to go to the coast with her, but they decided it was a bad idea. Too risky to be in such a small place with her boss so close at hand, with her husband visiting so soon. No, it would be much better to make a clean break in Rome. So they agreed to spend her remaining time there with each other, in whatever capacity.

"Lovers," he had whispered to her.

"Yes," she had whispered back.

They spent every day together that they could, every moment. Talking. Laughing. Touching. She skipped out on work more than a few times, burning the days away with him.

It wasn't always easy, though. His job kept him busy, and sometimes he would get called away in the middle of whatever they were doing. He left in the middle of lunch one afternoon, and she didn't hear from him for a whole day. One day out of their precious nine. She had thought she would go crazy, or that it was over, and he'd been transferred somewhere else—something he'd warned her could happen. But then he'd shown up at her hotel room at ten o'clock at night, looking haggard, as if he hadn't slept the whole time.

Her overly emotional state didn't help matters. When she was with him, nothing else existed. But when she was alone, reality caved in on her. Crying happened often, and for long bouts of time. Somehow, her picture of Mike had gotten kicked under the bed, and when she happened upon it, she'd stared at it for a long time, then burst out crying. She didn't stop for almost two hours. Tal had come over, and she'd tried to tell him to go away. But he wasn't a very good listener, and was very good at picking locks, it turned out. He let himself into her hotel room, then just held her.

*"It's not fair. You shouldn't make me feel better. I deserve to feel bad. I **should** feel bad,"* she stressed. He spooned up behind her and wiped her hair out of her face. Her tears from her eyes.

"I could never stand by and just watch you hurt. It kills me," he'd replied.

Then he'd undressed her, and she was high all over again, forgetting everything but his drugging touch.

Mischa bent over, fighting with the bottom drawer of a file cabinet. Her boss had just left, taking their Italian associates out to lunch. She'd been ready to go with them, but then they'd gotten a call—the main offices back in the U.S. were missing some of the permits required for the office to be opened in Italy. They needed that paperwork, pronto. Mischa had to stay behind and send it.

"Piece of shit," she swore, yanking and pulling at the handle on the drawer.

"Nice language, babe."

She actually screamed, leaping upright and spinning around. Tal stood on the customer side of the counter, smiling at her. All the lights were off in the front of the office, just sunlight spilling in from the front windows and light leaking out of the back offices. Misch pressed her hand to her chest.

"*Don't ever fucking do that to me!*" she yelled at him, trying to catch her breath.

"Oh, feisty," he teased, then he came around the counter and walked towards her.

"What are you even doing here!? How did you know where I was?" Misch asked, staring at him as he slowly moved her to the side.

"I wanted to see you. You said you were at work. Kinda seems like a no brainer," he told her as he bent down and jiggled the handle of the drawer.

"Yeah, but how did you know where this place was? I never told you. What are you doing?" she demanded as Tal squatted down in front of the file cabinet.

"This is locked, you dork, that's why you can't open it," he pointed out.

"Huh?"

He ignored her as he pulled something out of his pocket. It kinda looked like an Altoids tin, but without any label on it. He opened it, and it seemed to be full of wires, or paperclips that had been bent and unwound. He fingered through them, then pulled one out. She wasn't sure what his choice was based on, they all looked the same to her. He snapped the tin shut and put it away.

"No key, right?" he double checked.

"No. What are you doing?" she asked again. He bent the wire, then inserted it into the drawer's lock.

"Opening it."

And as if he'd said the magic word, the drawer popped open. There were a bunch of empty folders in it, and one at the very back that was full. He grabbed it and held it out to her, smiling.

"How do you always know what to do?" Misch asked, her voice full of suspicion.

"Man of many, many talents," he replied saucily. She narrowed her eyes and took the folder.

"Seriously, Tal, your man-of-mystery routine gets old," she told him as she walked back into her office.

"*Pffft,* bullshit, my mystery is what you love best about me," he laughed as he followed her.

She was in the middle of faxing the paperwork, so her back was to him when he spoke. She was glad, because she instantly blushed at his words.

Love!?

"Not hardly," she managed to say back, trying to clear her throat.

"You look amazing, by the way," he commented, then she felt him right against her back.

"Thank you."

"Red is a great color on you."

His voice had gotten husky, and they'd spent enough time together for Misch to pick up on his little tells.

"Behave yourself," she cautioned. He ignored her and his hand was suddenly on her hip.

"Kind of a racy dress, for just a day in the office," he said, pulling her back into him.

"It's a dress, Tal. Nothing racy about it," she told him.

"Oh really?"

His free hand was suddenly at her chest. Her dress had a deep v-neck, and his hand took advantage of it, diving into her bra without having to fight its way through any material. She gasped and reached out to grab some shelves, bracing herself.

"Only you would see a v-neck and equate it to easy access," she managed to laugh as he rolled her nipple between his fingertips.

"Me and every other man. You shouldn't dress this way in front of your dick-bag boss."

Tal's voice was almost a snarl, and it kinda surprised her.

"You've never met the man, why are you calling him names? He's always been nice to me, he -," her voice caught when his rolling fingers turned to pinching

"I can just tell these things, I'm very observant, and I don't like the idea of some jackass staring at your tits, storing that image away so he can jerk off over it later," Tal told her. She snorted.

"I seriously doubt that's going to happen."

"Shut up. You're so fucking clueless, you have no idea how sexy you are," his voice was a growl against her ear, and his hips rolled against her ass. "Feel that? How hard you make me? Every time you doubt your sexiness, remember this. Remember what you do to me."

Mischa moaned and let her head drop back to rest against his shoulder.

"Tal, we can't do this in here," she whispered as his free hand began lifting the back of her dress.

"Why not?"

"Because it's inappropriate. It's where I work. My boss could be back at any moment," she explained. His fingers snapped the edge of her panties, and she bit into her bottom lip.

"Don't worry about him. Worry about how hard I'm going to fuck you."

Her teeth clamped down so hard, she worried she'd draw blood, and she didn't say a peep as he pulled her underwear away from her. It fell to her ankles and she stepped free of them.

"You have to be quick," she panted. He spun them around and slammed her down over the desk, shocking her a little.

"I'd appreciate it if you didn't tell me how to do my job," he hissed before shoving two fingers inside of her. No gentle petting, Tal was on a mission to get her wet as quickly as possible.

It didn't take long.

"Please, please," she begged, clawing her nails down the desk.

"When you ask so nice, how could I say no?" he teased.

Every time they saw each other, they had sex—which basically meant they'd had A LOT of sex. Yet still, she was always caught off guard. His cock never ceased to surprise her, in size, in girth, in capability. She shivered and groaned, clenching and unclenching her fingers around the edge of the desk while he slowly worked his way inside of her.

"And here I thought it would just be another boring day at the office," she joked, after his hips met her ass.

"Baby, you'll never look at this office the same again."

Doesn't take a rocket scientist to figure that out.

He hadn't been lying, he fucked her hard. Hard enough to shake the computer monitor off the desk. Hard enough that she forgot where she was and began shrieking. Moaning and panting, begging him for something. Anything. *Everything.*

"Oh god, yes, please, yes," she whined when she felt his hand in her hair, pulling at the dark strands. She was forced to prop herself up on her hands, and she locked her elbows, holding herself upright. Dug her nails into the desk calendar, shredding the paper.

"I love it when you fucking beg. Such a good girl," he groaned, and his hands were back at the front of her dress. He yanked the material down, then pulled her breasts out of her bra. Kneaded her flesh with his fingers.

"I'm . . . I'm . . . I'm . . . ," she gasped for air.

"You're fucking amazing."

His words were always her downfall, pushing her over the edge. She came, shuddering and crying, her muscles locking down on him. He grunted and stilled, cupping her breasts as she exploded into a thousand pieces.

"Thank you. Thank you for that," she gasped for air as she broke away from him and laid back down on the desk. He leaned down over her, pressing against her back.

"Mischa," he said her name as he slowly, *so slowly,* pumped in and out of her.

"Hmmm?" she purred, circling her hips back against him.

"I want you to do me a favor," he continued, pulling almost all the way out of her, then sliding all the way in. She gasped in time.

"Anything," she agreed.

"I *never* want you to forget what this feels like," he told her.

"I won't," she promised.

"When I'm gone, I want you to remember. When you touch yourself, I want you to always think of me," his voice was as slow and soft as his thrusts.

"I will," she assured him.

"I want to be the only one you think of," he whispered.

"You already are."

His voice, his words, made her want to cry. Made her want to turn around and hold him. He must have sensed that, as he was able to do with most anything she was feeling, and he pulled away. Spun her around to face him before shoving her hips up onto the desk. She had barely caught her breath when he was slamming back into her. The sweet guy from a moment ago was gone, and he was all hard muscle and pumping action.

"You said we had to be quick," he reminded her, lowering his mouth to tease one of her nipples.

"Yes, you should hurry," she agreed. He shook his head and licked his way to her throat.

"*You* should hurry, cause I'm not stopping till you come again."

Bold words, but he made good on them. He grabbed her hand and forced it between their bodies, shoved her fingers into her wetness. Watched as she worked herself good, as the blush on her face spread to her chest. Her fingers couldn't keep up with him, though, and he was pounding so hard she couldn't keep her balance. Couldn't keep a fucking thought in her head. She wrapped an arm around his waist and held on for dear life while her second orgasm ripped her in half. He was right behind her, coming in a series of groans and twitches, his hips grinding against her.

"Holy. Fuck," she gasped for air. She let go of him and laid down, and he followed, laying his head on her chest.

"Fuck yeah," he agreed.

"Where does this come from? Did you wake up and think '*I'm gonna fuck her all kinds of right in her office*'?" Misch chuckled, combing her fingers through his hair.

"No. I thought we'd go have lunch, but when I saw you in this dress, pussy sounded like a better option," he replied bluntly. She snorted.

"You think I'm so easy," she teased.

"Maybe a little," he agreed, and she felt his hot breath against her nipple. Then he blew cool air over it, and she felt it tighten up. His tongue followed, sweeping across her areola, and she moaned low in her throat.

"We could go for a triple-play," she suggested, and this time, her voice was the husky one.

"Babe, I thought you'd never ask. First, though, you're going to get on your knees, and I'm not letting you up till you've fucking suck-," Tal started to get filthy, but he was interrupted by a noise.

A bell tinkled from the front of the building. It was the sound of the door being opened.

"*Oh fuck! Oh fuck! Get off me!*" Mischa hissed, shoving at his shoulders as voices filled the outer office.

Tal stood up casually, but she went into fast forward. She pushed him out of the way and raced around her desk before practically slamming the door to her office shut. She leaned back against it, thumbing the lock into place without looking. She had her eyes closed, and it was a moment before she realized Tal was laughing.

"God, I wish you could see yourself."

Misch opened her eyes and looked down. Her dress and bra were still yanked down, her breasts still exposed. She glared at him before putting the material to rights.

"You need to get out of here," she growled in a low voice as she dropped to her knees and began crawling around.

"How am I supposed to do that when you've got us barricaded in here? And what are you doing?" he asked as she shuffled under the desk.

"Climb out the window!" she told him, ignoring his question. She heard him moving around, and she figured he was working out how to get through said window, but then he cleared his throat.

"Looking for these?"

She stood on her knees and looked up at him. He had her panties dangling from his index finger, and he swung them back and forth. She rolled her eyes and climbed to her feet.

"Yes, thank you. Now this window, hurry and sneak out," she urged, overturning a trash can and standing on the bottom of it so she could reach the window. She unlocked it and pushed it open before hopping down.

"I've never seen you move this fast, it's almost impressive," Tal teased her. She glared at him.

"Shut up and leave," she snapped, grabbing for her underwear. He moved his hand out of reach.

"Oh no. No, no, no. Give me attitude? After the fucking I just gave you? Then I'm keeping these," he informed her, and she watched as her underwear disappeared into his pocket.

"What!? You can't do that! Give me those!" she demanded, reaching for his pants. He grabbed her wrists and held them behind her back, pressing his chest against hers.

"No. Good girls need to earn presents. Bad girls walk around bare assed," he told her.

"That is the stupidest thing I've ever-,"

He let go of her wrists and one had grabbed her ass, forcing her hips against him. His other hand went underneath her dress and grabbed the other side of her butt, his palm warm against her bare flesh.

"What were you saying?" he asked, his tone low and dangerous sounding.

"Please, Tal, we don't have time for this," she begged. He ignored her, and his hand stroked down to the underside of her ass.

"I always have time to make you come," he whispered, his fingers moving between her legs, trailing through the wetness that was coating the inside of her thighs.

"*Please,*" she breathed, pressing her forehead against his chest. The ignoring continued and his long, long fingers were making themselves at home.

"For the rest of the day, you're going to be thinking about me fucking you," he informed her. She nodded.

"Yes. Yes, I will," she agreed, panting as his fingers picked up speed.

"If you fuck yourself before you come home," he began, and his fingers slipped away. Made their way from her sticky wet center to the base of her spine. "Send me pictures."

Before she could say anything, he pulled away from her. He ignored the overturned trash can and simply pulled himself up to the window. She drooled as the muscles in his shoulders strained underneath his t-shirt. Then he was moving through the opening and he was gone. Not even a backward glance.

"*Mischa! You in there!?*" her boss yelled, followed by a banging on her office door.

She knew she must have looked weird. She'd finger combed her hair as best she could, but Tal had made a mess of it. Her dress was also stretched out, the v-neck now dipping down to show the top of her bra. She was red, she was out of breath, and she was jittery.

Her boss didn't seem to care, just wanted to know if she'd faxed off the paperwork and to tell her they'd brought lunch back for her. She smiled her thanks and followed him out to the main office. Was very aware of the fact that she was wearing no underwear, and was still very wet.

Fucking Tal.

She only lasted about twenty minutes before she excused herself to go to the bathroom. Luckily, it was a private room, no stalls. A space she could have to herself and a door she could lock. She went about cleaning herself up and was almost ready to head back out when her phone dinged. She picked it up and saw she had a text message from him.

Hanging in there?

She glared at the screen and banged out a response.

Barely. You're a prick.

Yes, but I'm your prick.

Still not a good thing.

Have you done it yet?

That threw her for a loop.

What?

Fucked yourself.

She was alone in the bathroom, and she still blushed. She would never get used to the way he talked to her.

Of course not! I'm at work. You're disgusting.

Not disgusting. Just incredibly turned on by a prudish woman. Do it now.

No.

Do it. Send me a picture of you touching yourself.

No!

I'll send you a picture.

That made her pause. This was all stupid—she'd seen the PSAs, she wasn't some teenager. Sending a nude selfie was a bad idea on a galactic scale. But on the other hand, getting one from him wasn't such a bad idea at all . . .

Misch glanced around, worried at her bottom lip. By the end of this little affair, she wouldn't have a lip left. She'd taken a seat on the closed toilet and she began to squirm. Rubbed her thighs together. Sought friction.

You first.

Please, I'm not a sucker.

She took a deep breath. She wasn't about to flash her vag, that just wasn't attractive, in any sort of lighting. But her breasts were a different story. She kinda liked her boobs, thought they were pretty okay. Tal spent a lot of time on her breasts, so he must have liked them, as well.

She ran her hand across her chest and dipped into her bra. Her nipples were still sensitive from his ridiculously attentive mouth, and when she touched the tip, she found it was already peaked. She pinched herself and hissed, relishing the feel.

Maybe this isn't such a bad idea.

While her breathing picked up, she worked the top half of her dress down. She cupped her right breast with left hand, trapping the nipple between two fingers, and then she took the picture. She didn't even look at it, didn't want to psych herself out, and just sent it to him.

It only took a minute for him to respond.

Fuck, you look good. Are you wet?

Yes.

Show me.

You owe me a picture.

A moment later, and she got one. It was of his crotch. He was still wearing his pants, but they were completely undone, and his hand was down the front, only visible from the wrist up. She panted as she stared at the picture, and then she noticed the caption—**"*I'll show you mine, if you show me yours.*"**

Mischa had never had phone sex. Had never *sexted*. Had never done anything like that—usually that kind of stuff made her uncomfortable. But with Tal, it didn't. It almost felt necessary. Something she *had* to do.

She stood up and faced the mirror. She worked the skirt of her dress up and held the material at her sides, pinning it with her elbows. Then she cupped her crotch, immediately sliding the tip of her middle finger inside her opening. Even she had to admit, it was a pretty sexy picture. Erotic—she was clearly touching herself. Not crude—nothing naughty was actually visible. She took a picture of her reflection and sent it to him.

Goddamn you're amazing.

Then she got a picture in return. Tal wasn't as shy as she was; it was a full on shot of his erect penis. But there was something different, and it took her a second to figure out what was going on.

He's got my panties wrapped around the base of his cock.

It wasn't easy to keep quiet, and texting dirty words and dirtier pictures with one hand proved difficult, but she managed to come in minutes. She whispered his name to the walls, wanted the foundation to feel what he did to her, even when he wasn't in the room.

That was amazing.

You're amazing.

You make me this way.

Don't go to Positano.

Misch was actually washing her hands when the last text rolled in, and she stared at her phone like it was some sort of poisonous insect.

What do you mean?

Don't go. Stay here. Stay with me.

I can't.

Why?

Because. My job.

Fuck your job. Stay with me.

I can't.

Why!?

I'm married.

Stay with me.

Why was he doing this to her!? And of all the ways to say that kind of shit, he chose to do it via texting!?

She didn't answer. She went back out, finished having lunch with everyone. Then she threw herself into work, didn't even look at her phone. It was six o'clock before she knew it, and she was the last one left in the office. She locked up and walked back to her hotel, dragging her feet.

Tal was waiting in her room.

"I was beginning to wonder if you'd avoid me all night," he said as soon as she walked in the door. She glanced at him, then took in the rest of the room. He'd had dinner ordered up for her—gnocchi in a garlic herb sauce, and a small bottle of pinot grigio. Her favorites.

She felt like she was going to be sick.

"No, I came here as soon as I got done," she assured him.

"Are you okay?"

"Sure."

"Misch."

"Tal."

"Cut the shit."

One of the things she loved about him, he always *"cut the shit."* There was no beating around the bush with Tal, no avoiding the topic or dancing around it. If she was in a bad mood, he demanded to know why. If she was being a bitch, he told her to cut it the fuck out. And whatever she said back, even if it was *"go fuck yourself,"* he just rolled with it.

One of the things you love about him. One of the things he loves about you. How many "things" does it take before it becomes the whole thing?

"I have to go, Tal," she said, toeing off her shoes before crawling onto the bed.

"Tell me why," he demanded. She turned towards him, then laid down and curled into the fetal position.

"Because I have a job and I have to go where it tells me to. Because I'm married, whether we like it or not, and I owe it to that marriage, to that man, to tell him what's going on," she answered.

"Fine, that's all fine. But then come back. Let's finish this," he urged. She shook her head.

"I can't. We're going to Turkey after this, to open a new office, remember? I have to go."

"Why? You don't even like your fucking job," he reminded her.

"But I made a commitment, I -,"

"Shut up. Just shut the fuck up," Tal suddenly snapped, and she was shocked.

"Excuse me!?"

"You're in a fucking marriage you hate—so much so that you took a job on the other side of the world so you could get away. You're in a fucking job you hate—so much so that you ditch it at every opportunity you get. Your problem isn't that you make bad decisions, Mischa. Your problem is that you're too much of a pussy to fix them," he called her out.

Everything he said was right. She knew that, knew it all. She was scared to leave her job, because she didn't know what would be waiting for her. She was scared to leave her marriage, because she didn't know what that would do to Mike. What it would do to *her.*

"You're right," she whispered, then cleared her throat. "You're absolutely right. I don't know how I became this person. This . . . *weak* person. I wasn't always like this, I don't know what happened. You shouldn't be with me, Tal. Find someone as strong as you."

He let out a groan, then knelt on the end of the mattress. He grabbed her by her hip and her knee and dragged her to him, so she was even with him on the bed. He laid down with her, propping himself up by resting his head against his fist.

"You're strong, Mischa. You've just forgotten how to be that way all the time. So fine, go to Positano, do what you have to do. Go to Turkey, do what you have to do there. But then *come find me,*" he urged. She sniffled and shook her head.

"And then what? What if I'm still this weak person? And even if I wasn't, what would we do? I live in a hotel room while you disappear for days on end, doing a job that you still won't fully explain to me? And as hard as it is to believe, Tal, I have a life. I have a home. I have friends, and family. You gonna move to Michigan with me?" she asked. He snorted.

"Fuck that."

She even laughed.

"Exactly. You're like . . . this free thing. So free. And I'm just not. It's been nice to pretend for a while, and I'll never be able to thank you enough, for what you've done for me."

She was crying in earnest now, not even trying to hide it.

"If you don't want to be with me, just say that, Misch. I'm a big boy, I can handle it. I don't want to be like Michael, living in your darkness. I wanna hear you say it," Tal urged. She cried harder.

"It's not that. I do want you, I do. I just can't hold you back. I already held someone else back, *for eight years,* and look at how that's ending. I'll never do that again," she told him.

"That won't happen to us," he insisted.

"Oh really? How? How do you know? How do you know you won't hate me in a year, when I'm still this crying, unsure, unconfident mess? How do we know this is real? What if in another eight years, it turns out we never really felt this way?" she demanded.

Tal laid down flat, so they were eye to eye. He pressed his hand to the side of her face. His large, warm hand, with his long, dexterous fingers. They pressed against her head, lightly massaging her skin. He stared straight at her, his black eyes pulling her into him. No one had ever looked at her like that before; it was one of the most intense moments she'd ever experienced.

"Tell me right now that this doesn't feel real to you. Tell me right now that you're not feeling the same way as me, and I'll walk out that door," he whispered.

Mischa cried out and shoved him away before she sat up. She got off the bed and began pacing back and forth.

"I can't do anything right," she groaned, her hands going into her hair.

"What are you talking about?" he looked bewildered as he stood up as well.

"I had a plan. A goddamn plan! I just wanted to feel special, to feel like someone wanted me. I wasn't trying to have an affair, I wasn't looking for you!" she yelled at him.

"Are you saying this is my fault?" he asked in a steely voice. She shook her head.

"No. God, no. You have been the most amazing . . . everything. *You're everything.* I'm saying that I'm not good enough for you," she stressed.

She was still pacing, and was near the door to the room. He stormed up to her and grabbed her by her arms, forced her against a wall. He glared down at her, and he looked *pissed.*

"How about you let me decide what is and isn't good for me, alright? Stop making fucking excuses. If you don't want this, say it," he snapped. She took a deep breath.

"I don't want this."

His glare grew more severe.

"*Liar.*"

"What do you want me to say!?" she demanded. "I don't trust you to be there! I don't trust myself to follow through! And Mike! God, Michael, I owe it to him to at least be there for him when I rip his heart out. I can't do that if you're in the background!"

"So that's it!? You just used me, this whole time, for a good fuck once in a while? I'm just '*background*' to you!?" he demanded.

"No, but Mike needs -,"

Tal slammed his hand against the wall by her head, three times, in rapid succession. She shrieked and ducked a little.

"*Fuck him!* I don't want to hear his fucking name!" he bellowed.

Mischa was blown away.

"But he's my -,"

"He got eight years with you. *Eight years!* Eight years to get it right! Eight years of you all to himself! I've only had this time, and all I ever got was half of you—the other half was always with him. *Always.* So you know what!? *I don't want to fucking hear about him,*" he yelled at her.

"I'm married!" she really was shrieking, slapping at his chest. "I don't know what you want from me, Tal! I'm fucking married! I wish I wasn't! I wish it had been you from the start! I wish everything was fucking different, but it's not! *I'm fucking married!* Of course he was always there—he's my goddamn husband! I'm married, Tal. I'm married, I'm married to him, I'm married," she sobbed it over and over. Kept repeating it, hoping it would sink in for him. For her.

He moaned and wrapped his arms around her waist, ducking his head to press it against her chest. She sobbed harder and coiled her arms around him, holding as tightly as she could. He sank down, and his weight dragged her with him, all the way to the floor.

"I didn't mean for this to happen," he told her, wrapping his body around hers.

"I know. Me, neither," she was having trouble breathing.

"I wish I had been there first, too," he whispered. She cried harder.

"God, me, too. So much. I'm so sorry. Please don't hate me."

"I don't hate you."

"Please forgive me."

"There's nothing to forgive."

"I wish I could stay with you. I really do. I wish we could just disappear, but I already did that to him once," she breathed, moving so she could push her forehead against his clavicle.

"No. Now you're just going to disappear on me," Tal replied. She took a breath. Nodded.

"Yes."

"Before you go," he began, and his voice was thick with emotion. So low, it made her heart vibrate. "I want you to know something."

"Please, don't say anything."

"I have to."

"It'll make it worse."

"It's already as bad as it can be."

"Please."

"You're one of the best things that's ever happened to me, Mischa. I'm glad I found you."

She took a deep breath.

"*Me, too.*"

Mischa

IT HURT. GOD, IT hurt. It hurt so bad. It hurt so much worse. It hurt the most.

I hurt and he hurt and we hurt.

Detox is the worst of part of being an addict.

Letting Go . . . ?

TAL DROVE DOWN A dusty road. The summer had gotten ridiculously hot, even for late May, even by Southern European standards. Everything looked like it had caught fire. They were surrounded by glowing embers, burning gold and orange and red. It was almost like a drought, everything had dried out and turned to sand.

If that's not an analogy, then I don't know what is . . .

He put his elbow on the side of the door, rubbed at his forehead with his fingertips. He had such a fucking headache. *A heartache.* What the fuck had happened!?

He could remember the first time he'd gotten a good look at Mischa. She'd been sitting at a high top table, wearing a long sleeved, low cut top and some incredibly short-shorts. And those legs. Goddamn, those legs. Crossed at the knee, one foot swinging idly back and forth. Her hair had been up in a bun, high on the back of her head, and she'd been reading a book. Her posture had been very straight, with her head bent to look down. He didn't need to know her background to know that she was dancer, her body language screamed it, and his next thought had been to wonder how she would feel dancing her ass in his lap.

That's all she'd been to him. Just a hot chick, sitting in a restaurant.

That first night, in his hotel room, he could admit it—she'd been a challenge. So unsure of herself. She had wanted to run away. He had wanted to stop her. Mission: Accomplished. Holy hot damn, she'd been incredible. So much pent up sexual energy, she'd run rampant all over him.

When she'd disappeared, Tal had given her space. It was just sex.

No big deal. She was gone, probably for the best. No, *definitely* for the best. He didn't need that kind of complication in his life, not with everything that was going on.

But he hadn't been able to stop thinking about her. The only reason he'd fucked his maid was because he'd had a hard on from thinking about Mischa. Made him sound like a horny douchebag, but he was a guy—and most guys were horny douchebags.

And he hadn't known her yet. Not really.

The speed and force with which he fell for her astounded him. Tal was a man's-man—he liked fucking, fighting, God, and his country. Matters of the heart were best left to pussies and women. Mischa was supposed to just be a good time. A challenge, a dare, a dirty secret.

But she'd turned out to be so much more. She was funny, and smart, and understanding, and . . . *and so much more.* He could tell that being with him made her feel like a better person. He knew because he felt the same way; she was making *him* a better person.

What the fuck.

He pulled into an empty field, put the car into park. The sun was setting, burning up the horizon. He felt like shit. He wanted to be with her, wanted to take away her hurts. But he couldn't, because not only was he the one causing them, but he had a job. A job that had called while she'd been crying on the floor.

How does a person choose between what they know, and what they love?

Another car came cruising from the opposite direction. Tal shut off his engine and took a deep breath. Well, apparently he'd made his choice. Two weeks lost in an Italian dream didn't cancel a lifetime of work. Didn't change the mission at hand. He had to keep that in mind.

No matter how much he didn't want to.

An older model Humvee came racing towards him as he climbed out of his car. The Humvee had long since been decommissioned, from the Italian or Greek army. All the gun mounts had been taken off, and at first glance, it just looked like an old Jeep. It screeched to a stop next to him and Ruiz got out of it.

"Hey, what's the status?" Tal asked, moving to lean against the front of his Range Rover.

"The mark is leaving the country. Intel says we have about a week, then we're back on," Ruiz prattled off. Tal nodded.

"Alright. What are we supposed to do during the interim?"

"We're getting pulled out."

"Seriously?"

"Seriously. We gotta take all the reports and pictures to HQ for a debriefing, they want to take this break as an opportunity to catch up, so everything will be ready when shit goes to trial," Ruiz explained.

Of course, Tal should've known this info first, but he'd been avoiding his e-mail updates. Making excuses, so he could stretch out his time with Mischa for as long as possible. He was the senior person on this mission, he was in charge, he'd been in the business a lot longer than Ruiz. Usually, he reveled in that information, took advantage of it to always be in charge. Now, he just wanted to defer everything to the other man.

Not enough time. Not enough time. Need more time with her. She's almost gone, why am I here?

"Fine," Tal sighed. Ruiz glared.

"You sure about that?"

"Did I fucking stutter?"

"Alright, man, just be at the chopper by 0600 hours," his partner snapped.

"I'll be there."

"You better."

Ruiz glared one more time, then stomped back to his car. Peeled out of the field.

Tal understood. It'd been just the two of them for a long time. Long winters in Moscow, quick fire fights in Rio, dangerous hidey-holes in Kuwait. Ruiz was jealous; his partner had found a *new* partner.

Lucky for him, it was a partnership that couldn't last.

Tal didn't want to go to HQ. He didn't want to go anywhere. He wanted to drive back to Rome as fast as possible. Kneel at the feet of a beautiful dancer and beg for forgiveness. Beg for mercy. Share all his secrets and lies, and see if she really meant it, when she said she felt the same way about him, as he felt about her. Of course, it was easy for him to think like that—he already knew everything about her.

She knew so little about him.

Lying normally came easy to Tal. It was part of his job, almost part of his being, at that point in life. He didn't think twice about it, used it to get what he wanted, to learn what he wanted. He virtually never took the time to wonder how it made him feel, to see if he felt any guilt or remorse. In fact, he usually made it a point to feel as little as possible.

Mrs. Rapaport had cured him of that, had given him a very healthy reminder of what both guilt and remorse felt like.

Maybe this is how it needs to be, Misch. For what it's worth, you were the best mission I ever had.

The Amalfi Coast

GOD, POSITANO WAS BEAUTIFUL.

Mischa soaked it in. Dropped her luggage off at the hotel and immediately went down to the beach. Buried her feet in the sand right at the water's edge and just stood there. Let the waves crash against her legs while she looked off into the horizon.

Tal had left her in that hotel room in Rome, though not on the floor—he'd helped her into bed, first. Gave her a slow kiss goodbye. So sad. He hadn't said what his phone call had been about, but based on his kiss, she'd guessed it. He had to go. Possibly for a couple days.

Mischa would be in Positano in a few days.

It was goodbye, without actually saying the words. Enough words had been said. Too many words, and they would break all the way. Misch was already cracked down the middle, she couldn't stand the thought of saying goodbye.

He didn't come back. She received a phone call, but she was packing when it came in, holding the picture of her and Mike. She let the call go, didn't answer. It was for the best.

Too many words. Don't let them in.

The night before she left Rome, she listened to his voicemail—two days after he'd left.

"Hey, dancer lady. I wanted to say this in person, but it just wasn't possible. I won't be back before you leave. I hate that, not getting to say goodbye for real. Not getting to see you one more time. Just . . . don't forget me. Don't forget us. Don't forget who you are, not who

you think you need to be when you're with him. Be nice to him, but don't be weak. You owe it to him. And don't be scared. You're strong, Misch. And stop thinking you're a horrible person. You're not. He's not. You're just not in love. That's not horrible. It's just sad. Don't confuse the two. Take care of you, take care of your heart. And just ... please don't forget us."

It had been very, very, *very* hard not to call him back. To not beg him to take her away from everything. She didn't care what his job was, or where he was going, she just wanted to be with him. Just wanted to be lost with him.

Come find me.

She took a train to Naples, then a driver took her to her hotel in Positano. She was supposed to be traveling with her boss, but he'd had to fly back to the U.S. to organize some other permits and licenses. He would meet her in Turkey. She was thankful for the time alone, even if it was only a couple days. Also, she was upgraded from her boring room to his two bedroom suite.

Made feeling like shit a little less horrible.

She was on her way back up to her hotel when her phone rang. It hadn't rung since Tal had called. She practically ripped her back pocket off trying to get it out. But it wasn't him.

"Are you excited!?" Mike's voice chirped down the line.

"Tired would be a closer approximation to how I'm feeling," Mischa sighed.

"Aw, poor sweetie. Long trip?" he asked, doing his baby voice. It used to make her laugh. Now it just made her feel like a horrible, god-damn monster, cheating slut-bag, fuck, such a horrible person, fuck, *FUCK*.

"Something like that. What time do you get in?" she asked.

"My itinerary says I should be at your hotel around six in the evening. I can't wait! Did you find somewhere for us to eat? It feels like it's been forever since I've seen you," he groaned.

"Me, too," she whispered, wiping at her tears.

"And I should probably tell you something," he started, and she could hear it in his voice. Another hour long *"Misch-doesn't-speak"* conversation was in the works. She couldn't handle that, not anymore.

"Oh god. Just wait till you get here. We have a lot to talk about. *A lot,*" she stressed.

Of course, he ignored her.

"I just want you to know before you come home. My mom has been rearranging. I think you'll really like it, she threw away the old couch and got us -,"

"She threw away my couch!?"

"C'mon, Misch, it was old. And she got us this cool leather sectional," he went on.

"I hate leather furniture. *You know that,*" she snapped.

"I know, I know, but you know how she is, and I really think you'll like it. And she took all your clothes to be dry-cleaned. That's nice," he offered.

What. The ever loving. Fuck.

"She touched my clothes!?" Misch hissed.

"Only the ones in the closet."

Only my nicest, my most expensive.

"Michael Rapaport. You know, *you know,* how I feel about this shit. *You know.* Why would you let her do that!?" Mischa demanded.

"Cause she's been really nice and taking care of me while *somebody* is on the other side of the world. And everything is fine, you can't even tell. Except for your one suede jacket, I guess that got ruined, but you never wear it anymore," he said.

Misch worked to control her anger. She never wore the suede jacket anymore because it had been a gift from a high school friend who was now dead. Normally, a huge screaming fight would ensue, with lots of colorful words pointed right at his bitch-face mother. But what he'd said stopped her, " . . . *while **somebody** is on the other side of the world.*" Tag on what she'd really been doing while there, and . . . she had no right to be mad. About anything. He could set fire to the house, and she'd have to smile and say thanks.

Cause I'm a horrible person.

He rambled on and on about the changes his mom made. Misch pretended to listen, all the way up to her hotel room. She sat on the railing of her balcony and made the appropriate responses at the appropriate points in the conversation. At the end of the phone call, he signed off with his usual "*love ya!*"; she didn't say it back. She wanted to feel guilty, but as she sat her phone down, another voice swept through her mind.

"*. . . stop thinking you're a horrible person . . . take care of you, take care of your heart.*"

But that was hard to do, when it was somewhere else.

The next day, she woke up feeling a little better. Tal's words were strong in her mind. She'd done a horrible thing, but that didn't necessarily make her a horrible person. She had to be strong. For her. For Michael. And even for Tal. He'd done something amazing for her. She would pay him back.

She spent the afternoon making phone calls. She had two days till Mike got there—after that she knew the shit would hit the fan. His friends were her friends, and vice versa. Her friend Lacey's husband was Mike's best friend, Misch was sure to lose her. And Mischa's own mother loved Mike. Like *looooooooved* him. She would be beyond upset. Of course, Mike's mom would be upset, but she'd never liked Mischa, anyway.

Maybe she knew something the rest of us didn't.

"Hey girl!" Lacey's voice squealed in her ear.

"Hey! How are you?" Misch laughed, pulling herself up onto the balcony railing. It wasn't so much a railing as a half wall, made of rock. She was able to sit flat on it and cross her legs.

"Good! So good. You'd be so proud, dancer lady, I've kept up with the work outs!"

Dancer lady . . .

"That's awesome, Lace, congrats."

"How about you? Has all that Italian food gone to your ass?" Lacey teased.

"A little," Misch chuckled. She'd actually gained around five or more pounds. She'd been upset at first, but Tal said he liked it. All her weight went to her ass.

"I haven't talked to you in about a week, how're things? Where are you now?" Lacey questioned.

"I'm on the coast, things are good. We go to Istanbul after this," Misch answered.

"I would kill to be you. And I was thinking, I've been looking at our schedules, and Bob and the baby are going to visit his mom—maybe I can get out of it and visit you! Is there anything fun to do in Istanbul?" Lacey questioned. Misch swallowed a groan.

"I don't know. Let's just put that on pause, Lace," she said slowly.

"You sound kinda sad. Is something wrong?" her friend asked.

"No. Yes. It's been a long trip," Misch sighed, running her hand over her face.

"Aw. You miss Mikey, don't you?" Lacey said in a sad voice.

"I . . . I miss a lot of things. Lacey," Misch breathed.

"What's up?"

"You love me, right?"

"Of course, doll! We're besties! Wherest thou go, I goest, and all that jazz," Lacey laughed.

"Good. That's good to know."

"Why are you asking me that?"

"Because right now, I need to know that someone loves me."

She managed to change the subject after that, though it wasn't easy. She really *really* wanted to confess everything, see if her soul was salvageable. But she wanted Mike to be the first to know, so she held off. Convinced Lacey that it was just home-sickness, and left off with a laugh.

The next phone call she made was at once harder and easier. She dialed her parents' house.

"Honey! I been dyin' to hear your voice!"

Oh thank god thank god thank god it's him.

Mischa had always had a close relationship with her father. She and her mother got along fine, but she and her dad were on another level. He probably knew her the best of anyone, even Mike. When she and Mike had problems—which was all the time—her father was the person she ran to, the person she cried to.

"Hey, Dad, how are you?" she said, finally smiling. *Really* smiling.

"Oh I'm good, I'm good. Damn hip is killing me, but that's life. How are you!? How is the Italian de Janeiro?" he asked, and she laughed.

"I think you mean *Italian Riviera,* and that's not where I am. But where I am is really super nice. You would love it. Sunshine, beaches, hot ladies," she told him.

"I do live for the hot ladies. Speaking of your mom, she's right here—wanna talk to her?" he offered.

"No," Misch replied quickly, then winced. "I mean, I don't have a lot of time, so you can just relay. How're things? Feels like I've been gone for a lifetime."

"*Pffft,* feels longer to this old man. I miss your face, sweetie. Things are good, real good. Retirement ain't exactly all it's cracked up to be, I'm bored most of the time. Should've come with you," he said. When Misch had first been offered the job, she'd asked her dad to go with her. Now she wasn't sure if she was glad he hadn't come, or if it would've been better if he had come.

*Don't say that. You're not a horrible person, and enjoying your time with Tal doesn't make you that way. If you had never met him, **that** would've been horrible.*

"Yeah, yeah, I'll be home before you know it. We're going to Istanbul next week, hopefully it won't take as long as Rome did, then Armenia, then home," she ran over her itinerary again.

"So far away. Mikey's comin' out there this weekend, isn't he?"

"Yeah. Yeah, he is."

There was a pause, and she could hear that her father was moving around. Leaving whatever room he was in and moving to another.

"You guys talk a lot while you're over there?" he asked in a cautious voice.

"Uh, no, not really. Haven't really talked much at all, actually," she was honest.

"Baby, you need to just say what you want, and mean what you say," her father's voice was soft.

"I know, Dad. I know. And he and I are gonna talk. *Believe me,* we're gonna talk," she groaned.

"Well, you know I love you, and I support any decisions you make," he assured her. She took a deep breath.

"Really, Dad? *Any* decision?" she challenged him.

"Of course, sweetie."

"What if I decide to shave my head and pierce my nose?" she

threw out there, and he laughed. "Or what if I quit my job and become a trapeze artist? Or . . . what if I joined a commune, shacked up with three different guys?"

The last one was as close as she could get to testing his fatherly love in regards to her indiscretion.

"If you wanna look stupid, that's your own choice, doesn't make a difference to me, and I always loved the circus, so I would be thrilled if you took that trapeze job. And while I don't think you're cut out for commune life, as long as those boys treat you right, I'm sure I could get used to it," he responded to all her suggestions.

Mischa took another deep breath and closed her eyes. Let her head drop back. Let the setting sun burn the side of her face. Let her thoughts run on and on, until her father asked if she was still there.

He was very intuitive, they were very close, and he knew something was up. Knew something was wrong. But Mischa wiggled around, made small talk, and eventually worked her way off the call. Made kissy noises in the phone before she said goodbye.

In Rome, she'd always been busy. With work during the day, then all her evenings with Tal. So her days and her nights had been filled. In Positano, the free time was killing her. She'd lain awake for hours the night before, her mind and heart racing. Going over and over what she would say to Mike. Going over and over what she wished she'd said to Tal.

Her next night was shaping up to be the same. There was some sort of festival going on in the town, but she wasn't about to take part. She planned on ordering up some room service and trying to find something, anything, to distract herself. Maybe pull her fingernails off with a pair of tweezers. *Anything.* The idea of talking to Mike made her want to throw up, but the idea of never seeing Tal again . . . it was actually worse. It made her want to explode.

When she'd been making her rounds with the phone, she had tried calling another friend, and the girl hadn't answered, so when her cell rang, Misch assumed it was her. She was laying face down on her bed, trying to suffocate herself with the pillows, so she didn't even look at it, just groped around for her phone and brought it to her ear.

"What time is it there? It's almost midnight here," she grumbled.

"Weird, it's the exact same time where I am."

Misch sat up so fast, her hand slipped on a pillow, throwing off her balance. She squeaked and tumbled to the floor, landing in a heap with the blankets. Her phone was buried under the comforter and she almost had a panic attack scrambling for it.

"Is this real?" she gasped when she finally had it again.

"Very real," Tal's voice was deep. It had only been about four days since she'd talked to him, but it felt like a lot longer. In her mind, it was *so much* longer.

"I'm sorry we didn't get to say goodbye. I'm sorry I missed your call. I'm sorry I didn't call you back. I'm sorry -," she began rambling.

"Misch, stop. It's okay. We're talking now," he said. She nodded.

"I miss you," she whispered.

"Good. Is he there?"

"No, not yet."

"*Good.*"

"How are you? How was work?" she asked, twisting her fingers in the blanket.

"Work was work. How are you?"

"Okay."

"Really?"

" . . . no, not really. But I'll be okay," she was honest.

"I won't."

"Excuse me?" she was caught off guard.

"I won't be okay until I see you again. I shouldn't have left like that, I had to come back," he explained. She closed her eyes. It felt so good to hear him say it, but it didn't make things easier.

"Tal, I wish we could, but I can't come back to Rome. I leave for Istanbul in four days," she told him.

"I'm not in Rome."

She stopped breathing.

"Where are you?"

"I'm in your lobby."

She leapt up from the floor and began pacing, another nervous habit. He was in her lobby!? What!? How!? He was supposed to be in another country! How did he even know which hotel she was at!?

"Don't do this. Don't do this to me," she moaned.

"I'm sorry, I couldn't help myself."

"I know it's hard, but you can't be here! Mike will be here in two days. I can't be with you and then be with him, see you and then see him," she babbled.

"You better not '*be with*' him," Tal growled.

"God, of course not! You think I could do that!? But I can't be sneaking off to see you during the days, and then coming home to him for the nights. I already hate myself enough as it is," she tried to explain.

"Stop it, you don't hate yourself. And I'm not asking you to do all that, just be with me tonight," he suggested. Her free hand went into her hair.

"You're making this so much harder, Tal. Why? Will it be easier to say goodbye tomorrow morning than it was Rome?" she demanded.

"No. It'll be hell. But I already went through it once; at least this time, I'll get to see your face when I say goodbye."

She closed her eyes.

"I can't see you," she whispered. "I can't see you, then go see him. I just can't. It wouldn't be right. I've already done so much wrong, Tal. I can't, I can't, I can't."

She'd thought about it a lot. Not being with Tal was horrible, but being with him and being with Mike was worse. Too many emotions, too many words. She was worried if she saw Tal, if she talked to him in person, it would be over. She would be hopelessly addicted, and she would follow him off the edge of the map, and there would be no going back. And she couldn't do that—she was still tethered to another person.

"*Come find me,*" he whispered back to her.

"I can't."

"You can."

"I won't."

"You will."

"Please stop," she begged.

"I can't stop.

"I'm hanging up," she threatened.

"Good. After you do that, come find me."

She hung up.

She paced clear out to the balcony. Then clear back to the front door. Back and forth, chomping on her bottom lip the whole time. He'd told her to be strong—this was the time to prove it. She'd told herself she wouldn't see him again. She would damn well stick to that promise. She owed it to him, even if he didn't realize it was better that way. She owed it to Mike, even if he didn't know it was going on. She owed it to herself, because . . .

Aw, fuck.

Mischa was in the hallway before she knew what she was doing. She halfway expected him to be out there, but the floor was empty. She would go down to the lobby, see him before he saw her, then she would sneak back up. That was it. She just wanted to see him one last time, burn his image into her brain. That was it, that was all.

Yeah, right.

As she walked to the elevators, she could feel her heart rate increasing. Feel her blood pressure rise. It was like a change in the ionosphere, a drop in the barometric pressure. She felt static electricity coursing through her body, to the ends of her hair. The closer she got, the more electric she felt, and when she hit the down button, there was a static spark big enough to create a tiny bolt of lightning.

This is bad. So bad. So wrong. So bad.

The elevator door immediately slid open, like it had been sitting on her floor. But it wasn't empty.

"*I knew you'd find me.*"

Tal was leaning against the side of the door, smiling down at her.

"I just . . . wanted to see you," she said in a small voice.

"You see me, Misch."

He yanked her into the elevator, then hit the floor for the lobby. She stared at him in awe, like they were meeting again after a long time apart. He didn't say anything, didn't even touch her, until the doors opened back up. Then he grabbed her hand and pulled her out of the elevator. Out of the hotel. Down the street.

She wasn't sure what was going on, but she went with it. He was walking so quickly, she almost had to run to keep up. They zipped down side streets, hurried down stairs, raced across squares. The farther they got, the more she started hearing things. Music and people, voices and laughing. When the smell of food hit her, she realized he was taking her to the festival. A second later, they came out of an alley and were right in the thick of everything.

"What are we doing?" Mischa laughed, ducking as a man carrying a huge bunch of balloons pushed past her.

"Having fun," Tal said back, leading her down the street at a more sedate pace.

She knew what he was really doing—it was a distraction. An interference, so they wouldn't have to acknowledge what was really going on. They didn't talk about their situation, about why they couldn't stay away from each other, or why they also couldn't be together, because those words that could break them were still floating in the air. So she followed where he led, traveled in his wake, basked in his presence.

They played games and ordered food, acted like teenagers. He won her a large stuffed tiger, which she turned around and gave to a little girl who had been crying. He got an ice cream cone for her, then held it for her while she licked at it as they walked. They told jokes and laughed and talked. And talked and talked and talked. They didn't touch each other, and they didn't ask any questions. But they talked.

"What a good time!" Misch called out, skipping ahead of him onto a beach. There were a couple groups of people hanging out, a couple fire pits roaring. Tal headed in the opposite direction of them, towards a rocky, craggy end of the beach.

"Yeah, I thought you'd like it," he chuckled, shoving his hands deep into his pockets.

"The hotel told me there would be booths and parades and stuff, but I was just gonna hang out in my room," Misch told him, walking in his shadow.

"How lame. I bet you're glad I showed up," he teased.

It was too close to truth speaking.

They gingerly climbed their way over rocks and discovered a small patch of sand between outcroppings of stone. A mini-beach, as it were. Misch hopped down and ran right into the water. Stood ankle deep and wiggled her feet into the sand.

"Heaven," she whispered, clasping her hands together on top of her head.

"You're welcome!"

She smirked over her shoulder at Tal before going back to the ocean. It was a clear night and the moon was strong, giving them a lot of light. And on top of that, light was filtering in from the town, so it wasn't completely dark. But the water was inky black as it lapped at her feet. As she stared into it, her thoughts sank down into the depths. It had been a fun night, but what about tomorrow?

Detox is a bitch . . .

"Tal," she said his name. Wanted to say it all the time.

"Hmmm?"

"Come stand with me."

"No thank you."

"Excuse me!?" Mischa was shocked and turned to look at him. He was standing far enough back that the water wasn't touching him.

"I don't want to get wet," he explained. She was surprised.

"Seriously? Tal, do you not know how to swim?" she laughed at him. He scowled.

"Of course I can fucking swim. Like a fish. But I don't feel like swimming right now," he told her.

"Why?"

"I'm wearing clothes, for one."

"Little miss priss afraid to get her clothing wet?" Misch teased him. He rolled his eyes.

"I've had enough of your sass, lady," he warned her, but his voice was teasing as well.

"Oooohhh, what're you gonna do about it? Nothing, not while I'm out here and you're over there!" she taunted.

"Don't push me."

"I can't believe you're actually afraid to get messy!" she laughed at him.

"Shut up."

"Scaredy cat. Miss priss," she continued teasing him.

"Someone wants a spanking," he threatened.

"Oh, please."

"I'm not kidding."

"Well, then I better make it worth it," she said, bending over and reaching her hands into the water, into the sand at her feet.

"Whatever you're thinking, don't," Tal's voice was actually serious.

"Don't what, Mr. Canaan?" she asked in an innocent voice as she

122

held up huge handfuls of wet sand.

"Don't do it."

"Oh, I think I have to do it."

"Don't."

"Can't stop now."

"Seriously, Mischa."

"Oh, I'm deadly serious."

"If you throw that, I'll -,"

Tal didn't finish, as a double fistful of sand hit him smack in the chest. Misch shrieked, laughing as he looked down at himself. When he looked back up, he was glaring. She kept snorting and laughing and waded backwards, farther into the ocean.

"I couldn't help myself!" she called out to him.

"You're going to regret that," he sighed as he reached down and pulled off his shoes.

"Probably, but it was *so* worth it," she assured him.

"We'll see if you still feel that way in a couple minutes."

When he began striding into the water, she realized he was serious. She shrieked again and waded deeper, reaching down to grab more ammo. Before she could turn to throw it at him, she got a handful of sand chucked at her ass.

Oh, it's on.

They flung sand and water back and forth, laughing and shouting as they circled each other. Tal kept warning her to stop, and she kept throwing more gunk at him. But when she finally chucked a huge pile of sand directly in his face, she pushed him too far.

"Okay, play time is over," he said in a steely voice as he wiped sand out of his eyes.

Misch turned and ran. Well, ran as well as she could in hip deep water. He was deeper than her, and she figured that would slow him down. But she was wrong. She hadn't made it very far when he tackled her. Full on tackled her. Arms around her waist, throwing all of his weight on top of her. She screamed as they went down and he pulled her under the water.

"Oh my god," she hacked and coughed when she broke the surface. Her hair was plastered across her face and she couldn't see anything. She went to move forward when her leg was yanked out from under her. She squawked and face planted in the ocean.

"I warned you," Tal was laughing as he dragged her upright, helping her to stand on her feet.

"You have no mercy," she coughed, trying to clear the salt water from her lungs while she pushed her hair out of her face.

"Never forget that, baby," she heard him say, then he smacked her on the ass and brushed past her, heading back to the beach.

Misch chuckled and followed him, straightening out her dress as she went—the same black sun dress she'd been wearing when they'd met. She got right to the edge of the water and stopped to adjust her sandal, which was hanging halfway off her foot.

"You could've drowned me, you know. How do you know I can't -,"

"Babe, look, look, look," he urged, and when she glanced at him, he was pointing to the sky over her shoulder.

Misch turned around just in time to see a huge firework explode. She gasped as a boom rattled across the beach, followed by a billion little red fires, flying through the air. Another light streaked across the sky, and then a green flower was blossoming within the explosion. She laughed and clapped her hands. She hadn't known there would be fireworks, what a treat. What a way to end the night.

As lights exploded all around them, she looked over her shoulder, smiling at Tal. He wasn't looking at her, he had his head tilted towards the sky, his arms folded across his chest. The different colors washed over his face. Red, green, blue, blue, red. He was in technicolor.

Misch stared at him, then turned to fully face him. Slowly walked towards him as she took in his height. His broad shoulders and black hair. His strong features and long legs. His kindness and caring. His thoughts and his words. So many words unsaid.

He didn't notice her till she was right in front of him, then he did a double take at her. He smiled and went to say something, then stopped. Just stared right back at her, with his heavy black eyes.

I want this night to last forever.

"Why did you come here, Tal?" she asked plainly. Such a simple question. Such a loaded question. He took a deep breath.

"I had to see you, Mischa."

"What happened to your job?" she pressed.

"I decided you were more important."

Warmth spread across her chest.

"What am I gonna do with you?" she chuckled.

"I can think of a few things."

"How long do you have?" her voice was soft.

"Not long," his voice was equally as soft.

"I only have two days," she whispered.

"Any time. I want any time with you."

The fireworks exploded, and her heart pounded, and she knew it was a bad idea. All the decisions she'd made in the last eight years had been bad ones, apparently.

So why not just roll with it?

She ran her fingers across his forehead as green light rained down on them. Down the side of his face while blue light washed over him. Pressed her hand flat against his chest as red light surrounded them.

"*Okay.*"

She all but leapt on him, pressing her mouth to his. His hands immediately went to her hips, his fingers squeezing. They were in fast forward, flying through time, trying to reach a speed where it wouldn't matter any more. He wrapped an arm around her waist and twisted her around, laid her on the sand. She yanked and pulled at his shirt, ripping it open, all while he pulled her panties over her hips and down her legs. She kicked them away while he undid his belt.

Words were still a danger zone, so they didn't speak. She just wrapped her legs around his waist and he put his hands under her ass, lifting her hips into the air, forcing her back to arch. She worked her hands between them, holding the base of his dick as he invaded her space. Conquered her body.

He kept one hand on her ass and moved the other to her breast. She put her hand over his and squeezed. Cried out as he thrust into her, over and over again. His hand slid out from underneath hers and worked its way over her throat, up her chin, two of his fingers sliding into her mouth. She moaned and wrapped her lips around them, ran her tongue over his skin.

He pulled his hand away abruptly, and before Misch could say anything, they were moving. She yelped as he swung her around, moving them so he was sitting flat, and she was sitting on his lap, her legs still around his waist. She was so impaled on him, she couldn't even think. Couldn't make a sound.

"*Look at me.*"

She opened her eyes and was reminded of the first time they'd ever had sex. He'd made the same command, told her to keep her eyes open. She nodded her head and began shivering on top of him, something she also hadn't done since that first time.

With his hands guiding her, she worked her hips back slowly, then slid them forward. He moaned and pressed his forehead to hers. His hips began jerking forward, and soon enough they were moving like a finely tuned machine. Like a pair of dancers.

The fireworks exploded around them and Misch pressed her hand to the side of his face as she gasped for air. She wasn't able to fill her lungs, she needed him to breathe for her. He stared straight into her eyes, and his lips were moving, but she couldn't hear anything over the explosions. Over her heart beat.

When her orgasm came, she didn't close her eyes. She shouted and shook and cried out. Called out his name, over and over again. He called back to her, and she finally heard what he was saying, over and over again.

"*Please.*"

By the time he came, Mischa knew. She knew it wasn't over. Knew two days wasn't long enough. A week wasn't long enough. Another month wasn't long enough. There wasn't enough time for her and Tal. Not nearly. A tear slid down her cheek, quickly followed by another.

"I don't want you to go away," she whispered, kissing his lips, his jaw, his cheeks.

"Then I won't," he was panting for air and kissing her back.

"I don't know how to be like this," she cried quietly.

"*Then I'll teach you,*" he promised.

Funny how things come full circle.

Boom Boom Boom

THEY SPENT THE NIGHT in the suite that was meant for her boss, and they talked. Said the words that were too scary to say before, said the things they felt. The things they wanted. Then they built from there.

"Did you really cut your job short?" Mischa asked, stretching out on her stomach on the bed. Tal was laying on top of the covers next to her, only wearing a pair of boxer briefs.

"Yeah. I was sitting in this room and I just kept thinking, '*I shouldn't be here, I'm not needed here,*' you know? I'm more of an in-the-field kind of guy, anyway," he told her.

"Isn't that kind of necessary, to be a photographer? Are you gonna get in trouble?" she wondered out loud. He shook his head.

"No. I said exactly that to them, that I wasn't needed there, why not just let me go, and call me back when I was needed? They said sure. I came straight here," he said.

"How romantic," she teased. He snorted.

"No shit."

"Ug, never mind, I take it back."

"Let's go over it again," he suggested, ignoring her. She cleared her throat.

"Alright."

"What are you gonna do when he gets here?" Tal asked.

"We're going to go to dinner—I already have reservations. Then we're going to go for a walk on the beach," Misch went over the plan she'd come up with earlier in the week, before Tal had reappeared.

"Not our beach," he interrupted.

"No, I wouldn't take him there. We'll walk on the beach, and I'm gonna sit him down and I'm gonna just tell him. I'm gonna make him listen to me, and I'm just gonna tell him," she said, making a decisive slice with her hand.

"And then?"

"And then, if he's understanding—eventually, obviously—I'll go to the airport with him and say goodbye, then I'll meet you back here."

"And if he's not '*understanding*'?"

"Then I'll apologize as best I can, as much as I can, but I won't . . . I won't let it deter me. I won't back down," she said it in as strong a voice as she could muster.

"*And then?*"

"Then I'll meet you back here, and we'll go to Istanbul, and we'll just see," she finished.

"We'll see where it goes," Tal agreed.

"Are we really doing this?" she double checked. He snorted again.

"You better believe it, baby."

"I wasn't looking for a boyfriend," she told him.

"Are you kidding? I was just using you for sex, left, right, and sideways. I think I've been brainwashed. That's it, I've changed my mind, the plan is off," he stated in a loud voice.

She hit him with a pillow.

"But what if this is just like . . . a rebound relationship?" she voiced her fears.

"Babe, you'd have to be out of your relationship in order to be on the rebound," he pointed out. She rolled her eyes.

"What if it's cause this is just new and exciting? What if this is just cause I was forbidden fruit to you?" she went on. He reached over and pressed his hand against the back of her thigh.

"You were never forbidden fruit to me—you were just an apple that needed to be plucked," he told her, and she swatted him in the chest. "And like I told you before, if you can look me in the eye and honestly say this doesn't feel as real as can fuckin' be, that it's just something '*new and exciting*' to you, then I'll walk out that door. Never contact you again."

Mischa leaned over and kissed him, working her tongue against his. His fingers clenched into her thigh, then raked their way up to her ass, moving under the edge of her underwear.

"I think it's real," she whispered.

She had to believe that. She had to have faith in that. If she didn't, then she couldn't believe in anything ever again, and her soul would be beyond saving.

"Whenever you get doubt-y, I'm going to fuck you. That seems to clear your head," he suggested.

"Oh, well then, I have *lots* of doubts. You snore, I don't know if I can be with a person like that. And you do this weird thing when you eat, where you scrape your fork with your teeth. I think my mom will hate you, and I -," she started rambling. He moved swiftly, rolling her onto her back and pinning her to the mattress.

"We need to work on your inhibitions. If you want me to fuck you, then just say it. Repeat after me—'*Tal, I want you to fuck me so hard, I won't walk right for a week*'," he instructed.

"Tal, I want you to—wait, for a week!? I wanted to go sight seeing," she complained, trying not to laugh.

"Whatever happened to my good girl? Who is this person? That's it, I'm going to teach you a lesson, Ms. -," his voice stopped, and they stared at each other. He cleared his throat. "I can't call you that." She nodded.

"I don't want you to call me that."

"Your maiden name," he said it as a statement, rather than a question, as he sat back on his heels.

"Duggard," she responded while he picked up her left hand. She had put her rings back on when she'd gotten to Positano. Tal took them back off.

"Ms. Duggard, it's lovely to meet you," he said, setting her rings on a night stand.

"Thank you, Mr. Canaan, the pleasure is all mine."

"It's certainly about to be."

⠑⠕⠑

Since she was now Ms. Duggard, Tal insisted that they go out on a real date, so he could get to know this woman.

"I hope she's not as neurotic as the last chick I banged," he said as he got dressed. His luggage had been delivered late the night before.

"Oh? And who was that?" Misch asked, leaning close to the mirror while she did her eye makeup.

"Mrs. Rapaport."

She threw a bar of soap at him.

They went on a day date, out to lunch at a fancy cafe. He got them a table on a balcony that sat over a cliff, looking out over the ocean. Misch breathed in the salty air, glad to be alive. Glad to not be thinking of what the next evening would bring.

"So, Ms. Duggard—*Mischa*—tell me more about yourself," he insisted. She sipped at her tea.

"What would you like to know?" she asked back.

"You're very exotic, you know," he told her. She blinked in surprise.

"Me? Boring old, insurance agent me!?" she exclaimed.

"God, you're annoying. You're not just an insurance agent, you twit, you're a woman, with tits and ass and legs for days and a smile that doesn't quit and a wit to match. Do you ever look at yourself?" Tal demanded. She blushed.

"No. Not really. Not anymore."

"See? Annoying. What's your dad like?"

"My dad? He's awesome. Grew up in Kansas, then moved to Detroit to go to school. Met my mom, and the rest is history. He's my buddy, I love him more than anything," she answered.

"What about your mom? Is she awesome?" Tal continued.

"Yeah, in a mom type of way," Misch responded, working around the question.

"What's that supposed to mean?"

"We don't quite get each other, you know? She's half Chinese, and her mom was super old school, and very strict. So here I am, this kinda mutt, a little Chinese, a lot German and Dutch, and all American. I wanted to dance and meet boys, she wanted me to study and become a brain stem surgeon, or something. She's super supportive and sweet, but it's kinda like, eh, I'm *that* kid to her," Misch tried to explain.

"*Chinese!* I was guessing Puerto Rican," Tal mumbled, his eyes wandering over her face.

"Excuse me?"

"Your ethnicity. You look amazing, your parents were a good blend—there should be more Chinese-German-Dutch babies in the world," he commented. She blushed again.

"Well, what about you, tall, dark, and verbally abusive? What's your deal?" she asked, leaning back as their waiter delivered their food.

"Me? Just a good ol' boy, raised in New York," he replied. But she already knew that, from their many conversations.

"If you're gonna badger me with questions, you've got to give some stuff up, too," she pointed out. He sighed.

"I was born in Jerusalem. My family moved to New York—Brooklyn. When I was thirteen, we went back to Jerusalem. When I was eighteen, I joined the Israeli Defense Forces," he covered everything.

"So your parents are both from Israel?" she prodded. He shook his head.

"No. My mother was from New York, she's mostly Italian. Catholic, her parents were not happy when she decided to marry my very Jewish father. They forgave her when I was born, that's why my parents moved back to the states. But my dad hated it, and my mom didn't really care where we were, so we went back to Israel," he elaborated.

"Oh. So when was the last time you were back in the states?"

"Never."

"Huh?"

"I've never gone back. I didn't like it in America, never really had a reason to go back. Both my grandparents died, so there was no one left over there to visit. I was busy with the army, then busy with my job. When you get to see all different parts of the world, America isn't so great," he told her. She scowled.

"It's good enough for me. I like it there," she pointed out. He smiled.

"You'll like it better in Istanbul. Or how about Tokyo? Ever been there? Maybe I'll take you to Dubai," he sounded like he was talking to himself.

"How about I take you to California, so you can see some of the most beautiful coast line in the world? Or maybe New Orleans, probably the most interesting place I've ever been in my life, *including* the places I've been here," she responded.

"Baby, if I'm with you, I'll probably love it."

Well, it's hard to keep arguing when he's being cute.

When they'd been in Rome, they'd already spent a lot of their time together just talking, but usually fun stuff. Favorite foods, movies they liked, books they hated, places they'd been—now it was interesting to get more into the nitty gritty. To hear about his time in the army, about how scary it had been, how secretly he'd been glad to leave it. For her to tell him about how she used to dream of opening her own dance studio, but had long since given up on it, especially after the knee injury. Her body scared her now, she didn't know if she could go back full time.

"You can."

They really hadn't known each other that long—Misch had always known the men she'd dated. They'd been acquaintances or schoolmates or friends. Tal had been sex first, ask questions later, but it seemed to be working. And what she was feeling with him was definitely something she'd never felt before; she wouldn't deny that, and she wasn't even trying to sugar coat her situation. If anything, she'd already spent a great deal of time trying to convince herself that it wasn't real. And she wasn't blinded by lust. It was fact. There was something strong between them.

Maybe it was fate. A really fucked up, long term play by fate. If I hadn't met Michael, we wouldn't have started dating, which means we wouldn't have gotten married, which means I wouldn't have become miserable, which means I wouldn't have come to Italy, which means I wouldn't have met the most amazing person. But why does my happiness have to come at his expense?

She asked Tal the same question, later that evening, while they were playing around in bed. They'd gone on a day date because Tal would have to leave early in the morning. Mike was due in the next evening, they didn't want to cut it too close. Tal didn't want to waste time not touching her, so they went back to her room. Explored each other a little more.

"Maybe fate's holding out for him, too," Tal suggested. She was laying on top of his chest, running her hand up and down his side.

"She's being a pretty big bitch about this whole thing," Misch replied, and he laughed.

"She isn't known for being nice."

"I don't want him to be sad," Misch whispered.

"It's unavoidable now, baby."

"It's going to be the hardest thing ever."

"Want to back out? Go home with him?"

" . . . okay, the second hardest thing ever."

"Good girl."

Mischa woke up to something tickling her. She batted at her leg and tried to go back to sleep. Whatever it was didn't go away, though, but continued its path up her leg. She was half asleep, and her body couldn't decide whether to wake up and investigate, or sleep and pray it wasn't anything nefarious.

She clued into the fact that it was fingers right around the time her underwear was yanked down.

"What are you doing?" she grumbled, shifting her legs around as the material slid down to her feet.

"Having breakfast," Tal said simply, his breath hot against her thigh as he moved between her legs.

"What time is it?"

"A little after six in the morning."

"Jesus, we just went to sleep a couple hours ago."

"I know. What a waste of a couple hours."

She went to argue with him, but he sucked on the inside of her thigh, hard. She yelped in surprise and he moved farther north, blowing cold air as he went. He always knew how to catch her off guard, and before she could get her bearings, he really was eating her like she was continental breakfast.

"Oh, wow, what a way to wake up," she groaned, fisting her hand in his hair, pulling a little.

"You're usually so grumpy in the mornings, I should wake you up like this more often," he chuckled at her as he pulled away, replacing his tongue with his middle finger.

"No one is stopping you."

While his finger worked in and out of her, he kissed his way up the side of her hip. Circled her belly button with his tongue. Her shirt covered her chest, and he frowned as he worked to push the material aside.

"We've got to break you of this nasty modesty habit you have," he complained, kissing the top of each of her breasts.

"I've always been this way," she replied, beginning to pant as his hand worked faster and faster.

"We're going to change that."

Then his mouth was on hers and he was kissing her hard, his tongue imitating his finger. She pushed her body up against his, rubbing her naked chest against his, creating heat. When his finger stroked particularly deep, she gasped and pulled away from him, only to have his teeth sink into her bottom lip.

"Please, please," she began to whimper.

"Please, what?" he asked, looking down the length of her body, watching his fingers move.

"I want you . . . inside me . . . now," she panted.

"I am inside you," his voice was mocking.

"Not like this."

"Like how?"

"Tal, just fuck me."

"Oh, feisty. *I love it.*"

He didn't move, though—he seemed determined to get her off on his hand. She was thrashing underneath him, literally begging for his cock, when the hotel phone began to ring on the night stand next to her.

"Who the fuck could that be!?" she exclaimed, moving her hips back against his hand, now striving to come on his fingers.

"Probably the front desk calling, asking you to keep quiet," he teased.

"I don't care, I can't keep quiet."

"Answer it. Let them hear you. Let them hear what I can do to you," he whispered.

God, it was so bad. So wrong. *So fucking hot.* She began to shiver, and she knew an orgasm wasn't far off, so she picked up the phone.

"Hello?" she breathed into the receiver.

"*Surprise!*"

Mischa sat up so fast, she smacked her forehead into Tal's collar bone. He immediately backed away and grabbed her by the shoulders, holding her in place. She felt like she was going to hyperventilate. Like she was going to pass out. *Like she was going to have a heart attack.*

No no no no no no no no no . . .

"*Mike!?*" she hissed, her eyes flying to Tal's. His eyebrows shot up and he stared at her for a second, then began moving. He crawled backwards off the bed and moved quickly around the suite, collecting his clothing.

"Yeah! I was able to get out on the early flight yesterday, isn't that great!?" her husband laughed.

"Yeah . . . great . . . where are you right now? Naples?" she asked, talking around her bottom lip, which was lodged between her teeth.

"No, I'm here."

"You're at the hotel?" Mischa looked at Tal, who paused in the middle of putting on his pants and looked back at her.

"I'm outside a room," Mike replied. Misch nearly fell off the bed.

"*You're at the door!?*" she practically shrieked. Tal's eyes moved to the front door of the suite, then he went back to putting on his pants.

"Yeah, I knocked on the door for like five minutes," Mike started. Misch scrambled to get off the bed, pushing her shirt back down over her breasts.

"Knocking? I haven't heard any knock," she replied, watching as Tal strode towards the door and peeked out the peep-hole. He looked back at her and shook his head.

"Well, yeah, cause apparently you're not in *this* room anymore. I tried your cell phone, but you didn't answer, so I called the front desk. They said you'd switched rooms, but wouldn't give me the new number, would only patch me through to the room phone," Mike explained.

Oh, thank god.

"I forgot to tell you," she let out a deep sigh and pressed her hand to her forehead. "I'm not in that room anymore." Tal went back to moving around, yanking on a shirt and then shoving the rest of his stuff into his duffel bag.

"Obviously. Why'd you get moved?" Mike sounded annoyed. Mischa watched as Tal went into the bathroom, and when he came out, he was carrying his toiletries. They all got dumped in the bag, which then got zipped up.

"Peter had to go to New York to get some stuff, he gave me his suite," Mischa explained about her boss.

"Oh, sweet! Upgrade! What's the room number?"

"Room 1816."

Tal finished putting on his shoes, then walked right up to her and kissed her quickly. Before she could respond, he hugged her close and put his lips to her ear.

"*I'm here with you. Be strong. If you need me, come find me.*"

Then he was walking out of the room, not a trace of him left behind.

"Sounds great, I'll be up there in a minute!" her husband said in a cheery voice. Then the line went dead.

Misch spun in about three circles, not sure what the fuck to do. Then she ran into the bathroom, ripping her shirt over her head. Tal's fingers had been inside her not two minutes ago. She just . . . couldn't meet her husband, not while she was stained with another man's skin.

What the fuck is going on!? How can this be happening!? I'm not ready. I'm not ready. I'm soooooooo not ready. I don't think I'll ever be ready.

She turned on the water and jumped underneath it, just long enough to run a washcloth over her skin and between her legs. Then she jumped back out and ran around the suite. Slipped on some underwear and a long, sleeveless, jersey knit dress. Very beachy, very non-sexy, very non-confrontational.

Is there recommended fashion for this? "What to wear when you break up with your husband" clothing?

She was almost to the door of the suite when she realized she still wasn't wearing her rings. She cursed and ran back to the night stand, and had just slipped them on when there was a knock at the door.

Be strong. You can do this. Be strong. Fuck. FUCK. I AM SO FUCKING FUCKED.

Tal shut the door to the suite behind him.

And then he waited.

Waited till he heard the elevator ding, down at the other end of the hall.

Then he slid his sunglasses on and walked forward, one hand casually in his pants pocket, his bag swinging in his other hand.

Of course he knew what Michael Rapaport looked like, he had seen plenty of pictures. But seeing someone in person is different, and seeing the husband of the woman Tal had just gotten done fucking, well, that was a whole new realm of different.

The other man was wearing board shorts and a tank, with hiking shoes on his feet. He was also wearing sunglasses, and he was smiling broadly as he made his way down the hall. Obviously excited. He was quite a bit shorter than Tal, but he was very wiry, and Tal remembered Mischa telling him her husband was a marathon runner, had gone to the University of Michigan on a track-and-field scholarship. It showed.

"Hey," Michael said as he passed, smiling and giving a head nod.

"*Ciao,*" Tal replied in a low voice, nodding his head as well. He could be polite to the other man, had no reason to be rude at all.

Fucker.

They passed each other without saying anything else. Just barely brushed arms.

Mischa had once told Tal that when she was with him, she felt like time would stop. Like they were in another realm, another dimension, something. "*A timeless existence,*" she'd called it. He'd written it off as romantic notions from a lonely woman experiencing passion, *real passion,* for the first time.

But now Tal understood, because that was *exactly* how he felt. As he turned to face the elevator, he could still see Michael out of the corner of his eye. Could watch as the other man knocked on the door, could see that door open, and had to witness as Michael immediately pulled Mischa into his arms. Wrapped her in a hug and picked her up off the ground.

Picked *Tal's* woman up and touched her body.

Except she's not yours. Not completely. Not yet.

Tal went down to the lobby and seated himself in a cushioned chair. Clenched and unclenched his fists. He and Mischa had come up with a plan, and originally, Tal would have left in an hour or two anyway. He'd booked a room at a different hotel. They figured it was safer that way, in case something happened and Mike refused to leave. Mischa absolutely did not want the two men meeting. It would be bad enough hurting Mike; she didn't wanna rub Tal in his face, and she didn't trust herself or Tal to keep away from each other if they were in the same hotel.

But Tal couldn't leave. Not yet. He kept his sunglasses on and picked up a newspaper. Read it forwards and backwards. Kept glancing at the elevator.

What are they doing up there!?

The problem with existing in Mischa's *"timeless place"*—fifteen minutes felt like an eternity, but that was all the time that elapsed between Tal leaving her floor, and the couple entering the lobby. He peered over the top of the newspaper, watching them pass in front of him.

He wondered how Michael could be so clueless. It would have been obvious to anyone with eyes and a brain that there was some sort of problem between the two. Michael strode across the lobby, all eager and excited to hit the town, almost marching in his haste to make it outside.

Mischa moved much slower, more languidly, and she didn't look excited at all. She looked somewhere between annoyed and going-to-her-own-funeral. She had a fedora shoved down low on her head, covering hair that looked damp, and she wore a large pair of sunglasses. Her dress was long and simple enough, but the thin material clung to her curves, and she held it up and away from her feet as she walked. So graceful. So beautiful. So out of place with the other man.

They don't even look like they're together. At all. Just two strangers who shared an elevator. That poor man. **That poor girl.**

Well, I Didn't See That Coming

MISCHA GLANCED AT HER cell phone, then glanced at her husband. Jet lag had knocked him out, like a baby. He was even still wearing his clothes, stretched out on top of the covers, snoring away.

She chewed on her bottom lip, debated whether or not to answer the incoming call, then grabbed the phone and tiptoed across the suite. She slowly opened the door, wincing at how loud it sounded. But when she glanced at the bed, Mike was still out cold. She slid out of the room and eased the door shut.

It was an all out dash after that; she ran to the other end of the hall, answering the phone as she went.

"Hello?" she panted, stopping when she got to a wall.

"What the fuck is going on?" Tal demanded. She grimaced. He sounded *pissed.*

"Nothing, I just snuck out of the room," she whispered, pacing back and forth, staring at the door she'd just left.

"You wouldn't have to sneak out *if he wasn't there,*" Tal snapped.

"I know, I know," she groaned.

"What the fuck happened to the plan!?"

"It's still the plan!" she snapped back. "It's just . . . *delayed,* alright!?"

"No! No, not fucking alright! Grow a backbone, Mischa!"

"*Hey!* I'm trying! This is hard for me, and you're not exactly making it any fucking easier!" she hissed.

"Well, excuse me, but I'm already very aware of how shitty you are at dealing with difficult situations. Why is he still there?" Tal asked. She chose to ignore his "shitty" comment.

"Because, I didn't get a chance to say anything yet," she started. She could hear him take a breath, a big one, probably so he could yell at her, and she barreled right through him. "He wanted to see all these touristy sights, and I couldn't exactly dump him at the *Grotta di Fornillo,* knee deep in tourists!"

"Did you spend all fucking day there?" Tal's voice was snide.

"No, but we did go just about everywhere else. The man can walk for days, Tal. I had to beg for lunch. Then he wanted to fill me in on everything that's gone on at home—everything I've missed out on because I was avoiding his phones calls for *somebody else,*" she threw back at him. If he was going to make her feel like shit, then he should feel that way, too.

"Don't you put this shit on me. You spent all day together. You walked around. You talked. All things that were in the original plan," he pointed out. Mischa rolled her eyes.

"Sometimes plans go differently when they're put into motion!"

"No. No, they don't. I live my life by plans, and you know what? You make a plan, you follow a plan, you execute a plan. So far, you've only accomplished step one," he informed her.

"You know what? Whatever, it's too late. Bitch all you want, the day is done, it's after ten o'clock. Tomorrow, I promise," she swore to him.

"Did you fuck him?"

She was shocked.

"Is that a real fucking question!?" she demanded.

"Of course it is. You cheated on him with me, who's to say you won't cheat on me with him!?"

She felt as if she'd been slapped. She yanked the phone away from her ear and hung up.

*How the fuck could he say that to me!? How **dare he** fucking say that to me! Who the fuck does he think he is!? What the fuck does he think is happening between us!?*

Mischa clenched her teeth together and let out a mock shriek, pacing double time between the walls.

It's a very valid point. You're the bad guy here. Not Mike. Not Tal.

Just you. Don't get angry. Understand where he's coming from, and move past it.

When her phone rang, she answered it.

"I'm sorry," Tal immediately said, his voice even and flat.

"I'm sorry, too," she managed to respond in an equally even, flat tone.

"Fuck, Misch," he groaned, the flatness falling away. "I'm just . . . I know it's hard for you, *I know.* But it isn't exactly fucking easy for me, knowing you're up there with him. Knowing he's gonna sleep next to you tonight. What if he touches you!? What if he wakes you up the way I woke you up!? I'll fucking kill him."

"Stop it, no you won't. And he won't do that, either, he's not like that. And even if he randomly decided to be, I won't let him. *I promise you.* You and me, right? You said that. *You said it,*" she reminded him.

"I know, I know. It's just . . . *hard.*"

They were both silent for a while and Mischa put her back against the wall before sliding down it, lowering herself so she sat on the floor.

"When I came to Italy," she started, her voice thick. "I had my plan. But nothing went according to that plan. When I slept with you, *that* didn't go according to plan. *Nothing* has gone the way I thought it would, and *nothing* was easy like I thought it would be."

"That's not true," his voice was soft.

"All of it's true," she sighed.

"Falling for you was the easiest thing I've ever done," he whispered. She managed a watery smile and picked at the edge of her dress.

"Yeah. Yeah, there's that," her voice was barely above a breath.

"*Promise me* you'll talk to him tomorrow," the hard edge was back in Tal's voice. She nodded.

"I promise. I've already told him that after breakfast we're going to the beach. Nothing else, no other stops, just the beach," she assured him, running her fingers up her leg and clasping her knee.

"If I don't hear from you by noon, I'm gonna call the room," Tal warned her.

"I don't appreciate being threatened," she snapped.

"I don't appreciate being shoved into the background."

Touché, Mr. Canaan.

"Alright, alright. If you don't hear from me by noon, feel free to call. Would it make it easier if you had his cell phone number?" she couldn't keep the sarcasm from dripping off her words.

"I already have it. *Noon.*"

Then the line went dead.

How does he know everything!?

Mischa's foot tapped out a staccato beat on the cobblestones. She chewed on her bottom lip and tugged at a lock of hair. A blind person would've been able to tell how nervous she was; Mike just kept shoveling eggs into his mouth.

"Hey, wanna go for a run on the beach?" he asked.

"Huh?" she hadn't been paying attention to him.

"A run, on the beach. You said you wanted to go to the beach," he reminded her.

The beach. The beach where I might have fallen in love. The beach where I'm going to end our love. I'll never be able to go to a beach again.

"Oh. Yeah. No, no running, Mikey," she told him. He glanced over his sunglasses at her.

"Remember how gung ho you were about exercising before you left," he said in a careful voice.

"Excuse me!?"

"I'm not trying to be a dick, babe, but you were so determined to lose weight. You don't wanna gain it all back while you're here," he pointed out. She sat up and put her hands on her hips.

"Are you implying that I've gained weight?" she asked, glaring at him.

"No. Well, I mean, maybe a couple pounds, which is fine, you look fine. But it only takes a couple more on top of that, and then you're right back where you were," he warned her.

Fuck this.

"Are you done?" she snapped, standing up from the table.

"What? I just started, I -,"

Mischa walked away from the table.

142

He caught up to her outside, laughing and giving her a quick sideways hug.

"C'mon, sweets, don't be mad at me," he begged in his baby voice, kissing the side of her neck. She resisted the urge to push him away.

He still thinks your skin belongs to him because you haven't told him that you gave it to someone else.

"I'm not, Mikey," she assured him, then let him hold her hand. Link their fingers together.

They chatted some more as they made their way to the beach. He talked about all the things he wanted to do while he was in Italy, and how excited he was that he was sharing the experiences with her. Mike had never traveled out of the United States. He didn't like to fly, and he'd once said he had no particular desire to travel. It was one of the reasons why they never went on vacation. Never even had a real honeymoon. Mike was a homebody.

"This is so beautiful," he groaned, letting go of her hand and jogging up to the water. Mischa trailed behind him and stopped a ways back. Glanced to her right, to an outcropping of rocks that hid a special beach. A special secret.

"It is," she whispered.

"And I'm so glad I'm here with you," he added, turning back towards her.

She smiled as he walked up to her. She had missed him, in her own weird, fucked up way. She enjoyed talking to him sometimes, he could be so funny. She had missed that. She would miss it so much.

"Mikey, there's something -," she began.

But she was cut off by him suddenly kissing her, wrapping his arms around her so tight, she found it hard to breathe. When he broke it off, she gasped for air, beyond bewildered.

"God, I've missed you, Misch," he moaned, kissing down the side of her neck.

"What are you doing!?" she exclaimed, wiggling under his touch as his hands wandered down her body.

"I know things have been weird at home, I know, but this time apart has made me think. We're gonna try, okay? We're gonna try. You put in all that work to get your body back, so I'm gonna be more attentive," he told her, kissing his way to her ear.

Wait . . . did he just imply that we weren't having sex because I'd gained weight!?

"Mike, stop, I need to talk to you," she said, pushing at his hands as they got grabbier.

"We talk all the time. *Shhhh,*" he replied, then his tongue darted in her ear. She literally jumped.

"*What are you doing!?*" she squealed, jerking her head away from him.

"Spicing things up, trying something new," he laughed.

"*Blech,* you know I don't like that! Stop it!" she demanded as one of his hands ran over her breasts.

"C'mon, there's hardly anyone out here. Let's be naughty," he suggested, his other hand moving to her ass and holding her against him as he ground his hips back against her.

"Let's not. I have to talk to you. *Michael, stop,*" she snapped, planting her hands on his chest and pushing. The use of his full name caught his attention and he finally leaned away.

"What? Are you okay?" he asked, ducking his head to look her in the eye. All the flirtiness from a moment ago was gone, and Mischa got the feeling he was finally seeing her. *Really* looking at her.

And it wasn't a pretty sight.

"No, I'm not okay. Not at all. I have to talk to you, about something important. Something big," she urged.

"Oh god. This is gonna be one of *those* talks, isn't it?" he complained.

Baby, you have no idea.

"Just sit down," she replied, before dropping to her butt. He sat in the sand next to her.

"Okay, what's so important that it can't wait till after our amazing holiday?" he asked, his voice snide.

Oh god. I can't do this. How am I going to do this?

"Mikey, we've got some problems," she started out slow.

"I know, babe. I just told you that I want to work on them," he said back. She swallowed thickly.

"I know you said that, but . . . we've had these problems for a while, and . . . I just . . . ," she struggled for words.

"What?"

"Sometimes things aren't fixable," her voice was so small, even she could barely hear it.

"What do you mean? Of course they are. You've just been gone, it seems weird, we haven't seen each other in a month. Have we ever gone that long without seeing each other?" he pointed out. She shook her head.

"It was weird before I left. It was weird before I even agreed to this job. It's gone too far. It's not fixable anymore, Mike," she told him, staring down at her knees.

"Wait," his voice was serious and he turned to face her. "Wait, wait, wait. What are you saying, Mischa?"

"I'm saying . . . ," her voice kept giving out.

"Tell me you're not saying what I think you're saying," he begged.

"I am."

"No."

"Mike."

"No."

"*Mike*. Things haven't been right for a while, and you know it. You're unhappy, I'm unhappy. It's gone too far," she tried to explain

"No! No, we can fix this! Just come home, and we'll fix this, I want to fix this," he told her.

"*I don't.*"

He gasped.

"Are you saying you want out!?" he sounded completely shocked.

"Yes."

"You want a divorce!?"

"Yes."

"Jesus, Mischa, we've been together forever! Just like that!?" he was yelling now.

"Not '*just like that*'!" she yelled back. "This was a long time coming, Mike! I tried to talk to you about it! So many times! You always pushed it aside, or patronized me, or promised to change, or ignored me! So many times! Not '*just like that*'!"

"Baby, baby, baby, you're upset. I get it. Whatever is wrong, I'm sorry. Just please, come home. Things will be better at home," he stressed.

"They won't. Things were *worse* at home. I *hate it* at home. I'm sorry, Mike. God, I'm so sorry. You have no idea how sorry. I'm just so fucking sorry," she started to cry.

"You hate it at home!? How can you say that!? You're the best part of home! You're my best friend!" he shouted.

"I should've been your wife!"

Her shriek settled around them, caused a few lone people on the beach to look up.

"What are you talking about?" he asked, looking completely lost. She wiped at her eyes.

"I've had a lot of time to think about this, Mike, and I think we've always been great friends. I hope someday we can be friends again. But I don't think we were ever . . . ever . . . *we were never lovers,"* she stressed, Tal's voice running through her head.

"*'Lovers'*? Is this a joke?"

"No. I wish it were. God, I wish it were. I just couldn't have this conversation over the phone with you. I had to tell you in person. I'm sorry," she sniffled. Mike's hands went into his hair and he bent forward.

"Had to tell me in person. *In person.* Why couldn't you come home? Why did I have to fly across the world!?" he demanded.

"I'm sorry. I couldn't come home, I just couldn't. I'm so sorry, Mike, I'm so sorry," she was having trouble breathing through her tears.

Suddenly he was moving, shuffling across the sand. He practically tackled her, resting all his weight on top of her. She fell backwards, giving a muffled yell as he kissed her again. His tongue dove into her mouth, aggressive and rough, not his usual style. She twisted her head away.

"Stop it!" she cried out.

"You've just forgotten what it's like. You love me, Misch. I know you do. *I know it,"* he whispered, kissing her jaw and her cheeks and her eyelids.

"I do love you, Mike. Just not that way. Stop it," she repeated herself, pushing at his hands.

"You do. And I love you. *I love you,"* he stressed, kissing his way down to her chest.

"*Stop it!"* she shouted, pushing at him hard enough to knock him off of her. He looked shocked.

"Jesus, what was that?" he asked, sitting up and examining his elbow. Misch sat up as well, folding her arms over her chest and drawing her knees up.

"I told you to stop," she replied.

"I was just -," he started, then broke off the sentence. Lifted his eyes to her. Stared at her. His mouth dropped open and she started shivering. But not in the good way.

"I'm sorry," she whispered.

"You keep saying that. Why do you keep saying that!?" he demanded.

"Because I don't want to hurt you," she cried.

"It's a little late for that! Why don't you want me to touch you, Mischa!? Why couldn't you come home, Mischa!? *What the fuck is going on!?*" Mike roared, jumping to his feet. She climbed to her feet right after him.

"I'm sorry, I'm so sorry, Mike. Please, I'm sorry," she babbled. He got up close to her, put his face right in front of her.

"*You cheated on me,*" he hissed.

Not a question. A statement. *Fact.*

"I'm sorry," she sobbed, putting her hands over her face.

Her eyes were covered, so of course she couldn't see, and it came as a shock when she felt his hands on her shoulders. Pushing her. *Shoving her.* Hard enough to knock her down. She landed hard on her ass and let out a shout.

When she finally got back to her feet, Mike was already off the beach. Mischa waited for a while, wanting to give him space. But they couldn't end it like that, not with his heart broken and her ass bruised. Eventually, she went after him.

She went all the way back to the hotel without a sight of him, and she halfway wondered if he would be there, or if he'd taken off somewhere else. As she approached the suite, she got her answer pretty quick. The door was wide open.

Mike was grumbling to himself as he carried an armful of clothing across the room. She didn't realize it was her clothing till after he'd flung it all over the balcony. She sighed and entered the room.

"I didn't think you'd show up! I figured you'd be busy *screwing someone else!*" he shouted at her, scooping another arm load of clothing out of her bags. She sat at the foot of the bed. Watched more of her clothing go over the railing. Did nothing to stop it.

I deserved that. I deserve this. I deserve so much worse.

"Can we talk?" she asked, her voice scratchy.

"Go fuck yourself."

"Michael, we have to talk about this," she begged.

"You should have talked to me about '*this*' before you *cheated on me!*" he full on yelled, dropping the clothing he was carrying and steaming up to her. She had never in their entire relationship seen him so mad.

"I know! I know that now! I do! I'm an awful fucking person, and I don't deserve kindness or forgiveness! But please, just talk to me!" she begged.

He dropped down into a squat and his hands went back into his hair. He was struggling for air, and she was pretty sure he was crying, as well.

"You're right. You're right. I'm sorry," he breathed.

"Don't be. You don't have to be sorry," she panted, struggling for air.

"This doesn't have to end us," he said in a quiet voice.

"What?"

"It really doesn't. I understand why you did it. *I do.* We can work through this," Mike went on.

Hmmm, not the direction I was hoping for.

"No, Mike. No working through it, I'm sorry. I really am, but it's too late," she said softly. He walked on his knees over to her.

"It's not. It's okay. It'll be okay," he stressed.

"*It won't,* Mike. It won't," she assured him. His hands gripped her wrists, held on tightly.

"I can learn to live with it! I promise! I can forgive you. We'll go to therapy, we'll take courses, whatever it takes."

"I don't want any of that. I don't want this. I'm sorry."

"You just slept with someone else, I understand. You got it out of your system, we can work past it," his teeth were clenched together.

"*No,*" she whispered, responding to everything. All of the above.

She could practically see the light bulb go on over his head, and his eyebrows shot up.

"You didn't just sleep with someone," he said softly.

"No," she repeated herself.

"You didn't get it out of your system," he added, slowly rising to his feet. He didn't let go of her wrists and she was forced to stand with him.

"No."

"You're still with him."

"*Yes.*"

The word had barely left her lips and he was shaking her. His hands moved to her upper arms and he really jerked her around. Mischa shrieked, her head whipping back and forth. She braced her hands on his shoulders, begging him to stop.

"Why!? Why should I!?" Mike was shouting.

Then he was moving her, dragging her across the room. She yelped and tried to pull away, tripping over her own feet. He shoved her against a wall, then pulled her back and pushed her again. And again.

"*Stop it!*" she screamed.

He did stop, but kept her pinned there, boxing her in with his hands on either side of her head. He pounded against the wall and she brought her hands to her face, screaming at him.

"How could you!? Eight years we've been together! Eight years! *You goddamn whore!*" he shouted as he kept pounding.

"I know! God, I'm sorry!" she yelled back.

Her hands were still over her face, and he grabbed her left wrist again, yanked her arm forward. She was shocked and she was thrown off guard and she was *scared*. She wouldn't have thought it possible, that Mike could scare her. He pinned her forearm between his elbow and his rib cage, his grip on her wrist like a vice. He began yanking at her finger.

"*You bitch.* I can't believe it. *Whore,*" he growled.

"You're hurting me!" she cried at him, shoving at his shoulder, trying to pull her arm free.

"You think I care!?"

He kept pulling, and at first she thought he was trying to pull her finger out of the socket. But then she figured out what he was doing, right as her rings scraped over her knuckle and came free. He let go of her and she was still pulling against his grip, so she stumbled backwards, hit the wall, then fell to the ground.

"Please, no, I'm sorry, stop," she sobbed, holding up her hands as he leaned over her.

"*You don't deserve to wear these,*" Mike hissed, holding her rings in his clenched fist.

Mischa sobbed on the floor, wrapping her arms around herself. She listened to him stomp around as he gathered his things. He hadn't unpacked much—he hadn't been there long. Then he was storming out of the suite, slamming the door as hard as he could.

Oh god. Oh god. This was worse. So much worse than I thought. Oh my god.

She felt like vomiting. She even gagged. She sobbed and shook and managed to get on all fours, so she could crawl into the bathroom.

Once she was in there, she turned on the shower and dragged herself into the tub. She didn't care that she was still dressed. She didn't care that she'd only turned on the hot water. She didn't care about anything, she just curled up in a ball in the bottom of the tub.

And she cried and cried and cried.

How Do You Fix
What's Broken

TAL STOOD OUTSIDE HIS hotel, pacing back and forth.
"Yeah, yeah, so what's next?" he barked into his cell
phone.

"Well, despite my best efforts to get us reassigned," Ruiz grumbled at the other end, "we're still on the job."

"I told you. If you ever try that bullshit on me again, we're gonna have a real fucking problem," Tal warned.

"We already have a real fucking problem. This is going to end, you know that right? What the fuck are you going to tell her then!?" his partner demanded.

"The truth."

"Fucked up, man. You have to know that. It's all gonna be fucked. The both of you have lied to each other and everyone else so much, there's no other way for it to end," Ruiz informed him.

"Then that's my problem, *not yours*. When do you ship out?" Tal asked.

"I'll message you. Canaan," Ruiz's voice got serious. "*Tell her before you leave.*"

"Mind your own fucking business."

Tal hung up the phone. He was angry—not because Ruiz was talking shit. He was angry because Ruiz was telling the truth. Tal was petrified of telling Mischa the truth, because he feared it would scare her away. Feared it would make her hate him. And he couldn't handle that, not anymore. He wasn't scared of much, but a beautiful dancer had him terrified. Somehow, she had managed to stitch her heart to his, and if she pulled away, she would rip his heart out when she left.

And so he postponed the inevitable. Told himself that after the *"Michael situation"* was dealt with, they could deal with Tal's issues. Fix her first, so she wouldn't break when he delivered his own blow.

I never meant to know her, but I've known her for so long. I never want to see her hurt, and I'm going to have to hurt her the worst. When did it get so complicated?

And on top of unraveling the never ending thread that was his feelings for Mischa, he had his job. The dark shadow she wasn't even aware of, yet it was looming over their relationship.

Dooming them.

Earlier that morning, he'd gotten a call from a buddy, informing him of Ruiz's attempts to get them assigned to a different job. Fucker. Tal had counterattacked and made phone calls of his own. Argued for continued assignment in their current position. Hadn't he provided stellar work? Hadn't he kept things running smoothly? Of course he had. Like a boss.

By the time he hung up on Ruiz, it was late. Just after noon. Tal scowled as he looked over his phone. No missed calls. He dialed Misch's cell phone, but it went to voicemail.

"Hey, this is Mischa!" her chirpy voice sounded happy. *"Leave me a message and I'll try my best to get back to you!"*

Beep.

"I'm giving you half an hour, and then I'm calling the hotel," he growled, then almost cracked his screen with how hard he pressed the end button.

Tal knew he wasn't helping matters by being an asshole. He knew she was doing something; something much harder than either of them were prepared for, he was sure. He knew it would take time, and that he should give her that time. Give her husband that time. After all, the other man had been there first.

Fuck that.

But Tal couldn't help the way he felt, either. And he felt like punching a mother fucker in the head. Her body belonged to him now, he'd paid for it in sweat. Paid for it with his tongue. His touch. The idea of another man touching her . . .

Mischa may have cheated on her husband to be with Tal, but that didn't make him doubt her, or her feelings for him. It sounded stupid, but she just wasn't that kind of person. At least, not when she was with Tal. He just *knew* that, he trusted that. He trusted her. If she said she wouldn't sleep with her husband, then Tal believed her.

But that didn't mean Mr. Rapaport wouldn't try, and that's where the "*punch a mother fucker in the head*" part came in to play.

He knew it was probably a bad idea, but he headed towards her hotel. He wouldn't go confront them while they were dealing with their shit, or even if they weren't dealing with their shit—Tal wasn't that type of guy. But he wanted to be close by for when she called.

A half an hour came and went. He called her cell phone again, got sent straight to voicemail again. He took a deep breath and called her hotel room. Prepared himself for a man to answer.

"I'm sorry," a woman's voice picked up, "the guest you're trying to reach appears to be unavailable. Would you like to leave a message?"

"Uh, no. Thanks."

Tal got to her hotel, then wandered down the street and sat at a cafe. Waited another half an hour, then called again.

"I'm sorry, the guest you're trying to reach . . . ,"

Tal didn't wait for the whole speech, just hung up.

Something felt wrong. It was one o'clock. Surely they had come back. Maybe she'd wimped out and they were having lunch. Or hanging out. Or . . . playing scrabble. Or . . . something else . . .

*She wouldn't do that, you trust her. She trusts you. This is real. You're perilously close to ruining everything for her, giving up everything for her. It **has** to be real.*

When there was no answer by one-thirty, Tal couldn't take it anymore. It was time for some recon. He headed back to her hotel. He still wasn't going to interrupt them. He was just going to *investigate.*

He didn't learn anything by prowling around the lounge and lobby. He finally went outside and headed to the pool area. Her balcony jutted out right over it, and he hoped to get a view into the room. But when he came around the corner of the building, he was a little stunned by what he saw.

There were clothes strewn everywhere. Floating in the pool,

draped on top of umbrellas, caught in hedges. A couple gardeners and housekeepers were scurrying about, trying to clean up the mess. A maid rushed past him and he grabbed her arm, pulling her to a stop.

"What happened here?" he asked, but she shook her head. He switched to Italian and asked the same question.

"Crazy guest, threw all these clothes off a balcony!" she exclaimed. Tal looked into her arms while she talked. She was holding a few items, but the one that stood out was a black sundress.

He had done very dirty things to that dress.

The elevator was taking too long, so Tal took the stairs. He practically lunged up them, taking them three at a time, yanking himself up using the railing. He slowed down before her floor, and composed himself before he went through the door. He just wanted to make sure everything was okay, he wasn't going to burst in like a jealous . . . *lover.*

I'm such a jackass.

He slowly walked down the hall, acting casual. He wished he had brought his gear, then listening through the wall wouldn't be an issue. As it was, he'd have to press his ear to the bottom of the door. Or maybe they'd be yelling. That would be handy.

Nobody was yelling when he got to the room. No one was even talking. He could tell because the door was wide open.

Fuck this.

He crept into the room, calling out in Italian. He could play it off as a concerned guest if he had to. But no one answered. He walked full into the living room and stopped at a pile of clothing. Misch's clothing. There were a couple items strewn about, laying in a trail towards the balcony.

"Hello!?" he called out. Fuck subtlety. He didn't care anymore.

The door to the main bedroom was wide open and he walked inside. The bed was made up and everything looked fine. Then he saw that one of her suitcases was on the floor, and the fold out tray for it had been knocked to the side. Something nasty had taken place.

"Mischa!" he barked her name, turning towards the bathroom. He could hear the shower running and he stormed in there.

She was curled into a ball, shaking on the floor of the bath tub. He hurried to his knees and reached for the shower knob, turning it off. The water was freezing, almost painful against his skin. He noted that it was the hot water faucet that needed to be turned, and wondered how long she'd been in there, for the water to turn to ice.

"Baby, what happened?" Tal whispered, slipping his arms under her and picking her up. He slowly stood and hiked her up against his chest.

"I was awful. Awful, awful, awful," she moaned, her teeth chattering so hard, her words were distorted. He sat down on the bed and held her against him.

"You weren't. You're not. Jesus, how long were you in there, Misch?" he asked, examining her pruned up fingers, taking in her almost blue lips. Mild hypothermia wasn't an unrealistic concern.

"Not long enough," she sighed. He pressed her hand between both of his and rubbed up and down.

"Tell me what happened," he urged.

"God, it was terrible. It was so terrible. It was so much worse," she started crying, pulling her hand away.

"What do you mean? Talk to me."

"Why are you with me!? I ruin things," she suddenly burst out, shoving at his chest. She was so slippery that he couldn't keep a grip on her and she fell out of his arms, hitting the ground hard on her hip. He went after her, dropping back to his knees, but when he grabbed for her leg, she scurried away and dragged herself backwards into the bathroom.

"What the fuck happened!?" he demanded, following after her. She put both her hands up, stopping him.

"Nothing! Everything! *God!* Just leave, please, just leave me alone," she sobbed, waving him away. He retreated and sat on the floor, leaning his back against the bed.

"Can't do that. You and me, remember? I'll always come find you," he said in a soft voice.

She curled to the side, shoving herself up against the cabinet under the sink. She sobbed for a while, and he watched. Just sat and watched. Let her work out her demons. Let her give some of them to him. Eventually, she quieted to just crying. Then just tears. Then sniffles and the occasional shiver. Finally, after about twenty minutes, she began moving around. Shrugging the straps of her dress off her shoulders and working the cold material down her body.

"What time is it?" she asked, her voice hoarse. Tal glanced at his watch.

"Almost two," he answered.

"Why are you still here?" she groaned, lifting her hips and pulling the dress away from her legs. She kicked it across the room, then laid down on her side, only wearing a bra and panties. She drew her knees up to her chest and wrapped her arms around them.

"Because you need me," he said simply. She closed her eyes.

"I don't need anybody," she whispered.

"Tough. Because it works both ways, babe. I need you, too."

She didn't answer, and soon enough he realized she'd fallen asleep. Completely worn out. Tal was careful as he moved into the bathroom, gentle as he picked her up. She wasn't as cold as before, but she was still shivering.

He carried her to the bed and laid her under the covers. Then he got behind her and wrapped his arms around her, draped his leg over hers. Tried to infuse her with his heat. With his soul. With his fire.

What did he do to you? What have you done to me?

Mischa woke up so hot, she was completely covered in a fine sheen of sweat. She sat up, shoving Tal's arm off of her. As it dragged down her own arm, she hissed. Something hurt. She looked down at herself, twisting her bicep. There were four bruises, marching down her skin in a line. Finger marks.

Mike.

What. A. Fuck show. Misch couldn't believe how badly it had gone. How it had gone, *period.* He'd been so upset, and she'd been so blunt. She should have done it differently. Taken him back to the hotel. Or actually flown home. Something. Anything.

I fuck everything up.

"Are you okay?" Tal's voice was thick with sleep. She shrugged.

"Not really. Sorry I yelled at you," she mumbled, staring across the room.

"Don't be sorry. Yell at me whenever you want," he offered, and she felt his hand rub against her back. It felt good, and that made her feel even more guilty.

It was so much easier when Mike didn't know. Then the guilt wasn't real. Not yet.

"You shouldn't be here," Mischa breathed.

"I shouldn't be anywhere else."

"I don't deserve this," she went on.

"Stop it."

"No. I hurt him so badly. I couldn't even picture it. I had no idea. It was so bad. I don't deserve anything good," she kept going.

"*Stop,*" Tal's voice was loud, and the hand on her back stilled. "Yeah, it was awful. Yeah, it hurts like hell. Yeah, you did a shitty thing—*we* did a shitty thing. But that doesn't mean you don't deserve happiness. You're not Hitler, you didn't kill people."

"Just someone's soul," she whispered. Tal sat up next to her.

"He'll survive," he stressed.

"I'm not so sure. You didn't see his face. You didn't hear what he said. God, it was so awful. I feel so awful, being here with you. How can I be with you now? Where is he now? Where did he go? Why do I get to be here, wrapped in someone's arms?" Mischa sniffled.

"He's at a hotel on the other side of town, he's flying home tomorrow," Tal answered. She turned to him, shocked.

"How do you know that!?" she exclaimed. He smiled sadly and brushed hair away from her face.

"Man of many talents, remember?"

Fuck you, mystery man.

"I just can't believe how bad it went. I never imagined, in a million years, that it would happen the way it did," she sighed, pressing her face into her hands.

"I'm sure it's not as bad as you -, *what the fuck is this!?*"

Tal's voice was sharp as he grabbed her arm and pulled it towards him. He examined her skin closely, his glare wandering over the little bruise marks. He let her go and shifted around her, looking at her other arm. She looked as well, and sure enough, there were identical marks on her other bicep.

"I'm fine," she assured him, trying to push his hand away.

"Like hell you are! That mother fucker put his hands on you!?" Tal shouted. She shook her head.

"No, it wasn't like that, really. He didn't hit me, he wasn't trying to hurt me," she said quickly.

"Well, he's fucking dead. What happened," Tal insisted, moving around some more till he was sitting in front of her.

"Tal, it's not a big -,"

"*What. Happened.*"

Mischa sighed.

"We went to the beach. He kissed me, I stopped him, he asked what was wrong, and I just said that . . . that we were unfixable. That it needed to end," she started.

"That doesn't get you bruises. *What else.*"

"He didn't listen, I kept talking, he started to freak out when I said I wanted it to be over, he tried kissing me again, and I . . . I kinda . . . I wigged out, I shouted at him to stop. And it was like he knew. He just knew. He asked if I had cheated on him, and I . . . I said yes," she stammered through the story.

"What did he say?"

"Nothing. He came back here, and I followed, and when I got here, he was throwing all my stuff off the balcony."

"You just let him!?"

"What was I supposed to do, Tal!?" she snapped. "'*Hey, fucker, I know I just pissed all over your heart and ripped our eight year relationship to shreds, but can you put my Victoria's Secret underwear down?.*' Yeah, no, I don't think so. He could've taken a shit in my luggage, and I would've let him."

Tal actually started laughing, which made her laugh a little, too. But it felt good. And feeling good was bad, and then the guilt was back. Suffocating her.

"What else," Tal kept his voice gentle. She took a deep breath.

"I told him that we needed to talk, and he calmed down. Said he understood, said we could work it out, he would forgive me, we'd go to therapy, blah blah blah. I kept telling him we couldn't work it out, and that's when he figured out that it wasn't just me having sex with someone else," her voice became smaller and smaller.

"He figured out it was an affair," Tal finished for her. She nodded, wiping at her nose.

"Yeah. Yeah, he did."

"How did it end? How did you wind up in the shower?"

Misch took a deep breath.

"He, ah . . . he was upset, at what I said, at what he'd figured out. He was yelling at me and, I don't know, trying to shake some sense into me. I think that's how I got the bruises. Then he kept pushing me against the wall, and he was calling me names," Mischa started crying again. "He just kept pushing me, then he yanked my rings off. Took them and walked out of here."

Tal stared at her for a second, then got off the bed. She watched as he pulled his shirt off the back of a chair—he must have taken it off while she'd been sleeping. He slipped it on and began buttoning it up as he walked across the suite.

"What're you doing!?" she demanded, sliding to the end of the bed.

"I'm gonna go kill him," Tal said simply, stepping into his shoes.

Misch was out of the bed and managed to get in front of him before he could reach the door.

"Stop it!" she yelled, pushing him away. "Stop. He was angry, and he did some fucked up things, but so did I. He hurt my skin. *I hurt his heart.*"

"I don't give a fuck. That doesn't give him the right to touch you like that," Tal was almost growling.

"It's my body, and I say it does," she snapped back. He suddenly leaned down and pressed his forehead to hers.

"Baby, I hate to tell you this, but it's not just your body anymore. It's belonged to me ever since that first night," he informed her.

"Tal," Mischa took a deep breath. "He was upset. I've known Mike a long time, and I have never seen him like that, *ever.* Please."

Before Tal could argue, the sound of Misch's phone chirping interrupted them. They stared at each other for a long moment, then she went back to the bedroom. Her cell was plugged in on the night stand, and she leaned over it.

"Is it him?" Tal asked, walking up behind her. She groaned and shook her head.

"No. My mother."

Worse. I think I'd rather be reliving my morning, than talking to my mom.

"Do you want me to wait out in the living room?" he offered. She grabbed his arm.

"God, no. Hold my hand. Just . . . keep quiet," she instructed, then she picked up the phone. She pushed the answer button, but wasn't even given a chance to say a greeting.

"What in the hell have you done, young lady!?" her mother was screeching. Misch moved to sit in the middle of the bed.

"Did he call you?" she asked. Tal crawled across the mattress and stretched out behind her, wrapping his arm around her waist.

"No! Belinda called me! The woman was hysterical! She thinks her son is going to kill himself!"

That's a bit much.

"Mom, don't say that."

"Are you saying he wasn't upset!?"

"Oh, he was upset."

"As any husband would be! Cheated on him! How could you do that!? *How could you do that!?* I thought we raised you better than that!" her mother's voice was reaching epic levels.

"You did, Mom. I don't know . . . I just . . . wasn't happy," Misch's voice fell into a whisper.

"Well, then you work it out! You get help! You talk to people! You don't go to another country and act like a common prostitute!"

"*Mother!*"

"I'm sorry, but that's what you acted like! I am so disappointed in you, Mischa!"

"I'm disappointed in me, too. I feel awful."

"As you should!"

"I know."

"Disgusting. I never thought I could be disgusted by my own daughter."

"I know. I am, too."

It just went on from there. Her mother didn't ask to hear her side, didn't question what had happened between her and Mike, or what was happening between her and Tal, or rather the *"filthy homewrecker,"* as he was dubbed by Mrs. Duggard. By the time her mom hung up on her, Misch felt numb, just nodding and agreeing with everything.

"That sounded rough," Tal said, rubbing his hand across her thigh.

"You have no idea. Have you ever been cursed at in Mandarin? Sucks," she grumbled. She had just sat the phone down when it rang again.

"You don't have to answer it," he pointed out. She shook her head.

"No. I deserve this. I should just get it out of the way," she replied.

"It's not like lashings, Misch. Give yourself a break."

"I don't deserve one."

The name *Lacey* was scrolling across the screen, and when Mischa said hello, she was hopeful that it would go a little better than her mom's call.

"Is it true!? Tell me it's not true," her friend was actually crying.

God, did Mike do a conference call!?

"Yeah, yeah it's true, Lace," Misch's voice was stuck somewhere deep in her throat, and it came out thick and watery.

"Why? Why would you do that to him? What did he ever do to you?" Lacey sobbed.

"Nothing. He didn't do anything. I'm just . . . a bad person, Lace, who made some bad mistakes," Misch offered. Tal's hand gripped her thigh.

"*We* are not a mistake," he whispered. "You're not a bad person."

*No, you're right. I'm the **worst** person.*

"Mistake!? *You cheated on your husband!* With some . . . *stranger!* Ew! You always said you hated cheaters!" Lacey reminded her.

"I know. I know what I said. Things happen, things change. I never knew I could feel this way, and I couldn't tell you how I was feeling cause I hated myself, and god, Lacey, I'm just so sorry," Mischa sniffled, wiping at tears again. There was a long pause, and then her friend sighed.

"Bob doesn't want me seeing you anymore," Lacey's voice was almost a whisper.

"Well, how do *you* feel?" Misch demanded, a little shocked.

"He's my husband, Misch. I'm not like you, I can't just do whatever I want," Lacey replied.

Ouch.

"He can't tell you who you can and can't be friends with, Lacey. If you don't want to be my friend because of what I did, then fine, that's your choice. But don't do it just cause your husband hates me," Misch snapped. There was an even longer pause.

"Was it worth it?" Lacey really was whispering that time. Misch glanced at Tal.

"I don't know. It's pretty awful right now. Way worse than I thought it would be, and I had already guessed it would be hell," she started, staring straight into his eyes. "But I think . . . I think maybe yeah, it was."

"God, you should've talked to me, Mischa. I could've helped you end things with him. I could've helped. You're my best friend. Why couldn't you talk to me?" Lacey was crying again.

"I don't know. I hated me. I didn't want you to hate me, too," Misch tried to explain. There was some noise, then a man's voice was talking in the background.

"I have to go," Lacey's voice was cold.

"Can I call you later? Like on your lunch break?" Misch asked, and she could hear the desperation in her own voice.

"No. No, I just can't be your best friend right now. Not after what you did. I'm sorry, Misch. I really am."

Then the line was dead.

Mischa dropped the phone and put her head in her hands. The cell started ringing again, and another friend's name scrolled across the screen. It went to voicemail. Then a text came. Then another. More. Tons. All the same.

"Is it true!? How could you!? What happened!?"

"What do you want me to do? How can I help?" Tal asked.

Misch's first thought was *"I want you to not be the kind of guy who sleeps with married women,"* but then an even heavier wave of guilt crashed over her.

He's the only good part of what's happening, and that's your first thought. You're such a bitch.

"I don't know. I don't know what to do," she whispered.

"The plan. Remember the plan."

Break up with Mike. Finish her job. Be with Tal.

"I just feel so bad. I honestly thought it wouldn't feel this bad. I'd already done the deed, how can I feel *worse?*" she asked.

"Out of sight, out of mind. Mike wasn't part of the equation, till you had to talk to him," Tal answered.

"God. I have to call him, I have to make sure he's okay," she wiped at her face and reached for her phone.

"Don't."

"Tal, I have to. Even if he hates me right now, I still care about him. What's the name of his hotel?" she asked.

"I won't tell you."

She glared at him.

"You can either tell me, or I will go out and visit every single fucking hotel till I find him."

He gave her the number and she quickly dialed it, asked for Mike's room. There were a couple rings before anyone picked up.

"Hello." His voice was low and gravelly, not normal for him.

"Please don't hang up," she rushed out. There was a heavy silence, and his anger was palpable through the phone.

"Why shouldn't I!? I don't owe you anything," he snarled.

"I know. I just had to make sure you were okay," she told him.

"No, I'm not okay! My wife is cheating on me! Nothing will ever be okay again!" he snapped.

"Mike, please. Please. I want to talk with you. Can I come see you?" she pleaded. Tal began violently shaking his head no at the same time Mike responded.

"No. I don't want to see you."

"Please, Mikey. Sleep on it, and I'll call you in the morning. Please?"

"I'm leaving in the morning. You better find a new place to live before you come home."

Then he hung up on her.

That's something no one ever tells you when you cheat on your husband and end your marriage—no one will say goodbye anymore.

"I told you not to," Tal pointed out.

"Shut up. Just shut up!" she snapped.

"Want me to order dinner?" he offered.

"No. I never want to eat again."

"Stop it."

"I'm just gonna sleep. Maybe when I wake up, things won't be so bad, and none of this will have happened," she took deep breaths, clawing her fingers through her hair.

"Stop. It's done, it's over with. Things are going to be shit for a while, but you're here. With me. We have each other," he reminded her.

"*I'm* the one going through shit! You're the one who gets a free fuck out of all this!" she yelled at him.

"Hey. You wanna take your anger out on me? Fine. If that's what it takes, fine. Yell at me, call me names, blame it on me. I can do that for you. I can take that for you," he said simply.

I don't deserve him.

Mischa suddenly leaned into him, pressing her face against his chest. He was surprised for a moment, then his arms went around her, holding her tightly. The guilt was still there, still clawing at her heart, eating her soul. But maybe, just maybe, if he held her long enough, it would fade away.

She had to believe that, or she'd go insane.

It was around five in the morning Italian time when Misch's phone rang again, waking her up. She'd been getting calls all evening, but it was really late in Detroit's time zone. Who would be calling at that hour? She crawled out from under Tal's arm and glanced at the screen.

Dad-a-rino.

"*Daddy?*" she answered the phone in a hurry.

"Oh, sweetie pea, what have you gotten yourself into?"

At some point, I've got to stop crying, or I'll never be able to open my eyes again.

"I'm so sorry, Dad. Please say you don't hate me, please, please, please," she cried. Behind her, Tal woke up with a start.

"What's wrong!? Are you okay!?" he asked, struggling with the covers. She waved him away.

"I could never hate you, baby, you're my sunshine. My reason for living. I knew something was up, I just couldn't place it. Now it makes sense. I gotta say, I don't approve of what you did," her father started. "I wish you hadn't done it. But I understand, baby. I do understand."

"I'm so sorry, Dad. I'm so, so sorry. I never wanted to disappoint you," she sobbed, crying so hard it was difficult to talk.

"Well, that's impossible in life, dear. I've disappointed everyone I know at some point. Hell, I even disappointed you a time or two—remember when I forgot you at soccer practice, and you slept in the dugout on the little league field? I still haven't forgotten that."

Misch laughed. She actually laughed, for what felt like the first time in forever.

"Oh wow, I had kinda forgotten," she chuckled through her tears.

"See? And you still love me. It's not the end of the world. You're not a bad person, baby, you just made some really bad choices," he informed her.

"I know, Dad. I know. I just . . . I felt trapped, and I did something stupid," she replied, trying to catch her breath.

"That's hitting the nail on the head. Now, I didn't actually call to talk to you," he said.

"Mike's not here."

"I don't want to talk to him."

"Then who . . . ," Misch's voice trailed off, and understanding dawned. She turned and stared at Tal.

"Yup. Put him on the phone," her dad instructed her.

"Why would you think he's here?" Mischa tried.

"Because I know you, and I know you wouldn't just go off with some random guy. If you went this far, then you must think he's a good guy. And if he's a good guy, then he sure as shit better be taking care of my little girl when she's hurting—even if he's part of the problem. Now put him on the phone," her dad demanded again.

"I can't do that, Dad. I can't. He -,"

Tal solved the problem by yanking the phone away from her.

"Mr. Duggard, sir," he said in a serious voice.

Mischa tried to grab the phone away, but Tal got up and moved to stand at the foot of the bed. She grabbed a pillow and hugged it to her chest while her teeth worked overtime on her bottom lip.

"Yes, sir . . . yes, I was aware . . . no, not necessarily . . . I'm sorry, sir, but your daughter is a very attractive woman . . . no, that's not all, I also think she has an amazing spirit and mind . . . it was very hard, I knew it was gonna be bad. Knew it was gonna be worse than what she thought . . . I do, sir . . . Tal Canaan . . . the army . . . New York, then

Israel . . . sometimes . . . oh, yeah . . . Mets!? Are you insane!? Yankees all the way! . . . no, no, no, we'll go to a game, and we'll see who's right . . . okay, that I can handle—as long as it's not the Pats . . . yes, sir . . . yes, I already do . . . you can trust -, well, I'll prove to you that you can trust me . . . one question—did he tell you that he grabbed her? Hard enough to leave bruises . . . yes, sir, I had the same thoughts, sir," Tal's voice started getting hard. The conversation Mischa had been over-hearing was surreal enough; she didn't want to listen to them bashing Mike, when he was the innocent party.

"Stop it! Give me the phone!" she hissed, knee walking to the end of the bed and holding out her hand. He batted her away.

"Yes, sir, I couldn't believe it either . . . pushed her around, called her names . . . I'd be happy to, sir . . . she wouldn't let me, or believe me, I'd be there right now, shoving his -," but he didn't get to finish, because Mischa grabbed his wrist and yanked as hard as she could. He hadn't been looking at her and he let out a shout of surprise, dropping the phone. She quickly grabbed it and put it to her ear.

"It's not as bad as he's making it sound," she said quickly.

"Michael hurt you!?" her dad was almost shouting.

"No. I mean, not on purpose," she replied.

"Bruising you is too much, Mischa, I don't care what you did to him!"

"They're tiny, on my arms, from his *fingers*. He just squeezed too hard, *he was upset*. Let it go, *both of you*," she made her voice stern as she glared up at Tal. "He's been through a lot, because of me, and on top of that, he was blindsided. He's allowed to be upset."

"Fine. But if he touches you like that again, I'm gonna tell that Tal guy to kick his ass," her dad threatened.

"Stop it. And '*Tal guy*'!?" she exclaimed. Her dad and Tal being on a first name basis. Unreal.

"He seems like a nice boy, Misch. Though he can't be all good if he chases married women, and likes the Yankees," her dad commented.

"Everyone likes the Yankees, you're the only who doesn't," she pointed out.

"I'm the only one with any common sense."

"You're really okay with this?" Mischa asked, sinking back down to sitting position.

"Hell no. But I love you, and I always thought things weren't right between you and Mike. Like I said, I wish things hadn't happened this way. I'm not proud of what you did. But I am happy that you seem happy," he answered. She closed her eyes.

"Thanks, Dad," she whispered.

"You are happy, right? He's taking care of you?" he double checked.

"He takes excellent care of me. I was very happy up until this morning," she chuckled.

"Well, I can't say that you don't deserve it. But don't beat yourself up too much—everyone else is gearing up to do enough of that on their own," her dad assured her.

"I know. I got it from Mom and Lacey today. I stopped answering the phone."

"Speaking of your mom, I made this call when I knew she'd be sleeping. She is one unhappy camper, sweetie. You're gonna be getting that for a while," her dad warned her.

"I know. I figured."

"You '*figured*.' If you knew it was gonna be this bad, then why'd you do it?" he questioned.

Mischa sighed and rubbed her forehead, not sure how to answer that question. It wasn't like she could say "*sexual frustration*" to her dad, that was just weird. Or that she'd only planned on having a one night stand and not telling anyone, that sounded worse. And she really didn't want to rehash all the bullshit between her and Mike that had driven her to it.

She glanced up at Tal, then stared at him. He was still standing at the foot of the bed, and he had his arms crossed over his chest. He was only wearing his boxer briefs, and he had braced his feet wide apart. He looked very dominating and intimidating, especially when combined with the intense look he had in his eyes. He looked concerned, and ready to jump in and save her at a moments notice.

"Because," Mischa whispered, not taking her eyes off him. "After Tal found me, I couldn't let him go. I didn't want to be lost anymore."

"Well, then hold on tight to that man, cause it's gonna be a bumpy ride."

They said their goodbyes after that, with her dad even shouting a goodbye to Tal. She chuckled and dropped her phone back onto the table.

"Your dad is a good man," Tal commented. She nodded.

"The best. And he likes you, which is kind of a shock," she laughed.

"Not to me—I'm fucking amazing," he replied. She snorted.

"Hardly. But really, I think he likes you. If I'd thought about it at all, I guess I would've figured that he'd like you. He's kind of a guy's guy, you know? He's always building something or working on a car or . . . spitting loogies, I don't know. He didn't not like Mike, but they never hung out or anything. Mike's more into runs, and trips to the lake, and concerts," she tried to explain.

"Your dad will love me, I can hock a mean loogie," Tal assured her as he moved to lay down next to her.

"Do you think you'll ever meet my dad?" Misch asked in a small voice.

Despite their connection, their chemistry, she and Tal hadn't really known each other that long, and they were involved in an illicit affair as opposed to a proper relationship, so she hadn't really thought about it. But if he and her dad didn't get along, a relationship was almost pointless.

"I hope I do. I hope you can introduce us someday. Maybe someday when everyone doesn't hate us," he chuckled, stretching his arm across her shoulders and pulling her to lay down next to him.

"The way today went, I don't think that day will ever come," she told him.

"It just feels that way now. It won't feel that way forever."

"How do you know that?"

"Because it can't. Things don't work that way. Your friends and family love you. They're hurt right now. They'll come around," he assured her. She took a deep breath and turned towards him.

"It always sounds so easy when you talk about it. Living it is so much worse," she whispered.

"It only seemed that way cause you were alone for the hard part. I'll be with you, from now on," he told her.

"Really?"

"I promise."

He leaned in and kissed her, and it was the first *real* intimate gesture they'd shared since Mike had shown up. She'd been feeling so guilty, and it must have been obvious, because Tal hadn't even tried to really touch her or kiss her. Just held her a lot.

The guilt was still there, the thoughts of Mike hurting and being alone were still there. But she couldn't deny it, Tal had always had a hypnotic effect on her. A *drugging* effect. She sighed against his lips and gave into him.

"*I missed this,*" she whispered as his lips moved down her throat.

"You'll never have to again," he whispered back, his lips lingering along her clavicle.

"It's not right, that we're here together. It isn't fair," she went on.

"*Life* isn't fair. Just be happy it's working out in our favor right now."

"God, that sounds horrible."

"We're horrible people, remember? Just embrace it."

"*Not funny.*"

His hands pressed her body down into the mattress, ran up and down the length of her torso. His fingers brushed away her guilt, and soon enough she was kissing him back in earnest. Straining towards him, holding onto him, *fiending for him.*

"I've been dying to do this since yesterday," he groaned, pulling her bra away.

"We shouldn't be doing this at all," she replied, working his underwear down his legs.

"We should *always* be doing this."

"Having sex?"

"Just being together."

Hard to argue with something that felt so right, even if it was wrong, and she let him remove her panties. They were gone with the flick of a wrist and then he was between her legs, parting them around his waist.

His tongue was hot and his touch scorching, she bit her lips between her teeth and went with it. When he pinned her hands to the mattress by her head, she abandoned herself to him. Let his hips ride her and guide her. His fingers moved through her own, linked them together. Squeezed so tight it hurt.

Kinda like love.

They came one right after the other, hips locked together in battle. Tal had his forehead pressed to hers, and even though her eyes were closed, she knew his eyes were open. Knew he was staring at her face. Knew he was looking into her soul.

"Say it now," he panted above her.

"What?" she was still coming down off the orgasm.

"He's not between us anymore. You can say it now."

"Excuse me?"

But she knew what he was talking about, knew what was going on. She kept her eyes closed, tried to keep the tears inside.

"Say it, one time. For the first time in your life, say it, and really mean it," he whispered. She took a deep breath.

"*I love you.*"

Mischa

I WANTED HIM TO SAVE me.

I wanted to be baptized in his skin, purified in his love. I was a sinner, or worse.

I wanted him to make me whole.

I wanted him to take away the pain and the guilt and the hurt and the wrong.

I was blinded by him, with him, to him.

I wanted him to save me.

Out of Time

S HE WANTED TO SPEAK to him. Wanted one last chance for some closure, before Michael left.

Tal warned her that it was a bad idea. That it wouldn't go well. That Mike wasn't ready for closure yet—he needed distance first.

But she insisted, so Tal drove her to the airport. Though he refused to wait in the car. He wouldn't interrupt them, wouldn't alert Mike to his presence, but he wasn't about to let the other man grab Mischa again, he didn't care how "*upset*" Mr. Rapaport was; Tal would kick his ass clear back to the coast.

It didn't go well, just as he'd predicted. There was a minor scene, with Mike yelling at her to get away from him. When he called her a slut, Tal stood up. But she backed away and Mike stomped off, heading through customs without so much as a backwards glance.

To her credit, she didn't break down sobbing again. She was crying, but she had on a large pair of sunglasses which hid most of the tears. Tal waited till they were outside of the airport to wrap his arm around her shoulders. He expected her to pull away at first, as she'd been doing ever since Mike came into the picture for real, but she didn't—she leaned right into his side, pressed her face into his shoulder, and walked the whole way to the car in that position.

We can do this now, whenever we want.

She was feeling depressed as fuck, so she went right back to sleep when they got to the hotel. He helped her undress, then he made her lay down on her stomach. She had acted suspicious, obviously assuming he was going to take advantage of her half naked form under him.

He really, *really,* wanted to, but he resisted—he gave her a massage, instead. Rubbed her aching muscles and her sore skin until she fell asleep.

Her phone rang not long after, and when he saw that it was her dad calling, Tal went ahead and picked up. It was strange, but much like with Mischa, he felt an instant connection to Mr. Duggard. Conversation should've been awkward between them—Tal had played a large part in breaking up her marriage. He was the "bad guy" by all accounts.

But it wasn't awkward. Tal gave him a rundown of how Misch was doing, and that he thought she'd be okay. Mr. Duggard told him everything that Mike had been saying, which it was all true, technically, but very colorfully painted and with graphic language.

Mr. Duggard liked hearing Mischa called names even less than Tal.

They bullshitted about baseball and football, discussed Ford versus Chevy. Both had served in the militaries for their respective countries, and they shared stories. And they both cared very deeply for a hazel eyed girl who was very lost.

Conversation was *very* easy.

"*Don't you hurt my girl,*" her father warned.

"*I'll try my best.*"

"*That's not good enough. I want your word.*"

"*How can you trust my word, when we've never met?*"

"*You're not making a good argument for yourself.*"

"*Just being honest with you, sir.*"

"*You hurt her, and I'll fly over there and break a lead pipe over your head.*"

"*Sounds completely fair, sir.*"

Of course, Tal wanted to say that he would never do anything to hurt Mischa. That he couldn't stand the thought of her being hurt, or in pain, because of him. That he would do anything to prevent that.

But Tal didn't like to make promises he knew he couldn't keep.

After he hung up, Tal pulled a chair up to the side of the bed and sat down. And stared. Let his eyes wander over Misch's body. Over her skin and lips and hair. He glanced at his watch, saw that it was dinner time. Then he stared at her some more.

"*I love you,*" she had whispered, shivering underneath him.

"That doesn't make you a bad person," he had whispered back. *"I think it does."*

Tal could try to kiss the pain away, try to touch the hurt away, but it would take a lot of time before she felt comfortable in her own skin again. A lot of time before she was strong enough to take another hit.

And time was something Tal didn't have. He would give her anything she wanted. Anything she asked for, he would find it and lay it at her feet. But time was a promise he couldn't deliver, not at that point. They had to stay caught in their moments, in her timeless existence, finding each other between the seconds. He just needed a few more of those moments, and maybe she'd never even have to know his secrets. She had run away from her life, and he'd found her.

Maybe he could run away from his secrets, and she'd find him.

I think I love you, too, dancer lady. Just have faith in me.

Shots Fired

"**I** CAN'T BELIEVE HOW BEAUTIFUL it is!"

"I told you."

Istanbul was gorgeous. And talk about being surrounded by history! Mischa loved it. She hadn't really expected to, or rather, she hadn't known what to expect. A language she couldn't speak, and a culture she knew literally nothing about; she had figured she'd feel lost, most of the time.

I don't feel lost at all.

Things weren't any better on the home front, necessarily. Her mom was still calling her disgusting. Her friends still weren't speaking to her. Mike was blasting her on any and all social medias.

But Mischa wasn't on the home front. She was *away from it all,* and that timeless feeling was slowly coming back to her. The ol' outta-sight-outta-mind trick. She knew better now, knew the come down would be harsh, but at least she was better prepared. And at least she would have Tal right next to her, holding her hand.

Such a surreal thought. She'd gone to Italy thinking she would cheat on her husband. She had never counted on finding someone like Tal. Love wasn't part of the equation, was a foreign feeling. She hadn't wanted it, hadn't been looking for it. But it seemed to have found her. She knew she should tread carefully, but the feeling was too immense. It was everywhere, all around her, blanketing her. It made her feel guilty to think it, but she could honestly say that she'd never felt that way before, with anyone. Only him.

Tal had come with her, actually flown on the plane with her. His home was in Istanbul, after all, so he told her he would stay in the city with her, for as long as he could. His photography job, whatever exactly it was, seemed to be something he could do from anywhere—she wondered if he was freelance and without work, and figured he was embarrassed to say he was essentially unemployed.

The only downside to Istanbul was she was forced to throw herself into work. In Rome, sneaking off and calling in sick had been easy, but not anymore. Her boss was gone from the office more than he was there, so the burden of getting things done fell to her.

"It's weird," Misch finally said, sitting down to dinner with Tal.

"What's weird?" he asked around a mouthful of food.

"I hardly see Peter. Like, at all. He's never in the office, or if he is, he's just dashing in and out. I don't understand what he's doing, I guess. How many business lunches can a person have in a day?" she questioned, stealing a piece of pizza from a tray in the center of the table.

"I don't know. A lot. I like lunch. Don't worry about it. Maybe you should play hookie more often, too," he suggested.

"But still. Maybe I should talk to him, ask him what -," she started when Tal stood up.

"Leave it alone, babe. The more distracted he is, the more time we get to spend together," he interrupted her before leaning down and kissing her on the forehead. Then he walked away, sucking pizza grease off his fingers.

She frowned as he went into the bathroom, then she shook it off and dug into her dinner.

They were in her hotel room. She had been demoted back to the standard room, no more suites for her—though her current room did have two double beds in it. While she was at work one day, Tal shoved them together, making a super bed for them.

The guilt was still there, of course. Sometimes she wondered if it would always be there, in a small way. Her and Tal's relationship was built on top of the still-beating-heart of her last relationship. Not too cute. But the guilt was lessening in intensity, and she was grateful for that; it had been hard, at first, to have sex again, and Tal was a very sexual person. He was taking it slow for her, he hadn't pushed her or asked for anything, but she knew it wasn't easy for him, and she was grateful for his patience.

"I e-mailed Mike again," she called out. That was another thing she was grateful for—they could talk about the dreaded "*him*" without that sense of doom anymore. No more hushed whispers or avoiding his name, like saying it would conjure him up, right in the middle of their dirty lie.

No, now it was just their dirty truth, so they could say whatever they wanted.

"Why do you keep doing that!?" Tal yelled back.

"Because, there's a lot of shit between us still. We shared an apartment, the car loan is in both our names, we have a joint savings account. We need to get divorced—that involves *some* communication. And believe it or not, I worry about him," she tried to explain. Tal finally walked back out into the main room.

"Seriously, Misch. Give him space. You spent so much time wishing for space from him—imagine that ten fold, and that's probably how he feels about you, right now."

Doesn't feel so good when the tables are turned.

"Whatever. Fine."

She glared at her food, pretending it was his face, but Tal ignored her.

"What should we do tonight? I know a great club, we could go dancing, I could finally see your moves," he suggested. She looked up at him.

"I know what we could do."

"What?"

"Go to your house."

He scowled at her before looking away.

"No."

When they'd made their plans to leave Italy together, Misch had honestly thought they would just stay at his house. She had planned on canceling her hotel room, till he told her not to, that she couldn't stay at his place. He said it was too small, too crappy. A total bachelor pad, and one that hadn't seen a duster in almost two months. Not worthy of her.

But a week and a half had gone by, and he still wouldn't let her go see it. He spent some nights there, claimed he was doing work around the place, but it still wasn't up to par. It all sounded very hard to believe.

"You're not keeping anything from me, are you? There isn't, like, a bunch of baby Tal's and a Mrs. Tal running around over there, are there?" Mischa even laughed, but she felt kind of sick, and remembered their conversation from when they'd first met.

"Would you care if there was a Mrs. Canaan?"

I most certainly fucking would.

"No. No Mrs. Tal. There hasn't really ever been a long-term-girl-friend-Tal," he joked back.

"What about the babies?"

"Oh, tons of those. It's like a baby farm at my house. Just crawling all over the place, piled one on top of the other."

"Great, I love babies. We should totally go over there."

"Mischa."

"Tal."

He sighed and finally walked back over to her. He squatted down next to her chair and took both her hands in his, pressed them together between his own. Making her pray.

"My darling little dancer, I swear to you, when the time is right, I will take you anywhere you want to go. Including my home," he promised her. She smiled at him.

"You're only sweet cause you know I'm a sucker."

"Totally. Now let's get out of here or get naked."

Mischa was brushing her teeth the next morning when her cell phone lit up. She glanced at the screen, then frowned. She'd gotten an e-mail, but she didn't recognize the address. She spit out the foam, then rinsed her mouth before picking up the phone. She got into her inbox and opened the e-mail.

"Oh my god," she mumbled, and headed back into the main room.

Tal was at the foot of the super bed, doing a ridiculous amount of push ups. He had a whole workout routine, she'd discovered. He paid homage to his body every single day, and she was very thankful for that—the man's body was *amazing*. But right at that moment, she didn't even notice it.

"What's up," he grunted, not looking up as she stepped over him and sat on the bed.

"He . . . ," her voice trailed off, as her eyes wandered down the screen.

"I can't hear you. Are you talking?" Tal called out.

"I'm getting divorced."

Tal stopped mid-push up. Held himself still. Then he pushed himself to his feet. Grabbed his discarded t-shirt and mopped his face and chest with it.

"I thought that had been established," he pointed out.

"Yeah, I know. I mean, it's happening *now*. I just got an e-mail from a man claiming to be Mike's lawyer, saying he wants to know where to send the divorce papers," she told him, her voice quiet.

"What address are you going to give them?"

She stayed quiet. Tal couldn't possibly understand what it felt like, though he meant well. It was the end of an era. A huge part of her life. She'd wanted it to be over, of course, but once again—nothing ever felt like how she thought it would.

"Probably the hotel," she finally answered, clearing her throat. "Maybe the office."

"Good. This is a good thing, Misch. It means he's been thinking things over. Eventually, he'll think his way back to you," Tal assured her, smoothing his hand over the side of her head. She looked up at him and smiled.

"What a nice way to think of it."

He leaned down and kissed her. It was hard and passionate, and she wondered if maybe she'd underestimated him and his understanding. This was a kiss to remind her of who she was with, and why she was leaving a different life behind.

Crazy boy, I could never forget.

Misch e-mailed the lawyer back, giving him the hotel's address. Then she went back to getting ready. Finished doing her hair and her makeup. Put on a dress and a pair of heels. Tal left with her, and as they waited for the metro, he pulled her into him. Kissed her. Made out with her. She felt stupid, thinking that at her age, but it actually made her giddy—when was the last time she'd "*made out*" with somebody?

Forever. She loved it and gripped his t-shirt, kissing him deeper.

When her train arrived, he smacked her on the ass and squeezed it, practically shoving her into the car. She stood near the door, waving goodbye to him as they pulled away.

I can't believe this is real. How is this real? I don't deserve this . . . but maybe I do . . .

Mischa could admit she was a little star struck by Tal. He was exotic, and he was different from anyone she'd ever met. He was beautiful, with his dark eyes and thick hair, his mocha skin stretched over toned muscles. He was sexiness personified, and he was able to make her body come alive in ways she hadn't known were possible. He'd swept her off her feet, literally, and she'd never quite found the ground again.

After she got off the train, she kept daydreaming about him while she walked to work. As she started to head into her office building, she glanced up, then did a double take. She could've sworn the man driving a car down the street was Tal. She laughed at herself for seeing him everywhere. But then she kept staring, her hand stuck on the handle of the door.

No, it really was Tal. Driving a big, black car. Very similar to the car he'd had in Positano. She had assumed it was a rental. *Range Rover,* that's what he'd driven in Italy, and there, in shiny letters at the top of the grill, was the same name. It couldn't have been the same car. Could it?

"What are you doing?" she asked out loud, even though she knew he couldn't hear her.

She was bewildered at first, but it quickly turned to panic as the car jumped the curb and seemed to head straight for her. She shrieked and leapt out of the way, backing into an iron statue that was behind her. The car swerved, whipping around in a fish tail, and screeched to a stop alongside her.

"*Get in!*" Tal shouted out the open passenger window. Mischa gaped at him.

"What the fuck are you doing!?" she demanded.

"Shut the fuck up and get in the car, Misch!"

"Tell me what's going on!"

"Just do as I -,"

There was a whining noise, and the glass door to her right exploded. Misch screamed again, throwing her hands up. She stared at the door—or where the door used to be—and tried to figure out what had happened. But before she could turn back to Tal, the other glass door exploded. Then a window.

Shot. That glass is being shot out.

The realization had just barely occurred to her when all hell broke loose. She screamed and ducked as an ungodly amount of gunfire was unleashed on the front of the building.

She wasn't sure how long she was down there before someone was grabbing her. Tal was at her side, all but picking her up. He dragged her to the car and stuffed her in the back seat before he got back behind the wheel. The car peeled out as he shot off down the street.

"Are you okay!?" he was shouting. There was a pinging sound, and Misch realized the car was being shot at.

"*NO I'M NOT FUCKING OKAY!*" she screamed at him, folding herself to sit on the floor between the front seat and back seat.

"I meant, are you hurt? Did you get hit!?" he demanded, stretching an arm between the seats and reaching for her. She slapped his hand away.

"No! No! We're getting shot at!" she kept shrieking.

"Don't worry, the car is bullet proof."

"*WHY THE FUCK IS YOUR CAR BULLET PROOF!?*"

Tal didn't answer anymore questions, no matter how much she screamed. The car raced along, and she was pretty sure they were air born at one point. She hugged the chair in front of her, screaming and praying for it to end.

What is going on!? How did I go from making out to getting shot at!?

They drove at breakneck speeds for about ten minutes. Then they broke away from the city. From her position on the floor, Misch could see the tops of trees out the window. But she still refused to get up. Not even when the car came to a stop. Not even when Tal told her it was safe. Not even when he got out and came around to her side, opening the door for her.

"C'mon, Mischa, you've gotta help a little," he grumbled, curling his arms under her own and yanking.

She still didn't budge.

He finally managed to wrestle her out of the back seat, and he carried her away from the car. She could hear gravel crunching under his feet. Then she was jostled around as he used one of his hands. A minute later, and they were inside a building. She finally opened her eyes, but couldn't see anything.

"Where are we?" she asked, nervous that they were in the dark.

"My place."

The lights came on and Misch glanced around. They were in a house. There were large, mismatched rugs everywhere, and everything was open. In front of them was a spacious, sunken living room, then steps up to a raised, exposed bedroom. Next to it was another room, but it was dark, and to their left was a kitchen that looked like it had been transported straight out of the 1980's.

This can't be anywhere but his home.

"Put me down," she grumbled, shoving at his chest.

When she was on her own two feet, she realized she was missing a shoe. She kicked her remaining one off, then moved down into his living room. There were two sofas stretching away from each other, and an end table between them. No chairs, no coffee tables. Just rugs.

"I'm sorry it's messy," he said from behind her.

Mischa slowly turned around to face him, holding her hands up. He stared back, his arms crossed. She was at a loss. They had been making out. They had gotten shot at. They were standing in his house.

"What *THE FUCK* is going on, Tal!?" she demanded.

"You need to relax. Go lay down, and I'll get you something to -,"

"*I DON'T WANT TO FUCKING LAY DOWN, I WANT SOME GODDAMN ANSWERS!*"

There was almost a wrestling style smack down, but Tal got her onto the bed. She stayed on top of the covers, curled against his pillows, while he went over to his kitchen. She glared at him when he came back, but she took the mug he was handing to her. When she sipped at the liquid, she coughed and almost spit it out.

"*Beer!?*" she exclaimed.

"Sorry, it was that or tea. I didn't want to boil water."

She chugged down the rest of what was in the mug.

"Alright. I'm relaxed. I'm chill as fuck. Now tell me, please, what happened?" she panted, wiping beer off of her chin. Tal took a deep breath and rubbed his hands over his face.

"*That* was a terrorist attack," he said in a simple voice, like he was explaining why the bus system was running late.

"I'm sorry. I'm kind of stupid. You'll have to be a little more specific. A *what?*" she asked.

"Dirty deals and trades have been going on, arms getting shipped through Syria, where they go mostly unnoticed because of the unrest going on over there. Guns, rocket launchers, ammo, all kinds of stuff, including information, has been flowing. But it's kinda like a phone line, you know? Turkey starts making calls to terrorists in Syria, and it was only a matter of time before they started calling back. Now al Qaeda and even ISIS groups are popping up. Sometimes, shit goes down," Tal explained.

Mischa was aghast. Of course, she knew about the trouble in Syria, but she'd been assured that Istanbul was well away from it. That she would be safe. There had been no "*hey, you might potentially get gunned down while walking to work*" clause in the paperwork she'd signed before agreeing to travel for her job.

"My office building was shot up . . . by terrorists . . . ," she couldn't even voice her thoughts properly. Probably because she couldn't think properly, period.

"Yes."

"Why?"

"Cause terrorists are dicks."

Mischa burst out laughing, so hard she dropped her beer mug. Tal chuckled and took it away from her.

"How do you know all this?" she asked, fanning her hand in front of her face.

"I have some friends who keep me well informed," he replied in a casual voice.

"Friends who are aware of imminent terrorist attacks, and they just call you up and randomly let you know?" she tried to clarify. He sighed and moved up so he was leaning against the pillows next to her.

"Look . . . I can't explain it all to you right now, okay? I know some people, who know some things. I knew that a terrorist attack, in the area of your workplace, was a possibility. And this morning, I got a call that it had gone from a possibility to a fact."

"You knew this was a possibility, and you let me come here!?"

"Hey, I tried to talk you out of coming here. Lots of times."

"Yeah, but never once was '*hey, you might get fucking shot*' said! I might have been easier to convince if that had been mentioned!" she snapped at him.

"I couldn't say that, babe," he sighed.

"Why not!?"

"I can't explain it."

Mischa felt herself getting worked into a fluster. She scrambled to get off his bed, grumbling to herself as she went.

"I'm getting really fucking sick and tired of that response," she informed him.

"I know. And I promise, I'll -,"

"*And* that one. I've heard it too much. When is it gonna be the right time, Tal!? Jesus, are you a terrorist!?" she suddenly gasped, staring down at him. He burst out laughing.

"*No*, I'm not a terrorist. Calm down," he snorted at her as he grabbed her wrist and pulled her back onto the mattress.

"Why can't you tell me anything? I thought we were in this together," she switched tactics, softening her voice and blinking her eyes at him. He frowned.

"We are. Look, it's been a rough day. You look exhausted. Why don't you relax, take a nap. I'll make some phone calls. When you wake up, I promise—*promise*—I will tell you anything you want to know," he offered.

Hmmm. Mischa was so wired up, had so much adrenaline pumping through her, that she felt like she could run a marathon. Sleeping was not an option. But she also really wanted to ask *a lot* of questions, and it was clear he needed some time to wrap his brain around answering them. She sighed.

"Can I take a shower?"

"Huh?"

She wanted to give him space, and to get the shattered glass out of her hair, so he showed her into his bathroom. She took her time in the shower, letting the hot water soak into her tense muscles. When it was time to rinse off, she was only able to shampoo her hair because that was all he had; stupid boy. There went any worries about a Mrs. Canaan—a woman needs conditioner. She wrapped a large, rough feeling towel around her body before heading out into the open area.

"Where are you?" she called out, rubbing a smaller towel over her head.

"In here!"

She went to his bedroom. It was a small space, more like a large nook, and the bed took up most of the room. There were little bookshelves along the walls on either side, and Tal was standing in front of one, holding a large scrapbook.

"What are you doing?" she asked.

"Just looking at some old pictures."

She went and stood next to him, looked down at the book. Then she laughed. He had the page opened to a bunch of pictures of when he'd been in the army.

"You're *adorable!*" she cooed. He grunted.

"Shut up."

Adorable probably wasn't the right thing to say, but "*sexy as fuck*" would have been appropriate. He was young in the picture, probably eighteen or nineteen. He still had his tan skin, even had dark stubble on his jaw. He had a bandana or a flag or something wrapped around his forehead, pushing his hair back, and he had a cigarette hanging out of the corner of his mouth while he gave a cocky, sly smirk to the camera.

The picture got slightly less adorable as she looked down, though. He was dressed in full military gear, camouflage pants and a matching jacket, with a flak jacket over it. He had a scary looking rifle in his arms—M16? Is that what they were called?—and other weapons strapped to his belt.

"Where were you?" Mischa asked, smoothing her fingers over the picture.

"A military base. *Biranit,* near *Galilee,*" he said, and he wrapped a thick accent around the words, something she'd never heard him do before. He spoke Italian with an American accent so obvious, even she'd been able to hear it—and she didn't even speak Italian.

"Do you know how to speak . . . ," she searched her brain to think of what was spoken in Israel. "Hebrew?"

"Yeah, grew up speaking it, and Arabic, and English. Learned Italian when we moved to America," he replied.

"You don't speak Turkish?" she questioned.

"Not really."

Mischa glanced back down at the picture. She kept honing in on the gun. Such a small part of the picture, such a big bang. She tried to picture Tal shooting a gun, with his easy manner and big smile. But then again, he'd looked pretty scary when he'd confronted Ruiz, in Rome. He'd probably look pretty scary holding a weapon, too. She wished he'd had one earlier, when they'd been getting shot at, but then that thought made her realize something else.

"God, what if you'd been shot today!?" she exclaimed, thinking of it for the first time. Tal rolled his eyes and sat the scrapbook down.

"I didn't get shot today," he assured her.

"But you could have," she pointed out, remembering the way he'd run around the car to grab her.

"Yeah, but I didn't. I have a better chance of getting shot while waiting in a subway station in New York," he pointed out.

She grabbed his arm and hugged it to her chest.

"I would die if anything happened to you," she whispered. He chuckled.

"I've been through a lot worse, trust me. It's gonna take a lot more than that to get rid of me," he teased her, turning so she was leaning into his chest.

Who is this man?

Misch pressed her hands flat against his waist, then slid them under his shirt. Pushed and pulled till he was forced to take it off. She smoothed her fingers across his chest, letting her eyes move over his skin. Skin that she'd only known for a month, yet she felt as if it belonged to her already. A possession she never wanted to lose, never wanted to see it hurt.

She stood on her tiptoes and pressed her lips to his. Even she was surprised by the ferocity with which she kissed him, but she couldn't help it. She couldn't waste one more second with him. What if he went out the door tomorrow, and never came back!?

She yanked his pants open and he pulled her towel away. Adrenaline shot through her and must have passed to him, because his hands started moving as fast as her own. He shoved her roughly onto the bed, then stepped out of his pants and followed her, laying down on top of her.

"I can't believe I was in a gun fight, and my first reaction is to have sex," she gasped as his tongue paid attention to her breasts.

"Not a gun fight. You'd have to fire back for it to be a fight," he corrected her. "And emergency situations can sometimes cause an overwhelming emotional reaction." Misch shoved at his shoulder, forcing him onto his back, and she straddled his waist.

"Well, I'm feeling very over-fucking-whelmed right now," she assured him, tracing her tongue down his sternum.

She'd been so upset, so scared, and he'd stayed so calm. Had protected her. An instant reaction on his part. She wanted to show her appreciation, so she kept working her tongue lower. Lower still. Low enough to lick a circle around the base of his dick, which was rock hard and pointing straight up.

"*Fuck,*" he hissed, when she tightened her lips around his head.

Blowjobs had never really been Mischa's "*thing,*" more a duty to be done. She put in her minimum time, then she was done. But not with Tal. She always wanted to rock him a little, the same way he did to her, so she gave it her all. Flattened her tongue against the sensitive underside of his tip, then worked it all the way down his shaft, and all the way back up again.

He was too big for her to get crazy with, and she was was no deep throat queen, but she gave it her all. Trapped him sideways between her lips and moved up and down him that way. Worked him in her hand while she gave her tongue's attention to his sack. Then she went back to the tippy top. Wrapped her lips around his head and her hands around his cock, then she moved them in unison, as one, her hand making up for what her mouth couldn't reach.

He cursed some more and his hand went into her hair. His fingers twisted in the wet locks, pinched and pulled, but he didn't yank her away. He begged her to keep going. Begged her to never stop.

She wanted to make him come, loved when she could do that to him with her mouth, but then he changed his tune and he really did pull her away by her hair. She started to ask him what was wrong, but he leaned forward quickly and kissed her. All hot, gasping air and dominating tongue. Then he rolled them, till she was underneath him.

"God, yes, please, like that," she begged when two of his fingers thrust their way inside of her.

Ever since Positano, sex had been soft, and sweet, and almost gentle. *Beautiful.* Anything else felt . . . *sordid* to her, after everything that had gone down. She had broken a heart, she shouldn't get to have multiple-sessions-crazy-animalistic-sex. Of course it didn't make sense, but it's how her brain worked.

But not anymore. Now she was feeling very fucking primal. His fingers had barely slipped inside her before they were being pulled away and a much bigger object was demanding entrance. She lifted her knees higher and Tal grabbed one, pulling her leg up so her calf rested against his shoulder.

"Goddamn, you're soaking wet. We should have '*emergency situations*' more often," he growled, working his hips towards hers.

"Not funny," she snapped. It was followed by a shriek, as he slammed his dick home.

"So good. You never stop feeling so good, Misch," he groaned, pumping into her hard and fast.

She couldn't respond. Just moved her hands to her breasts and squeezed. He was pounding the oxygen out of her. *She loved it.* She had missed it.

Just when she felt a monster orgasm blossoming, he pulled out. She whimpered and immediately reached between them, trying to find the piece of anatomy that should've been fucking her into another emotional state. But Tal backed away from her, then grabbed her legs roughly and flipped her onto her stomach. She started moaning low in her throat, almost a purr, and she didn't even need to be asked—she just hiked her hips into the air.

"Oh, *fuck.* I love this. I love it," she cried out when his hips finally met her ass.

"Then say it," his voice said from behind her.

"Say what? I love it. I fucking love it, Tal. Please, fuck me, god, harder, whatever you want," she begged. He chuckled and complied, slamming into her so hard she shrieked every time it happened.

"What do you love about this, Misch?" he demanded clarification.

"I love how you're fucking me."

"And?"

"How hard you are, how big you are. Fuck, so fucking big . . . ,"
"*And?*"

"And . . . ," she wondered if it was possible to get fucked so hard,
a person could get brain damage. "How good you are. So good."

"Not the answer I was looking for," his voice sighed.

She felt his hand on her ass, and he gave her right cheek a sharp
slap. She paid him back by tightening up on his dick, locking him into
place. She heard him give a gasp that time. Then he slapped her on the
right cheek one more time before both his hands came to rest on her
ass.

"I'm so close, babe. So close," she whined.

"I love you like this. It's so fucking hot, hearing you say what you
want," he growled, his hands smoothing over her skin, going lower.
Spreading her apart, tugging at the tops of her thighs. She wanted to
question what he was trying to do, but speech was difficult.

"What . . . are . . . you doing?" she managed to get out, laying flat
on her chest but managing to crane her head around so she could see
him.

"You have such a beautiful pussy, Misch. I'm going to give it a
treat that it deserves," he said, his voice almost soft as he slowed his
thrusts, pulling almost completely out of her.

"I think you already are-, *FUCK!*"

Both thumbs. The man had *both thumbs* on either side of his cock.
As he started to push back inside of her, she felt pressure at first, then
realized what was happening. He plunged back in so slowly, but with
his thumbs *and* dick driving into her. Fucking *spearing* her. Completely. Totally. Filling every last inch of her.

She screamed when she came, actually ripped a hole in his top
sheet. Normally Tal was a gentleman, he would wait out her orgasms.
Not that time. She'd only been caught in the explosion of it for about
three seconds when his hands went back to her hips and he began fucking her hard again. Actually *harder.* Harder than he'd *ever* fucked her,
his fingers carving into her hips as he pulled her back against him.

It was insane. Her orgasm regrouped and got bigger, spread farther. Her whole body went into spasms, and she couldn't do anything,
couldn't fuck him back. Could only try to breathe and be in awe of the
multiple-orgasms she was having. It had never happened to her before,

ever. Not with any of her ex boyfriends, not with Mike. Not even with herself.

A man of many talents, Mr. Canaan.

She thought she was going to pass out, the orgasms went on for so long. Finally, he came with a shout, and she could feel him pumping inside of her. She gasped for air, begged him to stop, not able to go on anymore. Her legs went out from underneath her and Tal went with them, not breaking the connection between them.

"Fuck. Holy fuck, Tal. *Fuck.*"

"Thank you?" he chuckled, kissing along her spine in between panting.

"Thank *you.* God, if I was unsure about loving you before, I'm damn sure of it now," she joked. He suddenly laid down flat, and all his weight was on her.

"Ah, there's the answer I was looking for," he sighed. She smiled. She had thought it was just dirty talk, and there he was, looking for some romance.

"I'm so in love with you," she whispered.

"*Not half as much as I am with you,*" he whispered back.

Mischa

HINDSIGHT IS TWENTY-TWENTY, THEY say.

Fuck them. Give me foresight.

Sometimes, I wonder what it was—was it willfully done on my part? Was I just so desperate, so needy, that I was willing to do anything? Believe anything?

It seems the obvious answer is *"yes,"* but I really don't think so. Despite all appearances, I don't like to lie. At least, not to myself. After all, I'm the one I have to sleep with every night. I'm the one I have to look at in the mirror. Lying to myself would just make me feel shittier, and I don't know how much shittier I could have possibly felt.

I think . . . I wanted to be liked. Simple. Something everyone wants, especially girls. And that's what I felt like; when I look back, it's like looking at a young girl. A little girl, so lost in her fantasies, just praying for Romeo to find her.

But no one warns her that Tybalt is lurking around there, too.

I just wanted to be liked.

The Trouble with Secrets

"*DON'T FUCKING MOVE! DON'T fucking move!*"
"*Keep your hands where I can see them!*"
"*I said don't fucking move!*"
"*Get out of the bed! Get down on the ground!*"
"*DON'T FUCKING MOVE!*"

Mischa had been sleeping. Tal had been next to her. One minute she'd been dreaming about the ocean, the next she was jerking upright to the sound of the door being kicked in. No, not kicked in; *rammed in.* As in with a battering ram.

It was like a professional football team had burst into the house. Large men dressed all in black were everywhere, running and shouting. They all had huge, automatic rifles with flashlights on them, and while Mischa screamed, she held up her hands to block the light.

Are we being kidnapped!? We're being kidnapped. I'm gonna be beheaded in the goddamn desert, and my father will watch the video on YouTube.

"What the fuck is going on!?" Tal demanded, leaping out of the bed.

"Just do what they say!" Misch screamed.

"Get the fuck down! *Get the fuck down!*"

Tal stormed out of the bedroom, right into the thick of their invaders. Mischa just gaped after him, wondering if he was really brave, or just really fucking stupid. There was more yelling, and several gun barrels were pointed directly in his face. But he didn't back down, he just kept demanding to know what was going on, not even a hint of fear

192

showing in his face.

The men were all wearing bullet proof vests, she saw, as well as face masks. They were like shadows moving around in the dusky home. She shrieked when one man grabbed her arm and began dragging her out of bed.

"Please! Please don't hurt us!" she cried as she was shoved to the floor.

"Hey! Don't you fucking touch her!" Tal turned back and began striding towards her.

It took four men to stop him and bring him to his knees. Mischa was shoved against the bed, her wrists held behind her back, her captor's legs pinning her in place. She sobbed.

"I'm okay, just stop, Tal. Just stop," she begged.

"Hey! I'm with *Ansuz!* I'm with *Ansuz!*" Tal began shouting, over and over again.

"Shut the fuck up!" was all he got in response.

Did they hit him? Does he have brain damage? Why does he keep saying that!?

"Look in my fucking wallet! On the table! Look! I'm with *Ansuz! I'm with you!*" he barked.

There was more arguing, more being told to shut up, more of him insisting that they look in his wallet. He was being kept on his knees, his hands clasped on top of his head. One of the men in black stood behind him, holding Tal's hands in place. And of course, the obligatory knee in the back.

Orders were barked in Turkish, then Tal began yelling in what could only be Arabic. Someone answered him, there was more shouting, and finally, someone went over to the table.

The men in black poured over Tal's wallet. Mischa watched everything get pulled out, one by one, and dropped onto one of the couch cushions. She thought the wallet was finally empty, but then they pulled out one last card. It was large, and laminated, much bigger than a regular ID card.

Everything seemed to quiet down at once. The men murmured amongst each other and passed the card around. Eventually one guy held onto the card and wandered off with it, speaking in hushed tones over a walkie talkie. Not that it mattered, it was in Arabic, so Mischa couldn't understand him, anyway.

"Alright," the man spoke in English as he came back to the group. "We take you now."

Tal growled back in Arabic, struggling against his captives.

"Where are you gonna take us?" Misch asked in a sniffly voice.

"You only want me! She has nothing to do with this!" Tal switched languages again.

"We have our orders. You may stay here for interview. She goes to *Silivri*," the other man stated.

Misch was abruptly yanked to her feet, and as if that wasn't shocking enough, Tal completely lost his shit. He surged to his feet, yelling and straining so hard she could see the muscles cording in his neck, chest, and arms. Two more men were added to the original four needed to hold him back.

"*You can't take her there! It's a fucking prison!*" Tal was roaring. *Prison!? I'm going to Turkish prison!?*

"You do not make orders!" the guy who seemed to be in charge started pointing in Tal's face. "I make orders here! She goes for questioning! You sit down and you shut up!"

Misch was dragged to the door, her feet barely touching the ground, her wrists still pinned behind her head. She had pulled on an old long sleeve t-shirt of Tal's and her panties before going to sleep, but that was it. She felt so exposed. She struggled against the hands that held her.

"No! No! I didn't do anything! I don't want to go!" she began shrieking.

"I will fucking shoot each and every one of you! Don't you fucking touch her! Let her go!" Tal was becoming unhinged, and he managed to knock one man to the ground.

"Please! Are you going to hurt me!? Am I going to be okay!?" Misch cried.

Everyone was yelling, and no one was answering, so she pulled an old childhood move. She let her legs go limp, forcing the man shoving her to carry all her dead weight. He cursed at her and dropped her to the ground. Before she could scramble away, though, he was grabbing her, his black gloves scratchy against her bare legs. He clawed his way to her hips and hiked her to her feet, then got a better grip and picked her up, throwing her over his shoulder.

She was crying. Tal was yelling. The last thing she saw as she was carried out the door was one of the men in black driving the butt of his gun into the side of Tal's head.

She started screaming again.

Mischa sat in a metal fold out chair, her legs bouncing up and down almost violently. Anything to release the tension that was running wild through her body. She'd finally done it, chewed her lip to the point it bled. She kept trying to stop herself, but mostly failed and just kept working at it, welcoming the taste of copper, the sting of pain. She kept her hands clasped in her lap, though she really didn't have anything else she could do with them.

She was handcuffed, and had been for the last eighteen hours. She was also still wearing the same clothing she'd been taken in—the panties and t-shirt. Her hair was crazy, her body was dirty, and every muscle she had was hurting; her brain, most of all.

*Am I gonna be here for the rest of my life? Do my parents know I'm here? Does the embassy? Does **anybody**? Is Tal okay? God, he has to be okay, **he has to be okay**. I'll die if something happened to him. **Please let him be okay**.*

Mischa hadn't been put in with the prisoners, and a translator had explained to her that she wasn't under arrest. She wasn't even necessarily in trouble. The handcuffs were just a precaution because of her behavior, when she had been brought in. Did she remember that during her extraction she had bit one of the agents? And that same agent had been forced to neutralize her?

"Neutralize"—translation, I got a gun rammed into my temple, too.

The agent had needed stitches, as Misch was often reminded. She explained that she'd been scared and upset for Tal. She asked about him, over and over again. Where was he, was he okay, was he alive, what had he been yelling about? *Ansuz.* What did that mean? What was he involved in? *What was going on!?*

Please don't let him be terrorist. Let him be okay and not a terror-

ist. Please please please.

They had told her she'd been brought in for questioning, but no one asked her any questions. She was originally locked in an old office that still had a couch. She slept fitfully with the handcuffs on, and was woken up for a disgusting breakfast that she couldn't finish. Then she'd waited, till some guards came and took her to another room.

It was almost cliché, the room she was in; large, all dark gray, with a cheap card table in front of her, a bare bulb hanging above her, and a huge mirror on the wall across from her. Obviously a two way mirror, she watched "Law & Order," she knew her stuff.

I'm going insane. Please, god, let him be okay, please, oh please, oh please.

"Mrs. Rapaport."

Mischa jerked her head up and was shocked at who was walking into the room. She hadn't seen him since Rome, and on top of that, he looked so different, wearing a suit.

"Ruiz!?" she exclaimed. He nodded his head at her, but didn't smile. He sat down at a second folding chair that had been pulled up to the table.

"How are you?" he asked, placing a folder in the middle of the table.

"Is he okay? Please, tell me if he's okay. They hit him so hard. Tell me he's okay," she begged, a tear slipping down her cheek.

"Canaan's perfectly fine. I'm sorry about our surroundings, they didn't have a safe house ready—the prison was the best option," Ruiz said, as if it explained anything. Mischa let out a deep breath and closed her eyes.

"Oh, thank god. I was so worried about him," she whispered.

"Mrs. Rapaport, please. We have a lot of ground to cover, and not much time. You need to answer some questions," Ruiz informed her. She opened her eyes again.

"What questions? What am I doing here? Is this because of the shooting!? Tal said it was a terrorist thing. Was he involved with it?" she babbled. Ruiz nodded.

"He was not involved. Yes, it was a terrorist act. We need you to explain some things to us. Tell us everything you know about Peter Sotera."

Mischa gasped.

"Peter? *Peter* Peter!? Peter, *my boss,* Peter?" she double and triple checked. Ruiz nodded.

"*That* Peter."

"What could you possibly want to know about him? He's an insurance agent, a uh . . . uh . . . field guy, he gets sent to start new branches. He sells fucking insurance!" Misch exclaimed. Her mind was unspooling, slowly but surely, becoming a pile of frayed memories and split ends.

"Yes, he does that. He is also the U.S. liaison for a very violent and aggressive chapter of al Qaeda. He sells them information—advanced intel on NATO and Interpol and the U.N., not to mention the U.S. . ."

Misch sat back, stunned. Peter. Her boss, Peter. Slightly overweight, generally smelled like salami. Got drunk and groped her tits at a Christmas party once. Wore Hawaiian shirts every Friday. *Peter.*

"You must be joking," she breathed.

"I wish I was. Mr. Sotera became involved with al Qaeda following the attacks on 9/11. He's actually spent a lot of time in Afghanistan."

"But . . . but . . . he's from *Hoboken.*"

"Yes. He was a very influential insurance lobbyist in Washing D.C. for a while, where he made a lot of political connections. Then he moved to New York, where he used secrets and blackmail to get the info he wanted. He is responsible for sending information that resulted in the bombings of at least four U.S. convoys, that we can prove. We suspect many more," Ruiz just kept going.

I'm having a nightmare. Wake up now, Misch. Wake up, and Tal will be trying to heat up waffles on the hotel's coffee maker. Wake up.

"Four bombings . . . ," all the breath left her body.

"We believe he moved to Detroit shortly after the failed '*shoe-bombing*' on Flight 253. Since then, he has been gaining more contacts within the terrorist organizations. He came on the C.I.A.'s radar a little over a year and a half ago, and that's how we were alerted to the fact that he was planning an overseas trip. Armenia, Turkey -,"

"*Italy,*" Misch finished for him, her voice barely a hint of a whisper.

"And Italy. Our contract is with the Turkish government. They knew he was coming here after Rome, so it was requested that we go ahead into Italy to gather more intel and to track his contacts," Ruiz explained.

"You knew," she gasped, her eyes finally meeting his. "You knew who I was. Before you met me, you knew who I was."

"Yes," he answered swiftly.

"That's why you were upset. That's why you didn't want us to be together," she began connecting the dots.

"Yes. Above all else, the mission could not be compromised."

"And I was part of the mission."

"*Yes.*"

She knew she should argue. Knew she should be proclaiming her innocence, shouting from the roof top that she didn't know, *she didn't know!* She'd had no idea. She'd been busting her ass setting up insurance offices. Peter had been busting his ass trying to topple governments.

But all she could think about was . . .

I was a mission. A mark. A way to get closer to Peter, to get closer to the mission. That's why he was so secretive. That's how he always knew where to find me.

"He knew me," she whispered, sniffling.

"*Yes.* Now, Mrs. Rapaport, can you tell me the names of every person Peter came in contact with while in Rome?" Ruiz questioned, pulling out a pen before opening the folder he'd brought in with him.

"Uh, no. No, I didn't spend a lot of time with him," she coughed out a reply. She felt sick to her stomach.

She hadn't spent a lot of time with her boss because she'd been busy spending all her time with a man she never really knew.

"But you did spend some time with him. There was a lunch meeting, and a dinner date," Ruiz went over some papers.

"I . . . ," she couldn't finish. Tal had interrupted, both those times. Both times, he'd assured her Peter wouldn't catch them. She had always wondered at his confidence. Now she wondered if he'd orchestrated it that way; if he'd *known* that they wouldn't be interrupted.

How is this my life?

"What about in Detroit? What kind of business expenses was Mr. Sotera making?" Ruiz pressed.

"How would I know that? I'm just an agent!" she exclaimed.

"You are one of the top selling agents in the entire city of Detroit, Mrs. Rapaport. You must be somewhat aware of your boss's movements," he pointed out.

"Yeah, when it comes to insurance! You wanna know how many policies he sold!?" she snapped.

"If you become difficult, the interview will stop. It won't start again till tomorrow morning. How long your time in this prison lasts is entirely up to you," Ruiz told her.

"Are you threatening me!?"

"Just explaining the rules, Mrs. Rapaport."

"I want to speak to a lawyer."

"I'm sorry, that's not possible, Mrs. Rapaport."

"Then I want to speak to the U.S. embassy."

"I'm not required to do anything you request, Mrs. Rapaport."

"A phone call! I should get a goddamn phone call!"

"This isn't America, there is no '*one phone call*' clause, Mrs. Rapaport."

"*DON'T CALL ME THAT!*" she screamed at him.

"*Hey!*" he jumped out of his chair. He immediately loomed over her and she shrank back into her seat, afraid of him. "Just answer the goddamn questions! Were you ever aware that your boss was knowingly involved with terrorist cells!?"

"No! I don't know anything! I don't know anything!" she yelled, pressing her hands over her ears as best she could.

"You know something! You *must* know something! I'll keep you here for a fucking year, it that's what it takes! A fucking year in this goddamn pri-,"

There was a loud alarm. It cut through the room like a buzz saw, startling both of them. Then it shut off, just as suddenly as it had started. Ruiz glared down at her for a second longer, then he grabbed the folder off the table. He strode to the door and yanked it open hard enough that it banged off the opposite wall. Then he slammed it shut behind him.

Mischa tried to catch her breath, shaking and shuddering in her seat. She'd barely started to calm down—well, calm down as much as was possible in her situation—when there was another buzzing sound. She clasped her hands together again and clutched them in her lap. Wished she could curl into herself. Disappear.

The door opened and a man started walking across the floor. Not Ruiz. She knew who it was the moment he stepped foot in the room.

"Are you okay?" Tal asked, sliding into the chair Ruiz had just left.

She stared at him, her eyes wide. He had a bruise on the side of his head, blooming around his temple. He hadn't shaved in a long time, even for him. But the strangest thing was the suit he was wearing. A Brooks Brothers style suit, with a tie that looked like it had been yanked on more than a few times. He looked rumpled and disheveled, which was almost bizarre. Not that he was normally clean cut, but he never looked harried, not the way he looked right then.

Who is this man?

"Not really," she finally replied, her voice scratchy.

"I'm sorry about all this, I didn't know that was going to happen," he sighed, rubbing his palm down his face.

"What happened?"

"Someone took down my license plate, when I grabbed you outside your building," Tal explained. "Those were . . . like policeman, S.W.A.T., the guys who came into my house. They thought I was a part of the shooting."

"But you weren't."

"No. Just the opposite."

"You track them."

"Yes."

"And me."

" . . . yes."

They looked at each other for a long time.

Wake up, Misch. Wake up, wake up, wake up, wake up, wake up . . .

"Who are you?" she whispered.

"Just Tal," he replied with a sad smile. "Same guy as before, I just know more about you than you realized."

"Obviously," she barked out a laugh, but it sounded hollow. Mechanical. He cleared his throat and glanced at the mirror.

"Look, Mischa. Your boss is in *a lot* of trouble, but luckily, it's obvious that you weren't involved. You were brought as a cover, to throw people like us off," he told her.

"Who are '*people like us*'?" she asked.

"I work for a security company—have you heard of Black Water?"

"Huh?"

"It's a private military company, it became kind of famous a couple years ago. They've since changed their name," Tal filled her in.

"Oh, yeah, I remember them. You work for them!?" Misch exclaimed. He shook his head.

"No, but I work for a very similar company, it's called *Ansuz*. Like Ruiz said, the Turkish government hired our company to help with the growing al Qaeda presence in Turkey. That included your boss, once it was discovered that he would be making a trip here. I have to ask this, Mischa, did you ever notice anything strange, in the U.S.? Hear any names? Meet anyone?" Tal questioned her.

How did I end up here? Oh yeah, I lied and I cheated and was a horrible person. Touché, karma. Tou-fucking-ché.

"No. I swear, Tal. I never spent any time with him at work, at all. I was actually shocked that I was offered this job, I figured it was because my sales had been really good that year," she answered him.

"Yeah. Okay. I know. I'm gonna get you out of here, don't worry. This never would've happened, if I hadn't come and gotten you from that shoot out. I'm sorry," he told her before starting to stand.

"So I never would've known . . . ," she let the sentence hang.

"I would've told you."

We'll never know if that's true, and you've already lied about everything else . . .

She refused to look at him, so he turned to walk away. But panic started clawing at her; she'd been alone for so long. She was upset and she was nervous and she was *scared out of her mind.* She dragged her nails up the table, reaching for him but not wanting to touch him.

"Please," she begged. "Please, get me out of here soon."

He groaned, noticing the handcuffs for the first time.

"Fucking Ruiz," he growled, digging something out of his jacket pocket. A key was produced and a second later her restraints were removed. He went to rub at the raw marks on her wrists, but she yanked away from his touch.

Tal stared at her for a long moment, his eyes sad. So sad. Worse than when he'd left her in Rome. Worse than anything, *ever.*

Don't. You don't know this man.

He turned and walked out of the room. Misch sat there, pulling her knees to her chest, making herself as small as possible. But his word was still good, and maybe twenty minutes later a female police officer came into the room. She murmured words in Turkish that Misch didn't understand, but they sounded comforting. She was given a blanket, which she folded in half and wrapped around her waist like a giant towel, then followed the cop out of the room.

The sun seemed ridiculously bright to her, and she blinked a lot as they drove across town. The other woman prattled on, not seeming to care that Misch couldn't understand her. When they got to the hotel, the cop walked her all the way to her room, then checked the room over.

Thorough.

Mischa had to all but shove the chick out the door, but finally she was alone. Not that she was even sure what to do with herself. She wandered around the room, the towel-blanket falling to the floor. She half-heartedly looked for her phone, but then realized it was in her purse. Which was at Tal's house. Which she would *not* be going back to.

She wound up sitting at the foot of the bed, just staring at the dresser across from her. An hour passed. Then two. Then she laid down flat, stared at the ceiling. She didn't know how many hours passed, how many thoughts went by.

He knew you. He used you. So many times. He was doing his job. And you never even questioned him.

The sun was beginning to set, casting a gold-orange glow in the room, when she heard a key in the lock. Remembered the time he'd picked the lock to get in her room, in Rome. Remembered him being everywhere, being everything.

Sad, sad, girl.

"Are you okay?" Tal's voice was soft as he lowered himself in front of her. She shrugged and sat up.

"Not really," she repeated her answer from the prison, staring over his shoulder.

"Misch, you have to know, I never -,"

"Tal," she whispered his name, then took a deep breath. "When was the first time you saw me?"

"At the -,"

"The first time, *ever.*"

There was a *long* pause. Enough time for her heart to sink even further.

"About ten months ago," he kept his tone even, his voice low. "It was a grainy surveillance photo. You were leaving your office building in Detroit. You looked different."

She shocked herself by laughing.

"I had just started my diet."

"You looked amazing, even in black and white. Your hair was a lot longer."

"I cut it for the trip."

"It looks good."

"How long? How long did you study me?" she asked.

"A long time. When we first got word that you had been chosen to travel with him, we did a general background check. When it got closer, and your tickets were bought, we did a thorough check, all the way back to high school," he explained.

She started crying.

"I hope you didn't see those pictures," she sniffled, trying to ease the pain with humor.

"You looked amazing even then."

"You said you were a photographer. You lied."

"I specialize in surveillance."

"Oh, excuse me. You twisted the truth till it was unrecognizable. Completely different, I apologize."

"I had to -,"

"You asked about school. You asked me so many questions. So many things you pretended not to know. You *pretended.* I feel so stupid. You were just pretending. You said I looked like a dancer, when we first met. I am such a sucker. You already knew. You just said it cause you knew it would work, you were just pretending, because you already knew," she babbled.

"Mischa -,"

"Were you '*assigned*' to me? To run '*surveillance*' on me?" she asked, lifting her head to look at him. He looked awful. Almost as bad as she felt.

"I was assigned to the case. You were part of the case. I wasn't necessarily supposed to make contact. That wasn't part of the job," he said quickly.

"Oh sure. God, I am so stupid. *So fucking stupid,*" she hissed, pressing the heel of her hand into her forehead.

"*Stop it.*"

He always knew where she was, he always knew how to find her. "*Come find me,*" their special phrase. But he'd always been cheating. That's how he'd known her phone number, that first time he'd called her. That's how he'd known where her office was, when he'd surprised her. That's how he'd known what restaurant she was at, when they'd had sex in the bathroom.

I'm gonna puke. Hopefully all over his lying face.

"That's how you knew, that's how, that's how, that's how," she whispered. "That's how you knew how to find me."

"I'll always know how to find you, Misch."

"Of course you will! You're a secret fucking agent! That's why, isn't it!? All those times! You were distracting me! God, so many times. What did you do!? Fuck me while Ruiz was sneaking into the office? Breaking into Peter's hotel room?" she demanded.

Tal suddenly stood up and walked across the room. He began messing with a lamp, and she thought he was trying to turn it on, but it never lit up. He pulled his hand out from under the shade, pinching something between his fingertips. Then he walked over to a night stand and reached underneath it, pulling out an identical object. He fiddled with them, then went into the bathroom. She heard the sound of the toilet flushing.

Oh. My. God.

"I just wanted to make sure we had comple-," he began as he came back out.

"You bugged my hotel room!?" she demanded. He nodded.

"I had to. If there was a chance Sotera came in here to talk to you, a chance he would say something, we had to catch it. *I had to,* Misch," he stressed. She started breathing heavily and pressed a hand to her chest.

"Oh my god. Oh my god. Positano. You just showed up. You knew exactly where I was, even what floor, even though I switched rooms," she gasped for air. He shoved his fingers into his hair, scratching back and forth.

"I had to see you. The only way I could get them to let me go was by convincing them there was a chance Sotera might show up, might use his old room, might call you, something. I had to be with you again, I had to have an excuse to come back," Tal said quickly.

"That room . . . oh my god . . . that room was bugged, wasn't it? And the other room, in Rome," she was almost panting.

"Yes. Before you even checked into the hotel in Rome, we swept that room and put in surveillance," he said softly.

"They saw everything?" she squeaked out.

"No one was watching, Misch. There wasn't a van down the street, or anything."

"But there's a recording. Somewhere, some fucking security company has a '*greatest hits*' reel of me cheating on my husband, breaking up with my husband. Fighting with you, fucking you, *oh my god,* I'm gonna be sick," she groaned, bending forward and putting her head between her knees.

"Baby, I swear, no one will see them. Sotera never came in your room, there won't be any reason to watch anything," Tal said, squatting in front of her again.

"I don't care. They exist. You used me. *You used me,*" she cried, putting her hands on the back of her head.

"*No.* I compromised the mission, almost lost my job, for you," he told her.

"Fuck you! You should've told me! You had so many times you could've told me! On the beach! Why didn't you say anything!?" she was shouting at him as she rocked back and forth.

"I couldn't, baby. I couldn't," he whispered.

"*You could.* But you didn't."

"I didn't."

"I was a job to you."

"No."

"A fucking job."

"*No.* You weren't, baby, really. I tried to shield you, tried to keep you out of it. That's why I got you out of certain situations."

"That's why you didn't want me to come to Turkey . . . I would've found out."

"No. I didn't want you to come for the same reason I didn't like you working in Rome—it was dangerous. Sotera's a dangerous man.

That's why I was always trying to get you to skip work," Tal reminded her.

Silly me thought it was because he just wanted to spend time with me.

"So I would come back to my room with you, where everything we did was monitored. God, oh god, oh god."

"I meant everything I said, baby, ever wor-,"

"*I am not your baby!*" she shrieked, sitting upright in a flash. He smiled sadly and pressed his hand to the side of her face.

"You're my everything," he whispered.

She lurched away from the bed, away from him. She sucked in air, but wasn't taking in any oxygen. She thought she might pass out, or throw up. Possibly both. In what order, she wasn't sure.

"You're a liar. You lied to me. Everything. You acted like you didn't know me. Introduced yourself, *fuck.* I can't believe it. You knew me, and I had no clue who you were. You had a mark, a mission, a job. All those days, all that time, just pretending," she went on and on.

"You know me, Misch. *You know me,*" Tal stressed, following alongside her as she paced.

"I don't. I feel like I'm just meeting you right now, and I don't like this man very much," she cried, pushing at his chest when he got close to her.

"You *love* this man," he reminded her.

"How can I love someone I don't know!?" she shouted, shoving and hitting as his arms came around her.

"You do. You know me, you love me," he kept repeating it.

She screamed and cried and shoved at him, but he held her tighter. Crushed her to him. Held her as she sobbed.

"I don't. I don't know you. I don't, I don't, I don't. I don't know this person. How could you do that to me? *I loved you.*"

She cried for a long time. He lowered them to sit on the floor, and she was reminded of their last day together in Rome, which just made her feel worse. She had thought breaking the news to Mike had been the worst thing ever?

Wrong.

"Mischa," Tal whispered, his breath hot against her ear. She wasn't sure how long they'd been sitting there for; long enough for her to stop struggling against him. "You lied to your husband, to be with me. Well, I lied *to you,* so I could be *with you.*"

"I want you to leave," she whispered back.

"No."

"Please."

"*No.*"

"I can't do this right now, Tal. First Mike, and then divorce papers, and now this. God, I always knew I wasn't a strong person, but fuck, you really wanted to nail it home for me," she cried against him.

"I didn't. You *are* strong," he assured her.

"I'm not. I'm weak, and you made me worse."

His arms got tighter for a second, then loosened. Fell away. They were just two people, sitting on a hotel room floor, not looking at each other.

Strangers.

"I never wanted to do that," he told her, his voice empty sounding. "I saw you in those pictures, saw you through a camera lens, saw you in Rome, and I thought to myself '*wow, what is this beautiful woman doing in this place?,*' and then I met you. Talked to you. *Touched you.* I'm selfish, Misch. So selfish. I couldn't stop. I wanted more. I'll *always* want more. Maybe that's wrong. Maybe I made a mistake. I've made a lot. But I'll always want you, always want to touch you. I have for a long time. I will for a lot longer. You own me, Ms. Duggard. Body and soul."

Ms. Duggard.

"I made the mistake, Tal. Not you. All me. I told a lie—it gave birth to more. You're right, I lied to my husband. I can't get mad at you for lying," she sighed.

"You can. I deserve it."

"*I deserve worse.*"

"Stop it."

"I want you to leave."

"No."

"*I don't want this.*"

"That's a fucking lie."

More tears.

"You know, Tal," she chuckled, wiping at her eyes. "For the first time in a long time, I'm gonna stick with the truth."

"*Fucking liar.*"

She finally lifted her eyes to his, smiling at him before she got to her feet.

"Mr. Canaan, it was very nice to meet you. Beyond words. But I've been playing around for long enough. I think it's time for me to go home."

Tal stood as well and loomed over her.

"You said you loved me," he growled.

"I know. I meant it."

"And I love you."

"I think you meant it, too."

"Then what's the fucking problem!?"

"Everything. I ended my last relationship in lies. I don't want my next one to be built on them."

Hard logic to argue with, even for Tal and his silver tongue. His jaw worked, clenching and unclenching. He looked like he was in pain.

"Please, babe. Please, *don't do this*," he begged.

"I have to do this. I'm in love with a guy I met in Rome. You're in love with a girl you met in Rome. Neither of us are those people."

He grabbed her hand and pressed it to his chest.

"Then get to know *this* man. You'll love him even more."

"It's time to go home now, Tal."

She walked to the door and opened it. When she turned back, he was still standing in place, glaring at her.

"Home is with you," he stated. She gave him a watery smile.

"Home is in Detroit. You hate the U.S.," she reminded him.

He strode towards her, eating up the ground. She didn't even have time to react, he just grabbed her and kissed her hard. They fell against the open door, moving backwards as it hit the wall.

One of his arms was completely wrapped around her waist, under his t-shirt, his palm hot against her skin. His other hand cupped her jaw, holding her head in place, like he was afraid she would try to get away.

She didn't. She kissed him back. She would have to feast on this fantasy for a long time to come, so might as well end it with a bang. She stood on her tip toes and gave as good as she got, moving her tongue against his while she raked her fingernails up his back, settling her hands on his shoulders.

She was pretty sure he would've kept going till they passed out, but when she got dizzy, she had to pull away. She dropped her forehead to his chest and took deep breaths through her nose, inhaling him. Memorizing him. She felt his lips on her head.

"*Don't do this, Mischa,*" he whispered.

"I'm no good right now. I'm broken," she replied.

"Let me fix you."

"I'm sorry, Tal."

They broke apart.

"This is wrong and you know it," he called her out.

"Maybe. It won't be the first time. But I'm getting better at dealing with it," she told him. He moved into the hallway.

"Do me a favor, Misch?" he asked. She turned towards him, but he wasn't facing her. He was staring off down the hall.

"Anything," she responded.

"Take care of you. Take care of your heart. And don't . . . don't forget us," his voice fell into a whisper.

"I could never. Not in a thousand years. Not at all."

He gave a curt nod, then walked off down the hall. She watched till he turned a corner and got on an elevator.

Mischa shut the door. Slid on the chain lock. Then she took a couple steps. Paused. Then walked into the bathroom and threw up; a particularly painful experience, since she hadn't eaten since breakfast the morning before.

The love of your life, and you didn't even know him.

Mischa

I MADE A CONSCIOUS DECISION to cheat on my husband.

I can't say that it went well. It certainly didn't go according to plan.

If I could do it over, I would have done things differently.

When I first accepted the job overseas, I would've talked to him then. Told him that I wanted to separate, and me working abroad would be our chance to explore life without each other.

I would've gone to Italy. I would've met Tal. It wouldn't have been scandalous. It wouldn't have been a secret. It would have been two people meeting, two people dating, openly. I wouldn't have been so nervous and panicky and overwhelmed and unsure. I would've been more aware, I would've noticed all the signs, I would've asked more questions.

I can only hope he would've answered them.

But I'll never know. And he'll never know. And Mike will never know.

Because I did it all wrong, and instead of cheating on my husband to feel better about myself, I upset three lives. Broke three hearts.

Oh, and was involved in a low key international terrorist incident in a foreign country.

But I feel that part was minor in comparison.

Home

T O SAY THINGS WEREN'T good at home would be a drastic
understatement.

And even just getting home had been an ordeal. The Turkish government hadn't wanted her to leave. Mischa was an employee of a known terrorist aider-and-abetter. That was frowned upon in the best of situations.

This wasn't one of those.

After arguing over her visa for days, suddenly, she was given permission. Just like that. She could only assume that Tal had intervened on her behalf, and she was grateful.

But she didn't see him.

She flew home, but she didn't have anywhere to go. She hadn't called Lacey ever again, and Mike still wasn't returning her phone calls. The apartment was half hers, of course, he couldn't keep her out, but she didn't want to be more bothersome than she already was to everyone around her.

Her little stint as an international-woman-of-mystery had become somewhat infamous. Peter got arrested in Turkey, and the story blew up.

"U.S. Insurance Agent Aids al Qaeda"

"Insurance Agent from Detroit Sells to Terrorist Groups"

"al Qaeda Life Insurance Policies, and The Man Stupid Enough

to Sell Them"

The last article heading was her favorite.

Her name was mentioned a lot, and she got requests for interviews about her relationship with Peter, about her detainment in Turkey, about her interactions with the super secretive military security company, Ansuz. About her interactions with a very specific agent within that company.

She declined all of them.

She stayed in a hotel at first. Another goddamn hotel. Her father picked her up at the airport and he drove her to the hotel, promising to help her find a place as soon as possible. He made good on his word, locating a shitty apartment in a decent part of downtown Detroit. It was small and it was old and it was ugly.

But it was hers.

They quickly found out that Misch's dad would have to loan her the down payment for the apartment—the savings account she shared with Mike had been cleaned out. Zero dollars. Her company had offered her a hefty severance package, which she gladly took, but she wouldn't get the money for a while. Her checking account was pretty close to tapped out. If she didn't find a job, pronto, she'd be living with her parents again.

How fucking depressing.

Mike wasn't speaking to her. Her friends weren't speaking to her. Her own mother wasn't speaking to her. Her father basically had to meet up with her in secret. The only interaction she had was with a corner grocer, and the few newspapers that kept calling her.

It took a while, but she finally got a job at a dance studio. At first just helping in the office, but eventually she was allowed to teach a toddler class. Simple stuff, but she enjoyed it.

Tal would approve of this.

She thought about him a lot, didn't avoid it anymore. He had earned it. Earned all her thoughts, all her memories.

"Have you talked to him, sweetie?" her dad came right out and asked one night.

"Who?" she played dumb.

"You know who."

"God, isn't this nice? An apartment with a terrace, I never thought I'd have one downtown," she sighed, leaning back in her lawn chair.

"Baby. We're sitting on a fire escape."

"Don't ruin it, Dad. It's gonna be bad enough when winter comes."

They were sitting on a fire escape, looking across an alley at another fire escape. But it was late July and a heat wave was ripping through the city—Misch's new bachelorette pad didn't have air conditioning. So they were trying to catch a breeze, knocking back beers.

"Stop being squirrelly. Have you talked to him?" her dad demanded.

"No, I haven't."

"But he's called."

"How would you know that!?"

"Because *I've* talked to him."

Misch sat up so fast, she knocked her beer over. She'd been home for almost two months, and she hadn't spoken with Tal at all. He'd called a couple times. She'd gotten a whole new plan, a new number, but of course he found that number. Not a shock. But he only ever left one message. One voicemail, and after that he never called again.

She still hadn't listened to the message.

"What!? When!?" she shouted, turning her chair to face her dad's.

"Oh, he calls every now and then, to check on me. Or really, you. But I haven't talked to him in a while, about two weeks. Usually I hear from him about once a week," her dad said it all casually, like it was something they talked about all the time.

"What does he say? What do you say? How is he? Why is he calling you!?" she was baffled.

"We talk about a lot of stuff. Ball games and women and work, things like that. I think he calls cause, well, he doesn't have a lot of family he's close to anymore, I think he's the black sheep. And I think talkin' to me makes him feel closer to you," her dad answered honestly. She got a warm feeling in her chest and she sat back in her chair.

She and Tal had talked a lot, so she knew about him feeling like a black sheep. Knew that he didn't get to see his family very often. It was a little weird, the dude she had an affair with that one time, calling her dad like he was said dude's own dad. But it was nice, too.

"Good. I'm glad," she sighed.

"He does seem kind of sad," her dad added on.

"He does?" she asked, keeping her voice soft. She'd worried about that, couldn't stand the idea of him hurting. Of him being sad. Of her being the cause.

"Yeah. Did you ever listen to his voicemail?" her dad questioned. She shook her head and took a swig of his beer.

"Nope."

"You should, honey. What he did wasn't right, but you didn't do a whole lot right, either. Just hear him out," her dad suggested. She shook her head.

"Don't you see? That's just it—we both did so much wrong. Both of us. And two wrongs certainly don't make a right," she pointed out.

"This is love, sweetie pea, not physics. Pull your head out of your ass."

She laughed at him.

They said goodbye after that and she walked him to the door. His words settled in her brain and she wandered through the apartment, thinking about Tal. She stretched out on her bed and stared at her ceiling. Remembered what it had been like with him, wondered what it would be like if he was there. She smiled. He'd probably be yanking and pulling at her skinny jeans, fighting to get them off her.

"God, why are they so tight!?"

"You love it when I'm in them."

"Yeah, but not so much when I have to get them off. They're impossible to get over your clown feet."

"I do not have big feet!"

"Don't worry, Boppo, I love your clown feet."

She actually laughed out loud, remembering him. Remembering them. Then she remembered what happened after the skinny pants were gone, and she stopped laughing. Smoothed her hand over her stomach.

She hadn't had sex since Tal. Couldn't really imagine having sex with anyone else. She went to work and she went home, that was it. Her heartless, *"I'm gonna find a man and fuck his brains out"* mentality was all gone; probably because the man she'd found had gone ahead and fucked *her* brains out.

Her phone started ringing, startling her fingers away from the waist of her pants. She glanced at the screen nervously. Maybe Tal had psychically tuned into the fact that she was about to touch herself while thinking of him and he'd decided to give her a ring-a-ding.

But she was almost more shocked by the name she saw on the screen.

"*Lacey!?*"

"Can you meet me somewhere?" her friend whispered down the line.

"Of course. Please. Just say where," Misch scooted off the bed and dashed around, looking for shoes.

"That pub we used to always go to."

"When?"

"Is right now okay? God, you're probably busy, we don't have to, I can just -,"

"I'm out the door. I'll meet you in five."

Misch actually got a little teary eyed as she saw her friend walking towards her. She didn't want to make it weird, so she stood lamely beside the table, just smiling. Lacey wasn't smiling, though. Her eyes were brimming with tears and her lower lip trembled. She walked right up to Misch and wrapped her arms around her, hugging her tightly.

"I'm so sorry," Lacey cried.

"What!? For what? You don't have to apologize, Lace," Mischa assured her friend.

"I do," Lacey sighed, finally pulling away. She brushed the tears away and sat down. "I wanted to call you, so many times. But I felt so bad for how I treated you, and everything, and I worried it would be weird. Then today I thought, just call her."

"I'm glad you did. It's not weird, and I deserved how you treated me," Misch slid into the booth as she issued assurances.

"No. You're my friend, I've known you longer than Bob," Lacey replied.

"He's your husband. You have to listen to him. Husbands come first."

"Not always."

Isn't that the truth.

A waiter took their order, then they chatted, caught up with each other. Lacey was so glad that Misch was dancing again, and Misch was excited to hear about how Lacey's baby was doing. They had a couple cocktails and relaxed. Slowly, the awkward tension began to fall away.

"So. What was it like?" Lacey finally asked. She was looking down at the table and blushing.

"What's what like?" Misch countered, slurping at a vodka-tonic.

"What was it like sleeping with someone else," Lacey said bluntly.

"Jesus, Lace, don't hold back."

"I've been curious for a while."

"Sex is sex, I don't know what you want me to say."

Lacey sighed and glanced around before leaning low over the table.

"I want to know everything," she whispered. Misch ran her teeth across her bottom lip.

"Everything?" she whispered back.

They stopped at a liquor store before they went back to Misch's place. Lacey squealed at the sight of the apartment, called it "quaint" as she walked from room to room. As in living room to bedroom to tiny bathroom, since that's all there was really.

"Your own apartment! We never lived on our own! Do you ever think about that? We didn't leave home till college, then we stayed in dorms, then we went back to our parents for the summer. Then you hooked up with Mike and I met Bob," Lacey sounded wistful.

"Yeah, the first night I slept here, it kinda hit me. This is my first place, on my own," Misch agreed.

"You get to do anything you want now," Lacey's voice was soft. Almost sad.

"Totally. I pee with the bathroom door open, whenever I want."

"Gross."

They made fruity drinks and curled up at opposite ends of the couch, burying their feet together under pillows.

It's little things that make life better. Like putting your feet on top of your best friend's and then putting a pillow over them.

"Do you really wanna hear all this?" Misch asked, grimacing when Lacey asked for the dirty details again.

"I'm *dying* to hear all this," Lacey assured her. Misch took a deep breath.

"It was . . . crazy. Awful and awesome, all at once," she started.

"How did you meet him?"

Oh, he was spying on me for months before I even went to Italy. Thought I had great legs, and apparently also thought I was stupid.

"In a cafe. I was going over a manual, and this creepy guy wouldn't go away. Tal appeared out of nowhere, chased the guy off," Misch smiled at the memory, at him holding up her hand, acting like she was his wife.

"Was it a while before you slept with him?" Lacey asked, obviously just wanting to get to the good stuff. Misch cleared her throat, blushed a little. This part never sounded good.

"Uh, not really, no."

"Really!?"

"Yeah. That first night. We got to talking, he was funny. We went to a bar in a hotel. Turned out it was his hotel. He kissed me in the bar. Kissed me in the elevator. Kissed me in his room. He's . . . a hard man to resist," Misch chuckled.

"That is so crazy! I can't, I just can't picture you kissing someone else besides Mike," Lacey breathed.

"I know. I couldn't either, for a long time."

"What happened next?"

"I had to go back to his hotel room a couple days later cause I -,"

"No, after he kissed you. Did you, like, jump on him?" Lacey questioned her. Misch laughed.

"Not at first. I kinda wigged out. I kept saying I couldn't do it, that I wouldn't do it, I was shaking. I was a hot mess, I don't know why he kept going. But whoa, man, did he keep going. Things almost went down right in the elevator," Misch snickered.

"That is so hot."

"Yeah. Then in his room, while I was still freaking out, he just kinda grabbed me and kissed me. Carried me to bed. Did things to me . . . I still get breathless thinking about them," Misch panted a little, fanning herself.

"Did you . . . ," Lacey rolled her hand for emphasis. They were besties, but talking about their sex lives wasn't something they often did, so Misch was surprised. But not embarrassed. Tal had actually cured her of a lot of her inhibitions involving sex.

Pity. I'm finally uninhibited, but have no sex drive.

"Oh yeah, like, multiple times. He went down on me, had me go down on him. We had sex in the bed, in the shower, on the balcony, all over that room. I came more times in that one night than I have in . . . I don't know, years? Forever," Misch stated. Lacey turned bright red.

"I know it's wrong, but that sounds *awesome,*" she whispered. Mischa laughed out loud.

"It kinda was. At least until the next morning. Then I went home and it hit me, what I had done. I hated myself, Lace. I think that's another thing, another reason why I couldn't stop it. When I was with him, I forgot to hate myself," Misch tried to explain.

"You don't have to hate yourself. Now c'mon, I wanna hear all about your sexcapades," Lacey clapped her hands together.

So Misch blabbed. She'd been dying to talk about her experiences, really. She told Lacey about the time on the beach. About the time in the bathroom at the restaurant, about the guy watching them. About another time, when Tal actually tied her wrists to the bed posts. She'd never been tied down before; it had felt amazing.

"I've never been tied down, either," Lacey confessed.

"Try it. I don't think you'll be disappointed."

"Do you have a picture of this sex god?"

Mischa worried her lip again. She actually did have a picture of Tal. She wasn't sure when he'd done it, but some time between leaving her, and her leaving Istanbul, he had gotten into her room. Put some pictures in her bag.

There was the one of him in his army days, the one she had seen at his house, and then another one. The "love-slash-hate" one, as she called it in her mind. Loved it because it was of the two of them. They were walking down a street in Rome. She was wearing her fedora and sunglasses, a fitted tee and shorts. Always showing her legs for him. He had his arm around her waist, his thumb hooked inside her shorts, and she was molded to his side, just the way he always liked to walk with her. Tal was smiling, his head tilted down a little, and towards her. She was looking straight ahead, and was smiling broadly, as well. It was a great picture, caught them in that timeless space where they had been in love for a moment.

She hated it because it was a surveillance picture. Hated it because it had been taken without her knowledge. Hated it because Tal had written on the back of it.

"***Don't forget us.***"

She brought the photos out to Lacey, who oohhed and aahhed over them.

"Good god, Misch, he's fucking gorgeous," Lacey sounded like she was about to drool.

"That he was. Even better naked," she assured her friend.

"Really!?"

"Oh yeah. Like *wow.*"

"Like *wow* wow?"

"Like *oh-my-god-it's-so-big-it-might-not-fit* wow."

Misch laughed as Lacey turned an even darker shade of red.

"That's, uh, that's good," Lacey coughed out.

"It was better than good. And his body, Lace, *UG,* his body. *Sickening.* He was in the army before and he worked out like a mad man, it was phenomenal," Misch groaned, flopping backwards over the arm of the couch. She had thought talking about Tal would be hard, but it actually felt good. If he'd been there, he would've gotten a kick out of it, would probably do a little strip tease for the girls. It made Misch feel close to him.

"Sounds great."

Misch realized her friend was almost whispering, so she sat upright. Looked over the other girl's face. Lacey was looking down at the photos, frowning. She looked sad. She looked about to cry.

"I'm sorry, Lace. God, me and my big mouth. I told you, I'm a bad person. And it's not like Tal being sexy takes away from Mikey being sexy—he's still sexy. He'll probably always be sexy, and he was great in bed," Misch babbled.

"Why'd you do it? Honestly. What made you decide to do it?" Lacey demanded, wiping at her eyes. Mischa winced.

"I was unhappy. I was lonely. I felt like I had nowhere to go. Mike wouldn't listen. I kept telling him something was wrong, he kept insisting things were fine. I'm not blaming him, I'm not. Not anymore. I should've had some balls. But I think . . . I mean, *I know,* I thought I could just get away with it. I know, I know, that sounds awful. I just finally gave up, you know? I wanted to feel desired. I wanted to feel sexy. So I decided to go out and find someone who would make me feel that way. I just didn't count on finding someone I'd want to hold onto," Misch tried to explain.

When she finished, she realized Lacey was crying in earnest. The glossy surveillance photo was pressed to her face and she was sobbing into it. Mischa leapt off the couch and pulled the photos away before grabbing some tissue. Then she sat down right at Lacey's feet and grabbed her hand.

"I'm sorry," Lacey hiccuped and cried.

"Don't be. I am. I'm sorry I was so weak. I'm sorry I hurt him. I really, really am. I'm sorry I did things the way I did," Mischa tried to say something, anything, that would calm the other girl down.

"I'm a bad friend," Lacey wailed.

"No, no you're not. Anyone would've reacted the way you did, you're not," Misch promised her.

"No, not that."

"Then what's wrong?"

"I wish you would've talked to me," Lacey sobbed. "About anything. About how you were feeling. I thought you and Mikey were perfect. So perfect. I just . . . I just . . . I just . . ."

Mischa got the other girl a glass of water. While Lacey sat up to drink, Misch squeezed in right next to her and wrapped her arms around her friend's shoulders.

"Nobody is perfect, Lace. No couple. No one," Misch stressed.

"When I got pregnant," Lacey started whispering, "I was so happy. I'm awful, but I thought '*Ha! We did something before The Mikes, before Mischa and Mikey. I'm finally gonna be the perfect one*'."

"Wow, Lacey, I had no idea," Mischa was genuinely shocked.

"But I wish I'd known. I wish you would've talked to me. I wish I could've . . . ," Lacey's voice trailed off.

"No one could have stopped me, Lace," Misch told her.

"No. *I wish I could've gone with you.*"

After Lacey calmed down, they moved to the bedroom. Had an old fashioned slumber party. She had resisted since moving home, but Misch figured if any night called for it, it was that one, and she put on the long sleeve shirt that had belonged to Tal. The only physical thing of him she had left. His smell had long since disappeared, she'd washed it several times, but she liked to think she could feel him when she was wearing it.

Lacey explained that things were not well in her own marriage, but for different reasons. Bob was a heavy drinker. Lacey was an enabler. Everyone knew this, it wasn't a secret, per se, it just wasn't talked about openly.

Lacey didn't want to cheat on Bob, but she figured it had taken strength for Mischa to do what she had done. Lacey wanted that kind of strength.

She wanted to leave her husband.

It wasn't much, but Mischa offered her home. The couch was a fold out, and it would do till Lacey could find a place of her own for her and her daughter. Lacey thanked her. Practically blessed her.

When the other woman fell asleep, Mischa stared up at the ceiling. Huh. Strength. She never thought of what she'd done as being strong. She thought of it as cowardly. As weak. As cruel and thoughtless and self-centered.

But if someone could actually benefit from her fucked up mistake, then maybe she wasn't such a horrible person after all.

See, Tal? I'm getting better already.

Is Everyone Hiding
Something!?

"WHERE IS MY SHOE?"
"Milk!"
"Just a second."
"Seriously! I just had it!"
"MILK!"
"I said, just a second!"
"I'm so fu-, er, ahhhh, -dging . . . so fudging late already, I need my fudging shoe."
"MILK! MILK! MILK! MILK!"
"I SAID JUST A SECOND!"

Mischa was glad she could help her friend out, she really was, but after a month of living with Lacey and her almost-two-years-old daughter, she was ready to shoot herself. She had thought that the little girl would stay with her daddy.

Turned out little girl's daddy was a frickin' douchebag.

Mischa finally located her shoe, hiding under three baby blankets and four stuffed animals. While the screaming continued, Misch slipped on her shoe and skipped out the door, hurrying out to the bus stop.

She had been given more classes to instruct at the studio. It was nice. No, it was *great*. She told herself that repeatedly. She had wanted to start dancing again, and now she was finally dancing. All was right with the world.

But it didn't feel right.

Mike still wouldn't answer the phone. All communication was done through lawyers. She still hadn't gotten any of her savings back. Her mother was unthawing, but not at a very quick rate. Her father plodded along, same as always.

And Mischa just existed. She got up, she went to the studio, she danced for eight hours, she went home. She got up, she went to the studio, she danced for eight hours, she went home. Rinse and repeat. The weekends she spent at the apartment, just chilling with the girls.

I depress myself.

When she got back from work that night, she expected more of the same, but was in for a surprise. No one was home when she got there. The sofa bed had been put away. The place had been tidied up. She walked around slowly, almost suspiciously. Then her phone dinged with a message, and it was Lacey explaining that they were having dinner with her parents. She would be out late, might even stay the night at their house.

Freedom!

Mischa took out a pint of ice cream and dug into it, all while sipping Baileys straight from the bottle. When the sugar became too much, she went down the street and got an unhealthy amount of Chinese food. Ate her weight in chow mein.

She was beginning to regret her choice of how to spend the evening when someone knocked at her door.

Did Lacey forget her key?

"Thank god you're here, I may have to be rolled into the -," she started as she opened the door. But she stopped in mid-sentence. In mid-breath. In mid-existence.

"Hi," Mike said simply.

She burst out crying. Just zero to sob, in nothing flat.

It's been so long.

He ushered her into the apartment. Sat her on the couch before rifling through her fridge. He poured a shot of vodka into the bottom of a tumbler and handed it to her. After she knocked it back, he automatically poured her another.

He still knows me.

"I'm . . . sorry, it's just . . . been a long . . . long time," she stuttered, trying to catch her breath.

"Yeah, I know. I needed time. A lot of time," he sighed.

"Of course you did."

"I've been seeing a therapist," he threw out there.

"That's great. Good for you, Mike."

"And we've been working on forgiveness," he went on.

"You don't have to forgive me," she assured him.

"No. Working on me asking *you* for forgiveness," he corrected her. He could have hit her and she would've been less surprised.

"For what!?" she exclaimed.

"For treating you the way I did in Italy. I've never gotten physical with anyone, you know that. I still can't believe I touched you like that. I kinda hated you and maybe wanted you to die a little, but I didn't want to hurt you," he told her.

"I know that, Mike. I knew it then. There's nothing to forgive."

"Yes, there is," he went on, taking a deep breath. "I took you for granted. I didn't listen to you. I pushed everything away, including you. I know you worked hard on us, and I know you tried to tell me, I do. I think . . . I think I was more obsessed with the idea of having the '*perfect marriage*' when I should've been trying to have the best relationship."

"That's awesome, Mike, and I gotta be honest, it feels good to hear you say a lot of that. But I still shouldn't have done what I did," she said softly.

"No shit," he stated loudly, and they both laughed. "You should've walked out first, before you even went to Italy. God, I wish you would've."

"Me, too."

There was an awkward silence.

"I've got a cashier's check," he blurted out.

"Excuse me?"

"The savings account. Sorry, I was angry," he said, taking a piece of paper out of his pocket. It was a bank check, made out in her name, for a lot of money. A lot of money she had worked hard for in a job she'd hated.

"It was understandable," she replied, taking the check from him.

"I don't know if I can be your friend yet. I just wanted . . . wanted you to know that I don't hate you anymore. I don't think I like you very much, but I don't hate you," he told her. She smiled.

"I don't like me very much, either," she whispered, wiping at her eyes.

"Is he . . . do you still . . . are you . . . ," Mike stammered. She shook her head and stood up.

"No."

She didn't elaborate.

"I'm seeing someone else," he offered up, his voice nervous sounding. She refilled her tumbler with water and sat back down.

"Really? That's great. Really," she gushed, and she meant it.

"Well, just a couple dates. Just going slow. You know?" he said, rubbing at the back of his neck. A nervous habit he'd had since they were nineteen.

"Of course. Slow is good. Slow is probably for the best," she assured him.

"Yeah. My therapist said I should talk about that with you, too," he went on, now rubbing his hands together. She thought it was cute, that he was nervous to tell her about his new girlfriend.

"Whatever you want, only if you're comfortable," she told him. He took a deep breath and she took a sip of her water.

"He's a music teacher named Dennis that I met while -,"

Mischa spit out her water. All of it, straight out. All of it, all over his face. They blinked at each other, water dripping from his nose and her chin. She gaped at him, and he stared at her like he was terrified.

"Um . . . ," she began, mopping at her chin. "I'm sorry. I must have misheard. *Denise*, you said?"

"The whole forgiveness thing covers this, too. I got mad at you for lying, and what you did was shitty, but I've been lying, too," Mike was almost whispering.

"About this? About a music teacher?" Mischa glanced around, like said music teacher was going to jump out of a dark corner.

"Yeah. I've . . . for a long time now . . . hell, since before you and I even hooked up, I've known I liked guys, too," Mike confessed in a rush.

"*What the fuck!?*" Mischa shrieked.

"I know, I know. I didn't know how to deal with it! You know how my mom is! And then you came along, and god, Misch, you were so hot and so perfect, I just loved you so much, so quickly. So I figured nobody ever needed to know. We'd get married and be together forever, and it would be enough," he explained. She gasped.

"Are you saying it wasn't? Mike, were you sleep-,"

"*No.* I'm not the cheater here," he growled, and she was immediately chastised.

"I'm sorry."

"But I did think about it. Fantasized about it a little. Not that you weren't enough. You just . . . ," his voice trailed off. She smiled sadly and placed her hand on his leg.

"Wasn't enough," she finished for him.

It was wrong and fucked up. Mike had kept everyone in the dark about his sexuality. It had effected their relationship and driven a wedge between them. Mischa had used that wedge as an excuse to explore her own sexuality.

We were so fucked up. We were doomed from the start.

"Do you hate me?" Mike whispered. She gasped.

"God, no! How could I? I mean, I feel bad, that all those years, we could've been having awesome threesomes," she joked, humor her ever-present armor. He laughed long and loud.

"Oh god, I missed you, Misch," he struggled to breathe. She smiled.

"I missed you, too, Mikey."

"Don't get me wrong. You were my wife. I never stopped thinking of you that way. I loved you. I thought . . . I thought we were going to grow old together. I still can't wrap my brain around it. When I wake up in the mornings, sometimes . . . sometimes I reach for you, like you're still next to me. Or I'll call out to you, thinking you're just in the kitchen. It's like someone died. You killed me in Italy, but then I came home, and you were the one who was dead. It's been awful. You were my wife. *My wife,*" he repeated the words, his voice trailing off. She worked hard to keep her tears at bay. She didn't deserve to cry, to release the pain. She wanted to bottle it up, remember it whenever she was feeling sorry for herself.

"I'm so sorry," Mischa whispered. "I don't think I'll ever stop being sorry. I do love you. I just wish I could've loved you the way you needed."

"I think we spent too much time talking about shit that didn't matter. Maybe we should've talked more about what we really wanted," he suggested.

She decided it wouldn't be helpful to point out to him that she'd done just that. Several times. *All the time.*

"I always thought of you as my husband, Mikey. I still do most of the time. I don't think it'll go away for a while," she told him. He chuckled.

"*The Mikes.*"

A nickname given to them by friends—Mischa could be Russian for "Michael."

"*Mischa. Russian, 'Who is Like God'.*"

"I love you, Mikey," she sighed, then panicked. "I'm sorry. I'm so sorry. Am I allowed to say that?"

"It's okay. I love you, too, Mischa. That's the worst part. Loving you so much at the same time as hating you," he told her.

"Tell me about it. I go through that every day when I look in the mirror."

They laughed together again, and she thought maybe, just maybe, they could get back to that place where they were good friends again.

"I gotta go," he sighed, pulling himself into a standing position.

"Okay. Just . . . I gotta double check. Dudes. You're dating a dude. You like dudes," she clarified. He blushed a little.

"Yeah. Yeah, I like '*dudes*'," he answered.

"*And* you like girls?"

"Very much."

"Wow. You're so . . . progressive."

"Shut up, Mischa."

Old habits die hard, and he playfully smacked her on the ass. They both froze for a second, then laughed some more.

Maybe even best friends.

"Stop by, anytime. Whenever. All the time. Or you know, take your time," she rambled.

"Time. Will definitely take some time," he nodded as he opened the front door.

"Thanks for coming over. Really," she told him. He stopped in the hallway.

"I talked to your dad the other day," he said quickly.

"Oh yeah? That's good," she guessed, though she couldn't be sure.

"Yeah. We talked for a while. It was actually good, which is weird, considering we didn't talk a lot when you and I were together. He told me a lot of stuff," Mike said. She raised her eyebrows.

"Well, that is good, I guess," she laughed. Mike took a deep breath. Wouldn't meet her eyes.

"You should call him, Misch."

"Huh?"

"I fucking hate him and I hope his dick rots off," Mike snapped, surprising her. He wasn't prone to being nasty. "But . . . he made you happy. And I know you, and I can't imagine how lonely you must have been, to have done what you did. So yeah. Call him."

"You're an amazing man, Michael Rapaport," she whispered, blinking away the tears.

"Ah, too late now. Now someone else is experiencing this awesomeness," he teased, but she could tell he was trying not to cry, as well.

"They better be worthy of you," she teased back.

"I hope so, too."

He nodded and walked off down the hall.

Wow. Woooooooooooow.

Mischa shut the door and immediately went into her bedroom. She went to lay on her bed, but saw that her cell phone was blinking with a new text message. She opened it up as she stretched out on her back. It was from Lacey.

Hopefully by the time you read this, he's come and gone. I hope it went well. Enjoy your freedom for the night. The tiny terror and I will be back in the morning. CALL ME if you need me.

Mischa laughed and cried a little at the text. She had the most amazing friends. That she could do what she'd done, and they still stood by her, still took care of her. Amazing people.

There was a little symbol in the upper left hand corner of her phone. A little envelope. A little picture, she'd been avoiding looking at it for weeks. Couldn't bear the thought of it.

"*. . . he made you happy. Call him.*"

She pressed the button before she knew what she was doing. She wondered if maybe it had been psychological—she'd been avoiding the voicemail because she'd been waiting for absolution. Forgiveness for her sins against her husband. Her anger at Tal had long since cooled, and she liked to pretend she had moved on into indifference.

"*Pining*" and "*depression*" were better words for how she actually felt.

The minute his warm voice filled her ear, she felt the tension wash away. The days, months, all the time. She was immediately back in that timeless space.

"*Hey dancer lady. Well, I guess it's official. You really don't want to talk to me. But I hope you'll listen.*

"*Whenever you hear this, I hope it finds you well. I hope you're dancing, because you were built for it. I hope you're smiling, because your mouth was made for it. I hope you're laughing, because it's the most incredible sound. And I hope you're being loved by somebody, because you deserve it.*

"*I know we lied a lot. To other people, to each other. About a lot of things. About most things. But I never lied about the most important thing—how I felt about you. I was always honest, from the very beginning. I didn't want to be attached to you. I kept pretending I wasn't. But we couldn't stop it. Your heart swallowed me whole. You know my real name, you've been to my real home. You always saw the real me. Not that guy on the job. I should've told you that when I had the chance.*

"*That's what you didn't get—you* **did** *fall in love with me. I AM that guy in Rome, not the agent in that interrogation room. You ARE that girl in Rome, not the insurance agent from Detroit. Those are who we really are, and I think that's why we found each other there.*

"*Fuck, I don't know. Maybe you'll never even hear this. Maybe you deleted it. Maybe you're listening to it right now, picturing that I'm next to you. If it's the last one, then please, please hear me.*

"*I'm in love with you. Right now, this moment. Back then, when you were here. In the future, whatever happens. It's love. I should have said that more. I should have touched you more, held you closer, never let you go. I should've quit my job, should've begged you to stay, should've come home with you. Gone anywhere with you. I would live my life in a thousand hotel rooms, a thousand double beds, if it meant getting to be with you.*

"You changed me, Ms. Duggard. You made me come alive, and I didn't even know I was dead. I was just some guy, before you. You made me a man.

"Please say you haven't forgotten us. Please say you'll never forget. Please say that sometimes at night, maybe sometimes, you remember what it felt like when I got to touch you every night.

"Never forget. Always remember. And when you do remember, when you're ready . . . **come find me."**

Mischa. Lost. Her. Shit.

She stumbled out of her bedroom, sobbing and crying, not even sure what she was doing. She rooted around in the closet, then finally found her laptop. She hadn't used it in a while, because she didn't have internet—couldn't afford it anymore. But she could steal it, so she went out onto her fire escape. She could pick up a neighbor's signal from out there. She sniffled and snorted, wiped her nose on her sleeve, and quickly turned on the computer.

Come find me.

She tried to call him, but he'd pulled a "her"—his number no longer worked. *Fuuuuuuck.* She googled his name, but hardly anything turned up. She found the Ansuz website, and he was actually listed in their employee directory, which kind of shocked her. Even more shocking was the branch he was listed under.

Ansuz. Office #349-A. 820 Lafayette Street, New York, New York, United States.

He's in America. Holy fuckballs, he's in America.

Mischa got up early the next morning and called the phone number for his building. She didn't get anywhere. He wasn't there, and they absolutely would not give out his private number or address.

Come find me.

He wasn't there the next day. Or the day after that, either. Or at any of the sixteen random times she called throughout the day.

She was suspicious. Something wasn't right. The receptionist was either lying, or not telling the whole truth, or something, but it was becoming increasingly clear that Mischa was never going to reach Tal over the phone at that building. Maybe he wasn't even really there . . .

Think. Think. He always knew how to find you. You should at least be able to find him.

She went to her parents house.

"Hey Dad," she called out, walking down into the basement. He was sitting at his workbench.

"What's up, sweetie?" he asked without looking up.

"Where is he?"

"Well, praise the lord," her dad chuckled, twisting around to face her. "Took you long enough!"

"Yeah, yeah—where is he?"

"Was it Mike? I thought that would do it."

"Less gloating. More talking."

"Well, honey, I haven't talked to him in over a month and a half. Last I talked to him, he was in New York, but he said he was gearing up for a big job," her dad told her.

"Big job?"

"Yeah, some long term gig. Something to keep his mind occupied, you know," he told her.

"Long term . . ."

"Yeah. But I don't think he's gone quite yet."

"Why? Dad, if he told you anything, I swear I'll -,"

"Nope. Just a hunch I have. New York. That's where he was last."

Then I guess I'm going to New York.

~~~ *ell* ~~~

Staying with him, staying in Istanbul, wouldn't have been right. She'd been telling the truth, she'd needed time to heal, to get over what he'd done and forgive him. Needed time to find herself, for once.

But Tal had been right, too. They had been in love, and not just for a moment between seconds. Not just in some timeless space. In the real world, in the now, in *every* moment. She should've trusted that, should've trusted him.

Now she had to trust that same love would help her find him.

Mischa wore her nicest power suit, did her makeup extra nice, put on her most expensive shoes, and she marched across the lobby of Ansuz Office #349-A, New York, New York.

"May I help you?" a pleasant sounding secretary asked.

I hope she doesn't recognize my voice.

Misch knew Tal wasn't there, because she'd called before going down there. She asked to speak with someone about hiring a security team. After five minutes, she was called into an office. A tall guy with blonde hair smiled big at her.

"Hello, Mrs. . . . ," he fished for her name.

"Duggard. *Ms.* Duggard."

She gave him the story she'd practiced all week. She was the assistant for a famous country-singer—who also happened to actually be her second-cousin, so she figured it was okay—and was looking over security companies, trying to find one that would suit them.

It wasn't normally the kind of security Ansuz handled, but the man seemed slightly enamored with her. Or her low cut top. He prattled off figures and numbers and success stories, listed off impressive clients they'd had in the past.

"I'm sorry, this may seem odd, but a friend of mine was involved in an incident in Turkey. Horrible situation, but I've heard nothing but praise for a certain agent . . ."

Yes, Mr. Canaan was an excellent agent, Misch was informed, but he simply didn't handle jobs like hers. He was originally a field man, though he'd been working a desk for the past couple months.

They put him behind a desk!? That's like keeping a tiger in a cage.

She replied that she didn't care. If he was the best, she wanted the best. Arguing happened, though she tried her best to keep it flirty. She pushed the man just far enough for him to snap at her. Just far enough to give her what she wanted.

"Look, I'm sorry, but Mr. Canaan simply can't work for you. His desk is here, but he's been working out of a field office."

And that's all he would say. He became a rock after that, wouldn't utter a word, and eventually asked her to leave. But that's all she really needed from him, anyway. She thanked the man for his time, then left.

She walked around for a while, frowning at the ground, dragging her feet. Maybe it was a sign. Maybe it had been too long. Surely, if he wanted her to find him, Tal would've made it possible. But this was impossible. He had no family, no friends in America. His job wouldn't say where he was, for obvious reasons. He'd changed his phone number. A call to her father revealed that he genuinely didn't know where Tal was, either. He was just . . . gone.

All pretty clear cut signs that he'd given up on her. That things were over between them. She couldn't blame him, not really. After all, she gave up on him. It was kind of fair. It was . . . *karmic*. Misch was sad, but she was understanding. She had tried her best, but it was too little, too late. He couldn't be expected to wait forever.

She'd fallen in love with him in Rome. She'd been in love with him when she'd left Istanbul. She was still in love him, right then and there. And she would still be in love with him tomorrow. And the day after. All the days. All those moments between those seconds. Timeless. Their love would always be alive; a living, beating heart, but just caught in a moment. Caught in *their* time. Maybe that's all they were. Just a time in love.

Just a time in an affair.

She wanted to hate herself. It was a feeling that typically came easy, after she'd left Turkey. But Tal had told her that she wasn't a horrible person. That her bad decisions didn't define her. She tried to think of what he'd say if he was there, and she was pretty sure he'd tell her that loving him, that him loving her, was proof enough that she wasn't horrible.

She would honor his memory, honor his words.

Don't forget us, he'd asked her. She wouldn't.

Remember me, he'd told her. She always would.

And she was still dancing, still smiling, and still laughing, just like he'd asked. Life wasn't so bad, and she could make it better. Being without him had already been hard when she'd been feigning indifference. It was going to be harder, knowing what she knew now about his feelings. About her feelings. But she could get through it. She *would* get through it.

For Tal.

Come find me . . .

Tal

WHEN I THINK OF Mischa, certain things come to mind immediately.

Exotic.

Smart.

Great legs.

Fun.

Sexy as fuck.

Love.

I know what we did was fucked up and what I did was fucked up, but honestly, none of it ever mattered. The only reason I ever talked to her was because of just that, *I wanted to talk to her.* I wanted to be close to her. Wanted to touch her, as much of her as possible, as much of her as she'd let me.

She let me touch *all of her,* especially her heart. That was the deal breaker, right there. That's when "*just sex*" flew out the window and "*holy shit, I need this girl to be a part of my life*" entered the picture. I never once cared that she was married—if he was taking care of his shit, she wouldn't be there, plain and simple. Maybe that's fucked up, but oh well. Cheating is just a symptom for something else that's wrong. Should she have cheated? Fuck, no. Weak move. But she had been a weak person.

I wanted to make her stronger.

Eventually, I also didn't care that I could lose my job. It didn't matter. She had never been about the job. I never saw her as part of it. *I didn't care.*

The only thing I cared about was her.

Probably the only thing I had ever *really* cared about, was her.

I needed more time. Time is an issue with me, I'm always going somewhere, doing something. Busy, busy, busy. I should've made more time for her. Given her more time to trust me, to trust herself. That fucking guy, I swear. Her husband fucks with her heart, makes her doubt him, in turn she doubts herself, so she doubts what's between us.

Then again, that doubt also brought her to me. I believe in fate, so if that's what it took to bring her to me, then that's what it took. Sorry, everyone, only not really.

But I have to wonder . . . why did fate take her away?

I miss her so goddamn much. I didn't even know her for that long, how can I miss her so much that it hurts every part of my body? Every part of my day?

All those years, bumming around, being an adrenaline junkie, being the job. I was actually looking for her.

But see, that's the scary part. It took me so long to find her.

What if she never finds me?

Epilogue

MISCHA SIGHED AND FLIPPED a page in her book, wiping sweat from her forehead.

Why does it have to be so fucking hot all the time!?

She was trying to get lost in the story she was reading, but her thoughts kept wandering. It was a common occurrence lately; she was distracted all the time. So she didn't even notice someone was sitting down at her table till the man was making himself at home in a chair. She was startled and jumped a little, dropping her book. She went to pick it up, but the stranger beat her to it.

"Sorry, didn't mean to frighten you," the man said, his voice friendly. She gave him a tight smile.

"No worries. Can I help you?" she asked, not wanting to be rude, but not wanting to encourage his little visit. She'd come to the outdoor cafe to sit and wait and read. Not to pick up random dudes.

"I just saw you sitting here, thought I'd introduce myself," he explained.

"Oh. Well, thanks, but I'm reading," Mischa informed him, holding up her book for emphasis.

"I'd love to hear about your book. Can I buy you a drink?" he asked, peeking at her cover before giving her a big smile.

"No, thank you, I'm fine, I'd just like to read," she replied, holding her book in front of her face.

It's too fucking hot out for this.

"How about dinner? It's just about dinner time, you must be hungry," he pointed out.

"Nope, not hungry," she replied, refusing to return his smile.

"Maybe we could go for dinner some other time, then," he suggested.

"I don't think so. It was really nice meeting you."

"But we haven't met. I'm Conrad."

"Hi, Conrad. I think I have to go now," Mischa sighed, giving up. He wasn't going away, so she decided she would go somewhere else. She slowly climbed to her feet, shoving her book into her tote bag.

"What about lunch?"

"No, but thank you."

"Breakfast."

"Seriously?"

"Coffee, then. Let me take you to coffee. I live near here, we must be on the same schedule—I've seen you eating here before," he told her, standing up as well.

Not creepy at all.

"I don't drink coffee. Just wine. Bye!" she tried to cut him off and edge away from the table. But he gently grabbed her wrist, stopping her as he moved to her side.

"Then maybe we could go to a wine bar I know. If you'd give me a chance, I think you'd like -,"

"*Hey, fucker, beat it, it's not gonna happen—you're hitting on a married woman.*"

Misch's left hand was grabbed and practically shoved into the overzealous admirer's face. Conrad turned a deep red and he nodded curtly before walking off down the street.

"You know," Misch sighed, "that trick only works when there's a ring on my finger, you idiot."

"I work all day in this fucking heat, and then I save your ass, *again*, and what do I get? Hassled about marriage. *Women.*"

Eight Months Earlier . . .

Oh, Mischa didn't give up.

Fuck that. Tal wouldn't have given up, so she didn't.

When they'd been together, he'd asked her to believe in them, to have faith in them. So she clung to that fact. She put all her faith in him, and went with her gut.

She bought a plane ticket to Rome.

Tal had lived in a lot of places, all over the globe. Rome was a long shot, really—he'd only been there for a job, just to follow her boss. Why would he go back?

Because that's where we became ourselves. That's where we found each other.

Ansuz was not always an easy company to track down, and they didn't exactly have an office building in Rome, the way they did in New York. It took a lot of digging to find out what kind of contracts they had in Europe, and then if any of those were even in Italy *at all.*

But she had faith.

As it turned out, they had a contract with the Vatican. The frickin' Vatican. She couldn't imagine Tal in a church. He was far too sinful.

It was a long shot, but she was willing to try anything that might lead to him. Mischa lurked around the cathedral for days. She toured it so much, she was pretty sure the security guards were starting to get suspicious. She considered finding a nun costume, but figured that was going too far. She was already a cheater. She didn't need more points to fast track her to hell.

Why would he even be here? Maybe he guards the Pope. Maybe he guards a bishop. Maybe he's in Tahiti with some pearl farm heiress-slash-supermodel and I'm wasting my time and money.

He was there, though.

The first time she saw Tal again, she felt like her heart stopped. She was in a crowd of people, waiting their turn to enter the cathedral, when he came outside. He was with a bunch of guys, all a lot younger than him, and he was barking what sounded like orders, all in Italian.

He looked so different. It was like dreaming about something for so long, then seeing it in real life. Had it all been a dream? Had she just imagined him as the smooth talking, long fingered, dirty man that she'd fallen in love with?

He was wearing a very fitted suit—she wouldn't be surprised to find out it had been tailor made for him. He was clean shaven, his hair neatly styled, and he had a radio piece in his ear, a curly wire trailing down the back of his neck. He looked so prim and proper.

Two words she never, ever would have used to describe a man like Tal Canaan.

A few seconds was all she got, then he breezed right past her. It took her heart a lot longer to start beating again, and by then she was shuffled inside by the crowd.

Tal would have been proud of her, she became an excellent stalker. "*Recon,*" she told herself. That's what Tal would've called it. She staked out the church. It took her about a week, but she finally learned his schedule, knew when he got off work, what door he left from, things like that.

She was being stupid, she knew. Her father *and* Lacey told her so every night, when she checked in with them. They told her to just go talk to him, to walk up and say hi. Ask how he was doing. Then just jump him.

"*Dad! I can't just* **jump him'***!*"

But they were right. She couldn't just watch him from afar, either. It was creepy and pointless. Not to mention the fact that she was living off of savings—she couldn't stay there indefinitely. She had to do something.

Mischa was scared, though. She'd left him. She'd made it very clear that she wanted nothing to do with him. She hadn't returned any of his phone calls. It had been three months. What if he was over it? What if he didn't feel the same way? What if he had failed to leave any sort of forwarding info because he didn't want her to find him? *What if he was with someone else!?* She couldn't bear that thought, not even a little. Maybe he hadn't contacted her again for a reason. Maybe it was time to let him go.

Come find me . . .

Tal lived in an old building that had once been a great home, but had long since been converted into apartments. There were HUGE wooden double doors, easily twice her height, and they were locked—a panel with buzzers sat to their left. "*T.C.*" was clearly labeled, second row, sixth button down. She knew exactly where it was because she'd stared at it a lot.

When she'd left for Rome, Mischa had bought a round trip ticket. She'd given herself one month to find Tal. One month to see if all they'd been was an affair. Just a moment in time. Or if maybe, just maybe, fate had something more in store for them. She'd spent the first two weeks looking for him. Another week and a half stalking him. Mischa had three more days before she had to go home.

Three days till she had to leave him.

It was night time when she finally screwed up the courage. It started raining on her way to his place, so she stopped in a shop and grabbed an umbrella. She felt ridiculous, wearing shorts and a tank top in the pouring down rain, but Italy in late September was still warm to her, so she'd packed for the warmth.

She huddled and shivered outside his door, repeatedly pushing his button. It wasn't exactly how she'd pictured it happening, her beating down his door. She'd been hoping for something slightly more subtle. Romantic. But the rain was torrential, she had to get out of it.

No one answered.

She scowled and pressed the buzzer again, letting her finger stay on it for a solid minute. Still no answer. She didn't get it. From what she'd seen, he always came straight home after he got off shift. Always. In that week and a half, she'd never seen him do anything different.

Really? Tonight of all nights, he decides to stay out!?

As Misch turned and scurried down the stairs, she saw something out of the corner of her eye. People, walking down the sidewalk. She turned her head and realized it was Tal. She was so startled, she slipped down the last two steps, almost falling on her butt. By the time she caught her balance, she realized something else, too. He wasn't alone.

Misch ducked behind a thick telephone pole a little ways up from his door, peeking around it to spy on him. She felt ridiculous. Her umbrella was jutting out, rain sliding off of it like a sluice, but she held her ground. She couldn't tear her eyes away.

He was with a woman.

A short woman, with amazing hips and long, thick black hair. She was chattering away, Tal smiling and laughing at her side. He was carrying two huge cloth grocery bags, long baguettes sticking out the top of one.

Oh my god. He's on a date. I'm gonna puke. I waited too long. I'm gonna puke. I deserve this. I'm gonna puke. I cheated on Mike, I don't deserve to live happily ever after with Tal. I'm gonna puke.

Tal and the woman stopped walking and turned towards each other. She was smiling up at him, and he was smiling right back down. His gorgeous smile, all his perfect teeth showing. Not even a hint of sly.

I can't watch this.

Tal deserved happiness, she didn't begrudge him that; she loved him. More than anything, she wanted him to be happy—even if that meant he wasn't with her. But that didn't mean she could stand by and watch it happen with someone else. She turned away, not wanting to see them kiss. She wiped at her face, took a deep breath. Took several more. Then she started walking the other way down the sidewalk.

"Mischa!?"

I can't do anything right.

She turned around, planting a big smile on her face. Tal had moved so he was standing in front of his own door. Mischa was a door down from him. The Italian woman was nowhere to be seen.

"Hi. How are you?" she called in a lame voice.

"Is it really you!?" he sounded incredulous

"Yeah. I just wanted to . . . to say hi," she babbled, feeling stupid. Beyond stupid.

"'*Hi*'!?"

"Well, yeah. I was here . . . and you were here . . . so I -,"

He moved so fast, she barely realized he had started walking before he was right in front of her. Just like their first time together, he swept her off her feet. Wrapped his arms around her and lifted her up, knocking the umbrella out of her hands. They were soaked in an instant.

"God, I missed you *so much,*" he was whispering in her ear. She hugged him back, as tight as she could.

"I've missed you, too. Since the moment I left," she replied.

"Then why'd you leave!?"

"So I could find myself," she whispered back.

He finally put her back on her feet and he stepped away, but only a little. His head was tilted so he was looking straight down at her, water running over his eyebrows and down his face.

"I thought I found you," he reminded her. She managed to smile.

"You did, but it was my turn to finally do some searching."

"Mischa. What *the fuck* are you doing here!?" he demanded.

"I . . . I also figured it was finally my turn to find *you,*" she answered. He stared at her like she was nuts. His black eyes opened so wide, she felt like she was going to fall into them. She chewed on her lip and glanced around. "I didn't mean to interrupt."

"Interrupt what?"

"Your . . . thingy. Your lady friend back there, I don't want to hold you up. We can catch up another time," Misch offered.

Tal laughed. Long and loud, from deep in his chest.

"You thought I was on *a date?*" he clarified. She shrugged, almost shredding her bottom lip between her teeth.

"I don't know. You were laughing and smiling, she was laughing and smiling," she rambled.

"Hey now, Ms. Duggard, not all of us are cheating bastards," he called her out.

She gasped.

"*Screw you!* I fly all the way out here just to see you, and you insult me and -,"

He kissed her, and Mischa didn't even care that he'd just insulted her. Didn't care that he'd just been walking down the street with another woman. Didn't care that they hadn't seen each other in months. Didn't care about anything, except touching him as much as possible.

"Thank god you're still feisty," he groaned, running his tongue along her bottom lip.

He grabbed her hips, pulling her towards him as he maneuvered them to his front door. It took some fumbling, but he managed to get his keys out and the door unlocked all while keeping his lips attached to her own. Then he yanked her into an elevator that was barely big enough for the two of them and hit the button for his floor.

"I wanted to come here sooner," she whispered, kissing along the side of his neck.

"You should've."

"Who was that lady?"

"Next door neighbor. Don't worry, she's married."

"She's married? Then I'm doubly worried."

That earned her a chuckle. Tal's hands were still on her hips and he gently pushed her back, forcing them apart.

"I'm not so into married ladies anymore. Single women only," he told her.

"Oh really?"

"Mmmm hmmm. And what about you, Ms. . . . Mrs. . . . ," he fished. She smiled at him.

"Definitely Ms. It's *Ms.* Duggard now, all the time," she assured him.

"Thank god," he groaned.

The elevator stopped, but there were still stairs, and he led her up them. His apartment was formerly the attic, but it had been remodeled. One bedroom, with a small kitchenette built into one wall. Seemed tiny, especially for such a big man, but he walked straight through it and right up to a large window, that she thought led to a Juliet balcony.

It led to a huge terrace—his attic apartment was actually on top of the building, and the rest of the roof was all open. He had potted plants and trees lining the sides, and some patio furniture scattered about, as well as a ridiculously huge barbecue.

"This is nice, Tal. Really nice," she commented, glancing around the space. Then, as if on cue, the rain let up. He stepped around her and went outside.

"You think? I thought you'd like it," he sighed, looking around as well.

"How'd you know I'd ever even see it?" she laughed at him. He turned to look at her.

"I knew. I had faith."

Mischa had always felt so overwhelmed by Tal. From the first moment she'd met him, when he'd been *"saving"* her, to when he'd reminded her what passion was that very same night. Even in Positano, he'd completely bowled her over with his presence. With the sheer force of his spirit. She'd never quite felt worthy of him.

But maybe she finally was . . .

"I leave in three days," she blurted out. He raised his eyebrows.

"Oh, really."

"Yeah. I wasted too much time, looking for you, and then trying to work up the courage to talk to you," she went on. "So much time had passed, and you had moved—why did you move? Why did you come here?"

"They wanted me back in the field, they wanted me abroad, I had no choice. So I asked them to send me here, and had faith that you would find me."

"You have an awful lot of faith in me."

"Always."

She felt like she was going to burst. He seemed so calm and collected. Like it was all a movie he'd already seen the ending to, but she had no clue what was going to happen next.

"I wish I was here longer, I wish we could catch up more. I have so much to tell you, and I want to hear everything that's -," she began rambling again.

"Mischa," Tal said her name in a loud, sharp voice, startling her.

"What?" she asked, watching him as he walked towards her.

"I want to hear everything you have to say," he assured her.

"You do?"

"And we'll catch up, believe me."

"We will?"

"Yes, because we'll have plenty of time to do it in."

"Huh?"

"You're not going anywhere," he informed her.

"I'm not?"

"No. You're home now. With me. Where you should have been this whole time," he said, coming to a stop in front of her. She sniffled. Tried not to cry.

Seems like I never cry as much as I do when I'm with him.

"You want me to stay?" she asked in a small voice. He laughed and cupped her face.

"Baby, I never wanted you to leave. *Of course* I want you stay. I never want you to leave again," he told her.

"You're not mad at me? Cause I left?" she double checked, a tear slipping out of her right eye. He playfully shook her head.

"I'm furious. It's been three months since I've had sex, woman! Three months! Do you know how long that is in man-time!? You have *a lot* to make up for," he warned her. She laughed as well, the tears falling in earnest.

"I was so worried. So scared too much time had passed, that it had all been in my head," she cried. "So many things. Worried you'd found someone else, or that you'd be over us."

"Mischa, there is no one else but you, and I don't think I'll ever be over us. I told you—it's love," he sighed, pressing his forehead to hers. "Stay with me. I got this place for you, so you could come outside every morning and look at the place that brought us together. Where we found each other. Where we came back together. *Stay with me.*"

Not "*come find me,*" not anymore.

Now "*stay with me.*"

How could a woman, who cheated on her husband, possibly deserve that kind of happiness?

When Mischa had decided to hunt him down halfway across the world, she hadn't really been sure of what to expect. She certainly had never imagined she would immediately move in with Tal. Straight from her hotel to his place—he actually went and collected her stuff. She missed her flight, and she didn't even care.

At first, she'd seriously wondered if it would work between them. Their relationship had been started on lies. She had cheated on her husband. Tal had lied to her the entire time. Not good building materials. Beyond that, his apartment was almost unbearably small, around six hundred square feet. *Tiny.* She felt like she was living in a dorm room.

She learned to love it. A smaller space meant they were always together. And the screwed up beginning to their relationship actually reenforced its strength. They had already seen each other at their worst, had already shared their worst secrets with each other. They had done what was wrong. Now they knew how to do it right.

Her family came to visit. Her mother was still cold towards her, so Misch wasn't expecting much, but Tal made quick work of the ice queen. He didn't give Mrs. Duggard a chance to not like him. When they picked them up at the airport, he simply grabbed the tiny woman in a bear hug, actually lifting her off the ground. Then he let his silver tongue go to work, and by the end of the trip, Mischa was pretty sure her mom was more than a little in love with him.

And of course her father loved him. Mischa was an only child—she got the feeling that Tal was a little like the son her dad had never gotten to have. The two would sit out on the terrace for hours, talking about baseball and basketball and football. Anything with a ball. It made her happy. Two parts of her life, fitting so seamlessly together. Her dad was also fascinated by Tal's life, by his secretive job, and loved hearing all the stories.

Tal's job was still crazy. He didn't work at the Vatican for long. Soon, he was back *"in the field,"* back doing missions with Ruiz. He tried to stay in Rome as much as possible, and tried to keep his time away brief, but still, it wasn't easy. One time he came home with a bullet hole in his bicep. That had almost ended it. Mischa nearly lost her damn mind, and a screaming match to end all screaming matches broke out between them.

But oh, wow, the makeup sex had almost been worth it.

After that, they reached a compromise. If he took an out of country job, he had to take her with him. She'd gotten a job at a dance studio, and her hours were flexible, so it was easy enough for her to sneak off, and it made him think twice about what jobs he accepted. It worked out beautifully. In the eight months they'd been together, Misch got to see France, Norway, Mongolia, Nepal, and South Korea.

Though nothing compared to spending every day with him. And nothing at all to spending every night with him.

After Tal scared away the over-eager gentleman who kept trying to get Misch to go out with him—seriously, a breakfast date!?—they sat down together. She'd been waiting for him to get off work. They ordered real drinks and chatted about their days before heading out.

"How am I so lucky?" Mischa asked as they walked away from the cafe, holding hands while they strolled along. Tal smiled.

"I have the same thought, all the time. I told you, fate. What a mother fucker."

"You're such a romantic."

"Only the best for you. Can we go home and get naked now?"

"No, I have plans for us."

Misch surprised him by picking up the pace, yanking him down the street.

"What are we doing? I was planning on deviant sex," he complained, following behind her as she led the way down a side street.

"You can have that any time. Can you hear the music? There's a big festival going on," she told him. She felt his hands slide over her hips, then he was pulling her back against him, even as they were walking.

"Any time, huh . . . ," he focused on the pertinent part of her statement.

A band was playing in a square, with speakers, and people were dancing and laughing. She'd been surprised to learn that Tal was actually a pretty good dancer—he'd made mention of her dancing, all the time, but had never mentioned that he had some rhythm of his own. Now every opportunity she had, she danced with him.

She always wanted to be dancing with him.

"This wasn't exactly what I had in mind for tonight," Tal laughed an hour later, when he finally convinced her to take a break. He led her away from the crowds, over to a bench nestled in some hedges.

"What did you have in mind?" she panted, still moving her hips and feet to the beat as she stood next to him.

"Something sexier," he replied, sitting down.

"*Pffft,*" she snorted, rolling her body, "my dancing is pretty goddamn sexy." He yanked on her hand, pulling her into his lap.

"So, dancer lady," he started, helping her to get comfortable on top of him.

"Yes?"

"Are you happy?"

"Exceedingly."

"Do you know what today is?" he continued with the questions.

"Tuesday," she replied.

"Duh. I meant, *what today is.* Like as in something special," Tal continued. Misch scrunched up her nose, confused.

"Uh . . . ," she tried to think of what holiday was being celebrated. He snorted at her.

"You dork, today marks one year since the day you came to Italy," he almost snapped at her. She sat up straighter.

"Really?"

"Really."

"Like the day we met?"

"No, like the day you got off the plane."

Mischa thought back. Over the winter. Last summer. So many moments.

"Wow, I'd completely forgotten," she gave a small laugh, staring off into the distance. "How'd you remember?"

"I was there," he replied in a soft voice, then she felt him kissing her bare shoulder. She glanced down at him.

"You were?" she was surprised. After they'd decided they were going to seriously make a go at having a real relationship, they established early on that nothing was off limits, and Mischa had asked *lots* of questions. But that had never come up.

"Mmmm hmmm. I wasn't supposed to be, either, I was supposed to be making sure all the equipment at the hotel was running smoothly. But something . . . I don't know, something made me go see you. I'd seen your pictures. I wanted to see you in person. You walked right by me," he explained, smoothing one of his hands over her arm. She smiled down at him.

"I didn't notice."

"Big surprise. You have the situational awareness of a manatee."

"Shut up."

"I was there. I watched you. I thought to myself '*I'm going to talk to her,*' so I remember that day very well. It was the day *we* started," he finished.

"Oh please, you just wanted to get in my pants," she teased.

"Very true. Pity I couldn't get rid of you after that."

"Hey!"

Mischa would have given another smart-ass response, but her mouth was suddenly indisposed, mainly dealing with his tongue. He kissed her hard, and aggressively, one of his hands moving to hold the back of her head. She moaned against his lips, kissing him back.

"So a year later—are you happy?" he asked her again, moving to kiss down the edge of her jaw.

"More than I've ever been in my entire life," she whispered, combing her fingers through his hair.

"Any regrets?"

"That I didn't find you sooner."

"Good girl, good answer."

His tongue was back in her mouth, his fingers were pulling at her hair, and his free hand was working its way up her thigh. Misch knew it was grossly inappropriate—they were in public and were behaving like horny teenagers. But that's just how they were, and she hoped they would never change. She was still drunk on his love, high on his love, and she never wanted to come down.

Though she wasn't so drunk that she didn't notice his hand moving underneath her skirt.

"Tal," she panted, grabbing at his wrist at the same time his fingers curled around the top of her underwear. He ignored her and began pulling at the material.

"Why you wear these is beyond me. How many pairs have you lost since you moved in with me?" he commented, tracing his tongue over her pulse. She shivered and he used the movement to his advantage, pulling her panties over her hips.

"Too many. We are in public, *stop it!*" she hissed, pressing her butt down harder against his leg, trying to hold the material in place.

"Do you think I care?"

It was too late, anyway, he'd gotten them too far. Plus, resisting him just meant his hand would stay up her skirt longer. Mischa finally let go of his wrist and he immediately dragged the underwear over her knees. She glanced around nervously, slipping her legs free.

"There, satisfied!? We're gonna get arrested one day, I swear, I -, *ACK!*" she was startled when he abruptly stood up, dumping her off of his lap. She stumbled, then panicked, scrambling to hold her short skirt in place over her ass.

"Want these back?" Tal asked, giving her a sly smile as he dangled her underwear in front of her face. She turned ten different shades of red and tried to snatch the material from him. He pulled away and her panties disappeared into his pocket.

"This isn't a game, Tal," she used her best no-nonsense voice. He stepped up close to her, completely invading her space, pressing his chest against hers. She held her breath, lost in his gaze for a moment.

"Baby, you are the funnest game I've ever played," he said, right before he kissed her again.

Mischa was just starting to get lost in his touch when he pulled away. Pulled away so quickly, she stumbled forward. He smacked her on the ass, hard. Hard enough that she fell into the stumble even more, tripping a few feet into the crowd.

She was glaring when she turned around, but Tal was nowhere to be seen. Usually his height alone ensured that he could be spotted in a crowd, but she didn't see his wavy hair bobbing along above everyone else. She turned in a circle, trying to figure out which way he'd gone.

"Tal?" she said his name softly at first. Then louder. Angry. "*Tal!*"

Mischa shoved her way through the crowd for a couple minutes, but the more she looked, the more obvious it was that she was alone. He'd kissed her stupid, stolen her panties, then ditched her.

How can I be in love with such an annoying man!?

Right then, her back pocket began to vibrate. She sighed and pulled her phone out, preparing herself for some sort of smart ass comment, or him laughing at how easy she was to evade, or some other stupid secret agent kind of talk.

But he wasn't calling. It was a text message. She smiled at the screen. Then laughed. Then smiled again, trying not to tear up. One year. She couldn't believe that it had been one year since she'd first come to Italy.

One year since a dirty man who kissed good had spied on her in an airport, and decided he would talk to her.

One year since she'd decided to become a horrible person and cheat on her husband.

She stared at her phone, cradling it in her hands.

Come find me.

Acknowledgments

So many people, so little end matter.

First and foremost, to the ladies in the street team. Always. You are everything.

Next—to Ella Fox. Before I ever "met" her, I read a blog post that she did, and it was about how she wrote a book thinking/knowing it wouldn't be well received, but she just had to write it anyway (it turned into a smash success). How brave. Then I joined a word count group in January of 2015, and who created it? Ella Fox. I was hitting writer's block hard, and I saw an encouraging post from her, then thought of her blog post, and I'd had this idea knocking around my head for a while (*"I can't write a cheating book, I'll be crucified, romance readers **hate** cheating!"*), so I thought—*"fuck it. Maybe everyone will hate it. But at least I wrote what was in me to write,"* and two weeks later I had 80,000 words and a rough draft titled *"An Affair."* So, thank you, Ms. Fox, for your thoughtful words, and the way you encourage and support all those around you.

Thanks to T.M. Frazier, for her beautiful personality and wonderful support, which she gives without thought to herself. A rarity in the word in general, and in this community in particular. I appreciate you more than you know.

To my beta readers! Deeeeep breath—Angie, Sue, Shannon, Rebeka, Letty, Beatriz, Bets, Rebecca, Lheanne, Ange. Your feedback helped more than words can say. And **big** thanks to Ratula! Eight million messages later, and we have an epilogue, and a lot of fixed typos. Your effort on this story was monumental and tireless and almost equaled my own. Thank you.

To Najla at Najla Qamber Designs—you never fail to sort through my semi-insane babble and come up with magic and art. This cover is *everything,* in my humble opinion. I love it so much more than anything I could've imagined on my own. Thank you for you talent and vision and patience.

To all the authors I've met on this incredible journey, your support and words of encouragement mean more than anything. Having the approval, and even better, the friendship, of your peers means the world.

To the people I've never met but talk to all the time, Rebeka, L.A. Cotton, Barbara Shane Hoover, and especially Jo. You let me bitch, whine, complain, vent, be crazy. You keep me sane. Thank you.

To the blogs. BLOGS. ARE. EVERYTHING. This is not kissing ass, this is FACT. Blogs change lives. Thank you to Yaya and the After Dark Book Lovers, for "getting me," and letting me be mean. Thank you to Milasy and The Rock Stars of Romance, for being bigger rock stars than any of us could hope to be. To Jessie—in case I didn't say it today, YOU'RE PRETTY. To Christine and Shh Mom's Reading, for always taking care of me during my reveals and tours and releases and just generally being the sweetest person I know. To Nina and The Literary Gossip, for your videos and posts and laughter. To ALL the Cover to Cover girls. To Deanna and her amazing reviews and graphics. To any blog that has ever posted for me, promoted for me, read for me, reviewed for me, *ever.* You made it possible for me to get this far. You make it possible for me to keep going. To any blog out there ever, that has ever supported their fave author, regardless of whether or not they've read me. Thank you for taking time out of your day to support what you love.

To any person *ever* that has shared something of mine, recommended my books, messaged me, fallen in love with the devil and Sanders, or maybe just now fell in love with Tal. *You* make it possible for me to keep doing this.

And last but most certainly not least, my husband. Writing erotica is already somewhat *interesting* for a married couple—"*I read your wife's book! WOW! I never knew you guys were so freaky!*"—so I know this book will bring its own lovely comments and assumptions. Thank you for understanding me and always letting me be me. Even when that means I wear pajamas and a headband ALL weekend. And thank you for bringing me waffles in bed.

Soundtrack

Songs that I listened to while writing, songs that just made me think of the story, and a couple that inspired actual scenes.

I Adore U—Adore Delano
Grown Woman—Beyonce
Lips Are Movin'—Meghan Trainor
Pretty Woman—Roy Orbison
Do I Wanna Know—Chvrches
Seaside—The Kooks
Love Somebody—Maroon 5
Can't Stop—Red Hot Chili Peppers
Firework—Katy Perry
Stay With Me—Sam Smith
We Found Love—Calvin Harris ft. Rihanna
Safe and Sound—Capital Cities
Paralyzed—Mystery Skullz
I Bet My Life—Imagine Dragons
Everything—Alanis Morissette
Gold—Neon Hitch ft. Tyga

About the Author

Crazy woman living in an undisclosed location in Alaska (where the need for a creative mind is a necessity!), I have been writing since . . . , forever? Yeah, that sounds about right. I have been told that I remind people of Lucille Ball—I also see shades of Jennifer Saunders, and Denis Leary. So basically, I laugh a lot, I'm clumsy a lot, and I say the F-word A LOT.

I like dogs more than I like most people, and I don't trust anyone who doesn't drink. No, I do not live in an igloo, and no, the sun does not set for six months out of the year, there's your Alaska lesson for the day. I have mermaid hair—both a curse and a blessing—and most of the time I talk so fast, even I can't understand me.

Yeah. I think that about sums me up.

CPSIA information can be obtained
at www.ICGtesting.com
Printed in the USA
LVHW090539151121
703355LV00018B/236